TREE OF LIBERTY

BOOK THREE OF THE HUMANITY UNLIMITED SAGA

TERRY MIXON

YOWLING
CAT PRESS

Published by Yowling Cat Press ®

Digital edition date: 6/21/2023

Print ISBN: 978-1947376069

Large Print ISBN: 978-1947376281

Cover art - image copyrights as follows:

DepositPhotos/innovari (Luca Oleastri)

Donna Mixon

Cover design and composition by Donna Mixon

Print edition design and layout by Terry Mixon

Audio edition performed and produced by Veronica Giguere

Reach her at: v@voicesbyveronica.com

ALSO BY TERRY MIXON

You can always find the most up to date listing of Terry's titles on his Amazon Author Page.

Note: the links below (ebook only, obviously) redirect you to my website where you can click a button to go to Amazon. This allows me to participate in Amazon's associates program and earn a little more. Sorry for any inconvenience.

The Last Hunter

The Last Hunter

Bonds of Blood

Alpha Strike

The Enemy Revealed

Command Authority

The Grand Conspiracy

Shield of Humanity

Fog of War

Ships of the Line

Operation Liberty

The Empire of Bones Saga

Empire of Bones

Veil of Shadows

Command Decisions

Ghosts of Empire

Paying the Price

Recon in Force

Behind Enemy Lines

The Terra Gambit

Hidden Enemies

Race to Terra

Ruined Terra

Victory on Terra

When Luck Runs Out

Gunboat Diplomacy

The Imperial Marines Saga

Spoils of War

Imperial Recruit

Enemy Action

The Humanity Unlimited Saga

Liberty Station

Freedom Express

Tree of Liberty

Blood of Patriots

Single Novels

Scorched Earth

Storm Divers

The Vigilante Series with Glynn Stewart

Heart of Vengeance

Oath of Vengeance

Bound By Law

Bound By Honor

Bound By Blood

Box Sets

The Empire of Bones Saga Volume 1

The Empire of Bones Saga Volume 2

The Empire of Bones Saga Volume 3

The Empire of Bones Saga Volume 4

Humanity Unlimited Publisher's Pack 1

Humanity Unlimited Publisher's Pack 2

DEDICATION

This book would not be possible without the love and support of my beautiful wife. Donna, I love you more than life itself.

ACKNOWLEDGMENTS

Once again, the people who read my books before you see them have saved me. Thanks to Michael Falkner, Michael Goad, Cain Hopwood, Kristopher Neidecker, John Naiser, Bob Noble, Andrew Olivier, Jon Paul Olivier, Bill Smith, Tom Stoecklein, Dale Thompson, and Jason Young for making me look good.

I also want to thank my readers for putting up with me. You guys are great.

1

arry Rogers examined the rolling landscape below his hilltop perch. The only sign of movement was the occasional four-legged scavenger darting between the parked cars. The lack of a police presence told him that—against all odds—the pitched battle fought below hadn't drawn anyone to the hidden base in the wilds of France.

Getting into the area without using the decrepit road had taken a few hours, but he hadn't wanted his team to stumble across any of Nathan's men or the people they'd been fighting. Or the police.

To all indications, the place was deserted.

Frankly, finding it at all had taken a lot of hard work and more than Harry's fair share of luck. His father, Clayton Rogers, had an extensive network of informants keeping an eye on the goings of his ex-wife Kathleen Bennett and his other son, Nathan.

Those people had pieced together where Nathan had been and where his mother had fled after the United States seized her holdings and tried to arrest her. That had gotten Harry to Paris.

The computers on *Freedom Express*, the mobile ship the human resistance to the alien Asharim had build a thousand years ago, had shown the general location of a nearby base and that had allowed

Harry to find this remote area once he'd convinced Brenda Cabot to bring him and his people back to Earth through their portable gate.

In all, it had taken almost half a day to locate the base and get here, which was pretty damned fast, considering they'd been out beyond the orbit of Pluto.

"It looks clear," Harry said softly. "Take your people around to the left. I'll go right. Those birds circling up near the big hill probably lead to the base and the heaviest fighting."

Rex Jamison, the lead scout in Harry's old private military company, lowered his binoculars. "Roger that. IR says none of the vehicles have been running in the recent past. As isolated as this area is, people might not have been able to pinpoint where the shooting came from. If they even heard it."

Sandra Dean looked up from the scope of a .338 Lapua Magnum. It was her preferred weapon as a trained and experienced sniper. "The flechette weapons are silent. We know your brother picked some up. If he were ready for the attack, the only noise would've come from the attackers. That could've been muted inside the base."

"We'll rendezvous there once we've secured the area," Harry said. "Keep an eye out for trouble, Sandra."

"On it."

He'd brought a dozen of his best men and women with him for this job. Here on Earth, it was their highest-priority task. His mother and brother, Kathleen and Nathan Bennett, had used a quantum tunnel in this base to get to the Asharim ship in the outer system.

They were still untangling the story of who the powerful aliens were, why they'd come to the solar system a thousand years ago, and what had happened to them. All he could say with any certainty was that they were the biggest threat humanity had ever faced.

That worried him, but there was nothing he could do about it right now. Best to focus on the problems he could actually deal with.

Nathan obviously knew how to use the gates. He probably had codes for the ones in this base. Harry meant to see them locked down tight to prevent anyone from sending waves of troops back through to Earth. He had to prevent that at all costs.

As he led his group around the area on his side, he considered how others might have thought he needed to be in New Zealand. The US had tried to kidnap his father in a wilderness area that, according to one of his people on the scene, was even more remote than this place.

Clayton Rogers and two local associates had disappeared before anyone had managed to call for help. The New Zealanders had gotten searchers into the area but found no sign of them or their attackers.

They'd sent ships to confront the US Navy destroyer that had launched the raid, but it had made it back into international waters. Even as badly as the US military had fallen, they were still far more advanced than pastoral New Zealand, so the destroyer had gotten away.

Either the US had his father, or his father had escaped into the base he'd been searching for. One way or the other, nothing Harry could do would change that situation right now. Besides, his father was a douche and deserved some trouble for being an asshat.

He'd head for New Zealand as soon as the France situation was under control. If nothing else, the people who'd vanished with his father deserved rescue.

Working slowly, they cleared the surrounding area over the next hour. No people or signs of conflict, though he smelled death and decay coming from the hill. This was going to be ugly.

He and his people had dealt with stuff like this far too many times in the Middle East. Mainly Iraq and Afghanistan. They knew what to do.

Harry slipped his nose plugs in. In the old days, people had put ointment on their upper lips. This was much better. It completely blocked the odor. That wouldn't do anything for his eyes, but he'd seen death before.

That's what they found in a cave up on the hill, too. Both outside and inside the well-concealed doorway. The attackers had left it open when they'd rushed inside. Parts of bodies littered the ground and corridor inside. Blood and other less savory bits painted the walls in a ghastly mural.

"It looks as if your brother made some new friends," Rex said as he moved inside, shooing the carrion birds away. "Looks like they headed for the elevator."

"Search every floor," Harry said. "Start at the top. I'll hit the bottom."

He stepped back out to get radio reception. "Sandra, we're going in. I'll leave someone out here to relay any warnings. We're going to move as much of the gore inside as possible. The birds will eventually draw official attention."

"Copy that. I've sent the drone out toward the main road. If anyone seems interested, I'll let you know."

Harry pointed to three of his men. "You guys drew the short straw. Get these bodies inside. Collect all the weapons and any other intelligence you find. Set aside any car keys. We'll be relocating the vehicles tonight, if no one finds us first."

Once he'd let Rex out on the next level down, Harry rode the elevator to the lowest floor. The people that had built these places liked to bury their power centers and the gates to the quantum tunnels deep.

There were a number of bodies and even more blood inside the elevator car. Nathan had fought for every inch of this place.

Harry didn't find the power room, but he did find a hangar even larger than the one on *Freedom Express*. Dozens of military-looking vessels sat there, waiting for someone to come along and use them. Black Jack McCarthy would be pleased.

The fighting down here had been brutal. Bodies littered the area around the elevator and stairs, and extended most of the way to the quantum tunnels. A particularly unlucky man lay in one of the arches, cut neatly in half from head to crotch.

That had to be the man Harry had watched die on the Asharim warship when Nathan had blown up the first gate.

"We're in the right place," he said, examining the arch. It didn't seem damaged on this side, but they would take no chances.

They'd probably used one of these vehicles to activate the quantum tunnel. The one with a raised canopy seemed like the best candidate.

Harry looked inside while his men searched the hangar and

watched the elevator closely. If there were any hostiles left alive in this base, they wouldn't be springing any ambushes on his people.

The screen came alive with a swipe of his hand. There was the gate controller. He tapped the button and brought up the code. That particular sequence wouldn't work with the gate destroyed, so he wouldn't try it. And if by some chance it could work, he had no intention of letting Nathan know they were coming before they were ready to pour through in force.

He started to pull back, but something on the floor caught his eye. An envelope.

Harry picked it up and looked inside. Then he smiled. His French was lousy, but this looked like a deed and a bill of sale. Probably to the very property they were standing under.

Nathan's name wasn't on anything, so he'd bought it under an alias. The bill of sale had his signature on it, though. Harry had seen the bastard's handwriting far too many times to be fooled.

Of course Nathan and their mother would want clear title to the find. Luckily, Harry knew people who could forge someone's handwriting so well that even the wronged party couldn't be sure they hadn't written the fake.

He'd accumulated a lot of his brother's papers over the years, so there were samples aplenty for the forger to use. By close of business tomorrow, he'd have a fresh bill of sale transferring the property to Humanity Unlimited. Or at least the name of someone untraceable that linked with the corporation.

In a way, they'd already paid Nathan and his mother for it. The two had stolen the spaceship Harry had found near the Mayan pyramid. He'd make sure the bill of sale indicated the base changed hands for the "Guatemalan ship." The irony was exquisite.

First, though, he needed to clear the place of bad guys. No time for gloating until the base was safe from discovery. He only hoped that his brother and mother didn't bring the wrath of God down on their heads while he secured all the pieces they'd left scattered around the globe.

The elevator doors slid open, and one of his men hurried over to him. "We have a problem. Sandra just spotted a couple of cars heading up the road. We're about to have company."

* * *

"YOU'RE ASKING us to take a lot on faith," General Jim Wayland, the senior Army commander advising the president, said. "This all sounds like some kind of drug induced fantasy. You haven't been smoking the wacky weed, have you, Mister Secretary?"

Secretary of State Josh Queen glared at the man in Army green. "No, but I came prepared to demonstrate this in a way that even you can understand, General."

He rose from the table where he'd just finished briefing the president, vice president, national security advisor, director of homeland security, and the senior military officers present.

"The scientists tore the wrecked ship apart and found a stash. It had this inside, among other things." The pistol he pulled from his case was sleek and dangerous looking. The Secret Service had thrown a kicking, screaming hissy fit when he'd forced them to allow it into the meeting. Only the president's stern insistence had allowed that to happen.

Queen laid it in front of the general. "I suppose I could blow a hole in something to demonstrate it, but that seems likely to get me shot. I'm sending it off with you to test for yourself. I have no idea how many shots it has left, so be sparing."

He cued the video of the weapon blowing a nice chunk out of a concrete wall. Everyone looked suitably impressed.

President George Blankenship shook his head. "Based on everything you've shown me, I'm inclined to believe this is as bad as you think it is. Until I say differently, we treat this as the most serious issue on the table. Everything we've seen is now classified top secret/SCI under the code word 'Prometheus.'

"It seems fitting, since we're stealing the knowledge of fire from the gods. Icarus was a close second, for obvious reasons. I want every effort expended to find the people who are spying on us and locate their little hidey-hole. Every bit of tech we can find and examine gets sent to Area 51 for secure testing."

General Weyland cleared his throat. "Sir, you do realize we don't actually have aliens there, right?"

The president smiled. "I'm not that far around the bend, Jim. It's a secure area with the brightest minds we have. That has to be where we keep this secret."

He looked at each of them for a moment. "Gentlemen, I want every angle examined. We have to get ahead of this, or you'd best start learning Chinese. Call Homeland with any breaks. Secretary of State Queen is in overall command. Dismissed."

Once everyone was gone, the president gestured for Queen to join him on the couch off to the side. He poured them both a stiff drink.

"Is it really as bad as all that?" the president finally asked.

"It's potentially much worse," Queen said grimly. "Former FBI Agent Cabot said this could be an extinction-level event. I'm inclined to think she was understating things. Rogers and the rest could very well bring an alien invasion down on our heads. One that we'd be powerless to stop."

"*War of the Worlds* bad? That's frightening. I want to know what you think of the main players. What kind of people are they? Who's in the driver's seat?"

Queen didn't need to look at his notes. "For the moment, that would be Jessica Cook. I looked her up before the meeting. An engineer with specialties in space construction. From what she said, she's also the number two in their company. She has a bigger stake than Harry Rogers does, in any case. I'm not sure why."

"What do you think of her?"

"She's bright and resourceful. She seemed like a straight arrow, but I'm disinclined to trust loose cannons not to roll over me. The same with Harry Rogers. He's not a twisty bastard like his father."

Blankenship sipped his drink. "What about Clayton Rogers?"

"I thought he was in it for the money. Now? Who knows? He's a bad one, though not as bad as his ex-wife and other son. They're lunatics."

"I thought you were going to pick him up. Where are we on that?"

Queen grimaced. "Nowhere. We weren't able to find him or the team we sent after him. It's as if they vanished off the face of the Earth. And with this technology, that's a very real possibility.

"Someone called in the local government to do a search and rescue mission, so we had to break off our examination of the area. Maybe, once the New Zealanders give up, we can find the gate they used."

The president sipped his drink without speaking.

Queen took that as a hint to keep speaking. "Frankly, those three don't worry me nearly as much as Cabot and her group. They could be anywhere and want anything. We know nothing about them."

Blankenship sighed. "A secret society of humans with ties to aliens. It's like something out of a science fiction novel. I can hardly imagine a group that has been active since the Middle Ages."

The president frowned. "This is more like a Dan Brown novel."

Queen would have laughed if the situation hadn't been so ridiculously dire. "That's the rub. Their organization has been active since around the time the Vikings found North America. They could have people anywhere in the country or be insinuated into anything.

"They could have someone in the Secret Service right out in the hall. They could have put taps into the NSA when it formed. They could literally have people anywhere, and we have no way of knowing."

"Trust only the people you have to," the president said as he set his half-finished drink down on the side table. "Put them through every bit of testing you can. We can only let paranoia make us so crazy.

"You're the man on point, Josh. I need you to get us a ship of our own before the Chinese find out about this. Or one of those gate things. Find someone in the secret society and make them talk. We can't be in the game unless we get a seat at the table. Make it happen."

Queen tossed his drink back and set his glass beside the president's. "You can count on me, sir."

2

Jess Cook craned her neck to stare out from the lifter's window as it passed over the immense buildings below them. Monumental snowdrifts covered everything, except that wasn't snow. It was the planet's frozen atmosphere. Not just the humidity in the air, but the gas itself, chilled into powder.

This far out beyond Pluto's orbit, the sun wasn't more than a bright star in the sky. It didn't provide any warmth worth mentioning. Or any illumination. Only the lifter's spotlights allowed them to see what they were passing over.

The view using *Freedom Express*'s telescopes was a lot brighter, but it had technology to enhance the ambient light. Her Mark One eyeballs thought of this world's normal light level as Stygian blackness.

"I'm going to pick one of the buildings for a closer pass," Black Jack McCarthy said from the pilot's seat. The ex-marine lieutenant colonel had really taken to the small craft.

No surprise there. He'd been a very talented pilot in atmosphere, and he'd been studying hard to learn how to use all their spacecraft. The copilot was the regular pilot, and she was watching his actions closely.

Jess knew that he wanted to get all the proficiency he could and then learn to fly the abandoned small craft they'd found scattered around the solar system. Particularly the fighters in the French base.

"Is there a place to land on one?" she asked.

"Maybe. Some of the roofs seem flat enough, but we won't know what's under the snow until I melt it off."

"How are you going to do that?"

He grinned. "I'm going to hover over one and dial the thrusters up. The heat and blast will clear us a spot."

She shook her head. "It'll also make for a really icy place to put our feet. Do you want me to slip and fall off one of those things?"

"No, but I'm a pilot. I just deliver the packages. Still, if you slip, the snow looks deep enough to save you."

"I'd rather not find out," she grumbled. "Make the blast long enough and the ice will convert to gas. It won't be completely safe, but that's better than risking a cracked helmet."

"Yes, ma'am," he said. "That one ahead looks good. It's taller than the ones around it, so we won't have to worry about dodging any unforeseen obstructions in the flight path."

"Make it happen, Colonel."

He smiled a little. "I'm just one of the boys, now. Call me John."

"Maybe I should've called you Black Jack. How did you get that call sign, anyway?"

"I'm really good at cards. Hang on. I'm going to hold us steady over the widest area on the roof."

The lifter came in slowly and stopped a dozen meters up from the snow. The exhaust blasted snow everywhere, blinding her.

"I have the radar altimeter keeping us at a good height above the deck," McCarthy said.

The white fog around them slowly thinned, and Jess found that she could see the actual roof. Part of it looked like some kind of landing area.

"Over there to the right," she said. "Is that a landing pad?"

"Might be. Let's clear it off and see."

The large slab of thicker material had a bright white circle that would hold the lifter easily. The small cross in the center made it look like a target.

"Well, unless they were asking for an orbital strike, this is indeed a landing pad," McCarthy said. "We need to be careful putting weight on it, though. We have no idea what its limits are or how much it might've weakened over time and under these conditions."

He moved the lifter over the probable landing pad and slowly settled down, never letting off the thrust completely until it demonstrated that it was up to the task of supporting them. Only then did he shut the thrusters down.

"Okay, we're down," he said. "Now what?"

"We see if we can find a way in and determine who used to live here," Jess said as she unstrapped.

"Good luck. This planet is too damned big to search in a meaningful way. Christ, it's about the same size as Earth and looks like it's covered by a single damned megacity. We won't even be able to examine the orbital in the near future because it's so massive."

That was true enough. The cylinder in orbit around the frozen world had an interior the size of Manhattan. Even with the quantum tunnel to bring people in from Earth, there just weren't enough bodies in the company to search it closely.

They had teams looking for the life support and power controls, but it might take months to find them. Or years.

The orbital had power, thankfully. The lights were on minimal settings, and the incredible quantum gate for spaceships worked. Unfortunately, the departed tenants had turned off the life-support systems. It was like an Arctic freeze inside the damned place.

The teams working inside it were in heavy cold-weather gear, much to Doctor Michael Crockett's annoyance. The archaeologist wasn't used to working under such trying conditions, and he wasn't shy about telling anyone who'd listen.

"We can only do what we can," Jess said. "You'll keep an ear on us?"

The ex-marine nodded. "The suit radios are good for quite a ways, but if you don't hear from me every few minutes, I want you to turn around and come back, no matter what interesting baubles you've found."

She smiled. "Yes, Mother. We're going to be careful. Don't come after us if we drop off for a little while. Give us an hour, and head back to orbit for more help if you can't get ahold of us for longer than that."

"They covered this kind of thing in the marines. We don't leave people behind. They also taught me to never give an order I knew wouldn't be obeyed, so I'll pass that lesson on to you now."

She stood and put her hands on her hips. "If we're not responding, one more person isn't going to make a difference. We'll need a full team for extraction. If you two don't go get them, they won't know where to find us."

He scowled. "You're annoying when you're right."

"So I hear. Don't worry. We'll be very careful."

Jess marshaled the team, and they exited through the airlock and onto the roof. The surface was still coated with a crust of ice, and the footing was treacherous. They all took care moving because a smashed helmet meant death.

Once she'd assured her footing, she stared up. The number of stars she could see above them was incredible. Vacuum did that.

There was an entrance off to the left. Wide doors of what looked like glass reflected the light streaming from the lifter.

No, they wouldn't be glass in this environment. Glass would never survive the intense cold. It had to be something else.

"This wasn't designed for vacuum," Ray Proudfoot said. The chief engineer of *Liberty Station*—their original ship—pointed at the handles. "These are for use in a shirtsleeves environment. There aren't even two sets of doors."

"That makes sense," she said. "No one would build a world-spanning city on a planet this far out of a system."

"How the hell did it get out here?" Everett Anderson asked. He was in charge of the tactical team Harry had insisted she bring along. As if there were anything more hostile than the environment on this ice ball.

"There's no telling," she said. "If the orbital station is any indication, the Asharim had something to do with it. I'm at a loss as to how or why."

The doors looked as if they were meant to slide open, but a tug failed to move them. They were frozen in their tracks. Doors like this could usually be swung open in an emergency, so she tried that and they rocked the slightest bit. Ray lent her a hand, and they popped open.

The interior of the building was pitch black, but their helmet lights lit the way in. More frozen atmosphere covered the floor a few centimeters deep.

"Uh-oh," Ray said. "That doesn't bode well."

His light had picked out a huddled form covered in frost and snow. A distinctly humanoid form.

"This isn't the first dead human we've found," Jess said sadly.

"Not the body," the engineer said softly. "The wall beside it."

She raised her eyes and stared at the sign. It welcomed them to Youngstown Emergency Trauma Center and pointed the way to the emergency room. In perfect English.

* * *

CLAYTON ROGERS WOKE with a stiff back. The stone floor inside the cave was the most uncomfortable surface he'd ever slept on. At least they'd let him and his companions sleep without restraints.

That had really pissed the CIA operative off. Agent Ulysses wanted them tied up hand and foot. Clayton had no idea where the man thought he and his people would get off to. They were all trapped on an alien world with an army of some kind camped only a few kilometers away.

Without a way to control the quantum gate deep inside the cave, they wouldn't be going anywhere soon. Since they'd brought the powerless controller from the other side along with them, odds were very good that no one would be able to come after them, either. They'd have to save themselves.

The special operations troops had made an early morning approach to the encampment they'd spotted yesterday. The people looked human enough, based on the descriptions that they'd brought back, but primitive. Maybe Revolutionary War tech levels.

As to whom they were fighting, no one could guess. Heavy-worlders were his personal wager. That seemed as if it would be a very short fight, though.

They were human enough to pass in society, but the Asharim had genetically modified them to be able to live in a three-gravity environment. The poor bastards had been military slaves to the powerful aliens.

A sailor came back with Penny Cash in tow. She'd just gone out to use the concealed latrine the men had dug.

She thanked the man and sat down across from Clayton. The third member of their abortive escape attempt, Mick Bird, was consulting with the Navy commander. His extensive outdoor skills might be critical in this situation.

"The army hasn't moved," Penny said. "That's what they tell me, anyway. It seems as though they might have been there for a while."

"That seems odd," Clayton said. "I know armies used to stay in one place over long winters, but why now? It seems warm enough to me."

She shrugged. "Damned if I know. Maybe they're waiting for their opponents to do something spectacularly stupid. Or maybe they're in hiding."

"Not with all that smoke from the fires. Speaking of which, how will we cook the food that they're hoping Mick can quietly kill? How do they even know that it's edible? With our luck, we'll poison ourselves."

"There are some animals being cleaned at the army camp. The scouts said they look like deer. Maybe they got through here at some point in the past and became part of the biosphere."

Penny looked back toward the entrance to their chamber. "While we're alone, we should discuss escape plans. First, are we even going to try?"

"No," Clayton said with a shake of his head. "All we know about this world is in the cave system here. Such as it is. We saw the dead alien city and the army. We haven't left this hill and have no clue what awaits us. Let's not jump out of the frying pan just yet."

"Then we need to make contact. We're not going to stay hidden for very long."

"That's not our call," he said dryly. "The men with the guns are in control now."

That answer didn't seem to satisfy her. "No disrespect to Commander Krueger, but I don't like leaving my fate in the hands of others."

"Believe it or not, I agree with you," a voice said from the dark tunnel leading toward the entrance. Commander Krueger stepped out of the passage and gave them a nod. "Voices carry in places like this."

The situation amused Clayton. Of course their plans had been overheard. That's the way things had been going for them.

"How are your people holding up?" he asked the officer. "This has to be a strain on them."

Krueger sighed. "It's sinking in, but we're special operations. We'll hold together. I know I wasn't the only one to lose sleep over the impossibility of our situation last night. I'm worried about Ulysses, too. Worried enough to detail someone to keep an eye on him."

Clayton nodded. "I hope we can find another way home. Hell, just a way to power the tablet would probably work for us."

"You said you agreed about not leaving our fate in your hands," Penny said. "What did you mean?"

"That the mission has changed," the officer said as he sat on a handy rock. "We can't get you back to Earth easily, so the new mission is to survive and learn about our new neighbors. If we reach an agreement, will you abide by it?"

Clayton smiled. "I'm a straight dealer, Commander—no matter what Ulysses might have told you. If I make a deal, I stick to it. You just need to be sure the details really mean what you think they do. Technicalities matter."

"Well, this is pretty straightforward," Krueger said. "I want you and your people to give me your parole. We all act as a team until we get back to Earth. If we can do that, then I don't have to guard you like prisoners, and Mister Ulysses can go piss up a rope."

"Colorful and vivid. I agree, but with one caveat. If we can get back safely, you have to let us go."

The officer shook his head. "I caught you fair and square."

"After we escaped to another world," Clayton riposted. "That seems to negate your point."

Krueger seemed amused rather than offended. "I have control now. That gives me the edge."

"Then release Penny and Mick. They have nothing to do with the charges against me."

The other man considered that. "Agreed. They weren't in my orders anyway. That just leaves you."

"Excellent. As for myself, if I can manage to do so without endangering any of your people, I reserve the right to depart once we return to Earth. Isn't that part of your creed as well? Escape and evade?"

Krueger smiled a little. "Once we get back to Earth, you're welcome to try. We have a deal."

"What happens now?"

"Breakfast. I'm afraid there are only MREs."

The sound of rapid footsteps in the tunnel interrupted them. It was Gunnery Sergeant Danvers. He stepped over to Krueger. "We have a problem, sir. A party from the army camp is headed our way. Maybe thirty people."

"Bring everyone back inside," the officer ordered. "We'll just have to hope they don't find us in here."

3

Kathleen Bennett didn't recall falling asleep, but she woke when the lid to the sarcophagus-like machine slid open above her. She sat up, trying to remember how she'd ended up inside the thing.

Nothing.

She remembered seeing it in the room her son Nathan had stuffed her into aboard the alien ship but not climbing inside. How odd.

After another moment trying to remember, she shrugged and stretched her back. She felt good. Really good. She must have really needed that nap.

Then the full memory of the day's events caught up with her. The fighting, the terrorists, and the way they'd tortured her. She looked down at her foot and saw that the bandages had fallen off. To her astonishment, her missing toe was there.

Feeling as if she were dreaming, she wiggled it. It moved just like all the rest. It was as if the bastards hadn't cut it off. How was that even possible?

Well, there'd be time to figure that out soon enough. First, she needed to find her son and see what was happening. They needed to secure control of this ship. It was the golden goose, and she meant to have its eggs.

She slid out of the device and noticed something else was different. Her clothes didn't fit properly. Her pants wanted to slide off, and her bra was like a clamp around her torso.

With a quick look around the strange room, she located a wall screen that would serve as a crappy mirror. She walked over to it, holding her pants up. What she saw stopped her dead in her tracks.

That wasn't possible.

Gazing back was a view of herself that she hadn't seen in far too many decades. She looked like she had in her mid twenties. The parts of her that life had filled out had slimmed back down, and the parts that age had deflated had ballooned back up.

Yes, this had to be a dream. A nice one, but she needed to wake the hell up.

The sound of the door opening made her turn.

Nathan Bennett came in and stopped dead in his tracks, his jaw dropping as his gun came up. "Who the hell are you? How did you get in here?"

"Try not to be more of an idiot than you have to, boy." Her voice was different, too. Less gravelly. Fuller. Younger.

Her son slowly lowered his gun, but he didn't put it away.

"Well, this is a surprise, Mother. You've found the fountain of youth. I can see you in there, now. You look younger than I do."

"How did I get into that machine?"

He leaned against the console. "You don't remember? The men I had guarding you said that you got into it under your own power."

"I remember coming into the room alone, so I won't rule it out," she granted. "What's happening out there?"

"Nothing as interesting as what's going on in here. You've been out almost twelve hours. The terrorists are still alive and kicking, though we have thinned the herd. I think there are two or three dozen left."

She'd have to do something about her clothes, but she had no idea what. They would have to wait.

"What about our forces? Do we still have guns?"

"Yes, but we're short on ammo. The new weapons are almost dry, but I might be able to find some more ammo somewhere on the ship. We have regular guns and ammo from the dead ragheads. Enough to finish the job, I think.

"But that will have to wait for a little while. We need to have someone look you over. One of my men is a medic."

She shook her head. "What would he see? You don't have any instruments that could look inside me. Forget it. I need something to modify my clothes. They fit like crap."

He grinned. "That's because frumpy clothes don't work on hot chicks."

"I'm your *mother*. Don't be more of a pervert than you must."

The deck under their feet shifted a little. Hardly enough to notice but more than it had before.

Nathan stood straight abruptly. "I think we better go find out what that was. Nothing good, I'll warrant."

No, probably not.

* * *

Brenda Cabot walked down the streets of Washington, DC, as if she hadn't a care in the world. No one would guess she was one of the most wanted fugitives in the country. The former FBI agent had no doubt she was number one on the most wanted list.

Her stylish hat and overly large sunglasses were more than enough to botch facial recognition programs on the numerous cameras watching over the nation's capital, but she made certain to walk in a different manner than she normally used. More of a sexy saunter.

Since that was completely out of character for her, it would screw with any of the more esoteric movement recognition programs running on the surveillance systems. Yes, that was actually a thing.

Piazza's, the trendy bar she breezed into, had a reputation as one of the hottest nightspots in the city, but it was early for the pretty people. The Families used the place as a means to keep an eye on what happened in the halls of power just over a dozen blocks away.

The Families had been part of an underground movement in the alien society after they'd taken primitive humans as slaves. They were as deeply buried in modern society now. They'd had a thousand years to become part of every organization that mattered, operating out of sight and with extreme subtlety.

The bartender was always one of them, so he didn't blink when she made her way into the back with a wave. A rack designed to hold wine bottles sat empty in the corner. It was old, and they'd upgraded one of the rooms to control the environment better for the expensive vino they stocked for the rich and powerful. It never drew the slightest interest during health inspections. That made it the perfect place to hide a secret entrance.

She bent low and found the hidden catch. It clicked softly, and the entire rack swung out, along with the wall behind it.

A newly revealed set of stairs led down into an abandoned portion of the old subway system, though not directly. There was a little walking through a dank tunnel to get to the station. That always set her into the right frame of mind for their secret lair: the Vault.

The Families had sprayed the crumbling walls with sealant to keep most of the seeping groundwater out, so the place was actually quite comfortable. The dehumidifiers and air conditioning routed in from buildings above the station helped a lot with that, too.

A massive door set in the wall of the abandoned station kept the lair secure. They'd bought it when a local bank had closed. Getting it down into the abandoned subway had been a chore, or so the older members of their group claimed.

In any case, it would keep any intruders at bay long enough for the people inside the Vault to escape by other routes if anyone ever discovered the place.

Two men wearing body armor and holding automatic weapons nodded to her as she walked past. They'd hold the door if trouble came knocking. Someone inside always monitored the bar to be sure no one raided the place.

Past the vault door, a wide room that looked like a CIA monitoring center awaited her. A dozen people stared at state-of-the-art monitors and listened to hidden bugs planted throughout the city —or in some cases, around the world.

A tall black man in a subdued suit gestured for her to come over to the raised platform above the rest of the stations. Cyrus Patterson had once worked for the CIA in a room very similar to this one, so he'd been the perfect choice for their intelligence chief.

"Brenda, I'm glad to see you made it here safely." He gripped her hand for a moment. "I'm so sorry you had to come out into the open like this."

"It's okay, Cyrus," she said as she set her purse, hat, and sunglasses onto his desk. "This is way more important than what I was doing before."

His smile widened. "Actually, I said that because the FBI is sweeping all their buildings and we've lost a number of bugs. It won't be long before they turn their attention to other critical areas. That's what I'm sorry about, not your loss of a social life."

She swatted his arm. "Ass. You never change. Now that we have the portable gate set up in the house over by the river, what is our situation like?"

"The government has gone all paranoid, which makes sense since we still have them penetrated six ways to Sunday. They're kicking off the king of all witch hunts. Everyone is a suspect, so everyone is keeping their heads down. It'll take them weeks to vet the critical people. We're safe enough for the moment."

Cabot pulled up a chair and sat. "What about our assets? Are they likely to find anyone? Do we need to start pulling people out?"

"I think not. Just like you, we made sure they had no links back to the Families. Some of them have been in place for decades. They're often the people doing the vetting. This has to be a nightmare for the alphabet agencies."

"We can't be complacent," she said firmly. "They have smart people working hard to find us now that they know we exist. They won't stop looking."

"Exactly, so we've picked out a number of bad apples to throw their way. People we've been aware of for a while that have dark little secrets they'd rather keep to themselves. We've left careful and subtle clues linking them together.

"The counterintelligence teams will unravel quite the conspiracy when they find them. One that doesn't lead back to us. Best of all, none of our people have to 'discover' them. A couple will pop up in a day or so without endangering any of our folks."

Brenda looked around the room while she considered that. A massive witch hunt was to their advantage. It wouldn't last forever, but it would put the opposition into disarray. Right now, time was a critical factor.

"Okay, that sounds good," she finally said. "What are our top issues right now?"

"We've had someone keeping an eye on Harry Rogers since you brought him through our gate. He found a hidden base in France, just like you said he would. Dammit, but I wish we'd known about it. Think of all the equipment that has to be there."

She shrugged. "The Families have been looking for just that kind of thing for centuries. We missed this one, but there are other bases scattered around the world, I'm sure. Rogers knew about the one in France. He'll know about others. We can trade our assistance for one."

He grinned. "I like the sound of that. In any case, we used our man in the French national police to be sure no word leaked about the site. No one has uttered a peep about it, so he hasn't had to smother any awkward information. It's still clean."

"It makes me mad, too," she admitted. "Centuries of hard work and some guy just waltzes into what should be our hidden fortress. Still, you're right. We'll manage to get on his good side. We just have to gain his trust so he doesn't poke the Asharim."

"I might be able to help with that. There was a big national security meeting at the White House. We don't have the full details, but one of our people picked up some of the fallout. They're going to use the military to solidify the US claim to the Yucatán Spaceport in Mexico and fortify it."

"That's not a big surprise," she said. "The US doesn't have a space program anymore. Idiots."

"True, but that's going to change. They leaned hard on the Indians and 'bought' their Mars ship. It's almost ready to go, so Roger's people there can expect company in about three months."

That wasn't unexpected, but she'd hoped it would take longer. "What about the Chinese?"

The Indians and Chinese had been engaged in a race to Mars. The US co-opting the Indian ship would definitely gain the attention of the most powerful nation on the planet. With their powerful military, they could potentially act out in unexpected ways.

"They're monitoring the situation. The fact that *Liberty Station* made it to Mars in a matter of days and that the US is now heading after them isn't lost to their senior people. They still don't know about the Asharim, but that won't last forever. One of their spies will pick up something eventually."

The Chinese would have no problem using force to take any advanced technology. They'd rightly see it as a direct threat. That could get very ugly in record time.

"We'll need to let Rogers know," Brenda said. "He'll want to get weapons to Mars so they can defend themselves. Thank God there are only those two ships. Any chance we could sabotage them both?"

"It's possible we could do something to the Indian ship but not the Chinese. It's too well guarded."

She sighed. "I want options on my desk as soon as possible. Too many people know about the technology for it to stay quiet much longer. If we have spies that are hearing about it, the Chinese will, too.

"Rogers and Cook will need someone to hack the big gate soon. They'll want to track down where that ship went. Do we have anyone that might be able to help?"

He considered that for a moment. "I think I know just the man. Kevin McHugh. He's one of my guys. A real hacker."

Brenda raised an eyebrow. "One with skills in Asharim tech?"

"He told me there had to be similar ways into those kinds of systems. He's built up a number of tools and techniques over the last few years. He's your guy, but he's based out of Virginia."

"Call him to Washington. If I'm right, he'd best pack for a long trip."

4

Chen made his way into the depths of the Chinese Embassy in Washington, DC. A room there was proof against any external monitoring, and he wanted no one to be aware of what he was about to pass on to his superiors.

Even though the guards knew him well, they were thorough in checking him for listening devices. It was always possible that someone would manage to plant a device on him, so he approved of their caution and diligence.

He left his cell phone and other electronics in a lockbox on their desk. That kept them safe from either of the guards getting their hands on them. Paranoia ran both ways.

Inside, the secure room was much as depicted in various entertainment programs: high-tech gear off to one side and a large screen dominating one wall. A technician awaited his pleasure in front of the controls.

"Leave me."

The man rose, bowed, and retreated without a word.

Chen secured the door behind him, activated the jamming technology built into the walls, and disabled all the recording devices. He manipulated the controls and opened a channel to Beijing.

The man who appeared on the screen was of lower social rank than Chen, but that didn't stop him from virtually sneering. "Imperial Palace. How may I assist you, Ambassador?"

"I must speak with the president's secretary. The matter is urgent."

The other man made a show of checking his watch. "She has most likely been asleep only a few hours. It would be best to call her back at a more reasonable hour."

"It is not your place to question my judgment. Wake her."

The man's expression subtly indicated he thought Chen was making a mistake, but the screen blanked.

Fifteen minutes later, the screen once more cleared, and Chen saw the president's secretary. She'd obviously risen hastily and looked somewhat peeved.

"Ambassador Chen," she said coolly. "The hour is early."

"Are you alone in the secure room?"

She glanced to the side. "No. The technicians are here."

"Send them away."

Her eyebrows rose. "They have the highest clearance."

He said nothing.

She searched his face for a moment before nodding. "Everyone, leave me."

The man Chen had spoken with earlier shot a disgruntled look at him as he crossed behind the president's secretary. A second man kept his face blank as he followed him.

The woman watched them until they were gone and then turned to face Chen. "I am alone."

"Be certain that no recording device is activated."

"I have already done so. Proceed."

"This is a matter for the Dragon, not the president."

Her eyes narrowed. "You are not supposed to contact us through official government channels. This is dangerous."

He nodded. "The information is too critical to use my normal courier. Only this heavily encrypted line will do. The United States government has come into the possession of Asharim technology."

The woman's eyes widened. "Are you sure?"

"I am. One of our sleeper agents has seen it with his own eyes. An independent source intercepted a message about the acquisition, as well. There is no doubt."

"Forgive my misgivings, but this could be a trick of some kind."

He shook his head. "The technology was a flechette pistol of the standard design. Our man saw a video of it blowing a chunk of concrete the size of my head out of a wall.

"The Americans confiscated it from Kathleen Bennett, and it is merely the smallest of a sizable cache of similar equipment. The largest appears to be an Asharim cargo lifter in questionable condition but also recognizable. There is no mistake."

The woman considered him for a moment before nodding. "I will see that the Dragon is made aware of these developments in the morning. It would be too conspicuous for me to contact them any sooner. Watch for a special courier in the next day."

She wasn't genetically one of the Dragon's members—it only took one look at her petite frame to realize that—but she was still one of their leaders. The Dragon needed people of non-heavy-worlder extraction in many areas of their work, so some families had been with them for many hundreds of years.

"I will have as detailed a report as possible ready at that time," he said. "My people are still gathering data. One complication is that it will not be long before spies outside our control become aware of these developments."

Her expression darkened. "That is unfortunate. Can we seize the trove?"

Chen shrugged. "Possibly, but I would not count on it. The Americans are moving it to a secure facility under extremely heavy military guard. While they are not as strong as they once were, they can defend themselves here in their home quite well."

"Pity. I will need a story to tell the president when she wakes. Someone will report your call."

"That will be no challenge. The Americans have sent military forces to secure the Yucatán Spaceport and cajoled the Indians into selling them their Mars craft for a significant—perhaps even ruinous—premium. The US seems suddenly desperate to get to the Red Planet. That tells me there must be more technology on Mars."

"That is troubling but not really a surprise. The rebels were scattered all across this system when we suppressed them. I do not recall specific mention of anything on Mars, but it would shock me if there were not.

"The Chinese vessel incorporates more powerful engines than the Indian ship, but it is less powerful than the fusion drive Rogers employed. It will still take us months to get to Mars, and the forces we can send will be small. His mobile station is far larger than our ship, so he will outnumber us."

"True, but we can send crack military forces with heavy weapons. Roger's ship is unarmed. He could not smuggle anything serious through the Yucatán Spaceport."

"Such as a stolen fusion reactor?"

Rogers had powered his Mars ship with a prototype fusion reactor stolen from his ex-wife. That briefly made Chen wonder if Kathleen Bennett had used Asharim technology to build it. No matter. They'd find out soon enough.

He inclined his head to grant her the point. "We can stop the Indian ship. Rather, the American ship, I suppose. We have weapons in orbit capable of destroying the thing. That will generate unfortunate consequences here on Earth, however. In the end, that decision is not mine to make."

The corner of her mouth quirked up. "No, I suppose it isn't. You have done well, Ambassador. The courier will have further instructions for you. Good night."

The screen went blank, and he took in a deep breath to settle himself. The great game was entering a very dangerous phase. If it came to war, China could crush the Americans but only at a terrible cost.

Well, so long as the Dragon triumphed in the end, it was worth the blood and fire. Let the world burn. They would soon be leaving it behind anyway.

* * *

JESS WANTED to rub her face, but her helmet prevented that. This situation was not only impossible, it was ludicrously so.

Time travel? Where someone brought another Earth with them? Yeah, preposterously impossible.

They'd need to get a good reading of the continents to confirm everything under the global ice sheet matched Earth, but it was hard to dismiss a frozen planet filled with huge buildings and the bodies of people that sure looked as though they'd come from the future.

They'd examined dozens of bodies so far, and the majority of them had IDs from Virginia or the surrounding states. All with dates corresponding to more than two centuries in the future.

"We're going to have to wrap this up," she finally said. "I want everything documented in a way that won't make Doctor Crockett lose his mind. We'll take a few bodies back with us for the medical team to examine. Let's finish searching this floor, and we'll put a beacon on the roof to lead some follow-up teams back. Stay in pairs."

She gestured to Ray Proudfoot and led the way deeper into the offices just off the landing platform. They'd made a single pass through, so their footprints marred the perfect sheet of frozen gases that covered everything.

This level had probably housed senior executives, if these people followed anything like the practices on her Earth. Those in power seemed to think they needed to be higher up than anyone else and have a better view.

The central area was an open space filled with desks. Probably people that supported the movers and shakers in some way. The latter were probably in the offices along the perimeter of the building, with the most powerful having corner offices.

There were some bodies here, but not as many as one might expect on a workday. Whatever had happened to them, it had come at night, or it had taken time. Not too long, though. Otherwise, there'd have been no one here at all.

"What do you think happened?" she asked Ray as she headed for the largest of the corner offices.

"I've been running possibilities through my mind. It's hard to speculate on something this crazy."

She opened the door and looked into a spacious and luxurious office. One that Clayton Rogers would've been proud to occupy. "Well, we're going to have to speculate on what happened here, impossible or not," she said. "After all, we just found out we can travel across the universe via quantum tunnels."

"Point."

The office contained three bodies bunched together on a couch, two larger forms with a smaller one between them. This was the first child they'd found, and it made Jess's heart ache.

Ray moved to the spacious desk while she stepped closer to the dead. "Since we're talking the impossible, I suppose that a planet that suddenly lost its sun might die this quickly. I'd have to run some numbers, but just look at how quickly temperatures at home fall overnight.

"Without any solar radiation, that trend would keep on going as heat radiated into space. Faster, really, since the heat on the other side of the planet wouldn't be there to help smooth things out. The US would be like the Arctic in a matter of days at most. Perhaps even quicker."

She nodded, knowing that he couldn't see her. "That would jibe with the cold-weather clothing. Whatever it was didn't happen all at once. These people were inside a building that presumably had power, yet they're dressed in as many layers as possible."

Like the rest of the bodies they'd found, these three were dressed for extreme cold but not with dedicated gear. Just whatever they could put on in layers.

The two larger forms turned out to be a man and a woman. The child was a girl based on her braided hair and bright hair clips, perhaps ten. Definitely prepubescent. She had something in her lap.

Jess brushed the snow off the girl's lap and found a small black cat curled up there. That made her choke a little more. She loved cats.

She couldn't cry now. She had no way to wipe her eyes.

A search revealed an ID on the man, and there was a purse beside the woman. They had the same last name and address in Youngstown. This was a family.

"There's a fairly advanced-looking computer over here," Ray said.

"It might only be a terminal, but there's a possibility I can get something from it."

"Take it with us, then. I've got a family over here. I think we should take them with us as a unit. They died together, so we should keep them that way."

A search of the short table beside the bodies revealed a pill bottle. They'd probably taken a lethal dose of something before the intense cold froze them. She also found a pet carrier on the floor.

"We're going to need to be very careful moving them," she said as she turned to face Ray. "They're completely frozen, and I don't want to break parts off them."

"That's gruesome. I've got the computer and monitor—or what I suspect is the monitor. It's a strip that sat on the desk at about the right place. Maybe a projector of some kind."

"Let's get it out to the lifter, then. I'll send someone back to get the bodies."

She was able to lift the cat free. The poor thing was just as stiff as one would expect but small enough that Jess could carry it easily. It took a little work to angle the small body so that it went into the carrier, but she managed it.

The two of them retreated to the roof. She tagged some of the other team members to secure the bodies. They'd put the family in the cargo area in back of the lifter. That way the family could stay in vacuum until the medical team collected them.

Half an hour later, Jess's team was ready to go. They'd barely made a dent in the exploration, and definitely had more questions than answers. Doctor Michael Crockett was going to go nuts.

She filled McCarthy in as he took them up.

He looked at her and shook his head when she finished. "That's just crazy. Of course, at this point, it's getting to be a whole new level of crazy for everything.

"I spoke with Harry while you were in there. He's secured the base in France. They locked down the gates so that his asshole brother couldn't come back unexpectedly, but they have someone snooping around. He can't head for New Zealand until they take care of them, one way or the other."

Jess sighed. "We have so many things we have to do. I'm not sure we can handle this all by ourselves. We need more people. People that we can trust."

"You need to set up a recruiter on Earth. One that can quietly find people with useful skills. With the base in France, we can get them to where we need them. Of course, if we could find a portable gate that we could set up in the US, it would be better."

"Add it to the list. Until then, I suppose we need to formalize an agreement with Cabot and her people. I'm still not sure I trust them yet, though."

"Having backup plans are good," he assured her, "but you have to work with the tools at hand. From what I hear, she might be able to shed some light on this stuff. Surely that's worth having a discussion over terms."

Jess couldn't argue with that kind of logic. "I'll clean up and make the trip to Earth to see them."

The lifter made it back into orbit, and McCarthy landed it outside the base entrance next to the other lifter they'd brought from *Liberty Station.*

Freedom Express had ships inside, but they didn't know how to fly them yet, and there was no easy way to get them out. The gates they used led everywhere imaginable but not to the surface of the extinct comet, which seemed stupid, so they'd probably missed an external gate. They were still looking for any on the surface of the dormant comet.

Jess left the team to handle the work of unloading everything and made her way inside. She stripped off her suit once the pressure and temperature came up.

She'd take the cat down to the lab and leave it with the team there to examine. Then she'd clean up and go have a long talk with Brenda Cabot.

That plan lasted right up until she reached for the pet carrier and saw a pair of green eyes examining her from inside it.

5

Clayton waited patiently for the scouts Commander Krueger had left outside to report. Their tactical radios gave the special operations team a distinct advantage over the more primitive folk that were coming up the hill, as did the video feed from the small drone that the Americans had brought with them.

Commander Krueger and he watched the feed from it over the operator's shoulder. The slow-moving craft was almost coasting over the hill and had a great view of the string of men climbing a disused and rocky path toward the summit.

Ulysses—the CIA agent—sat glaring at them from a handy shelf of rock. The Navy officer had cut him out of the command loop now that they were no longer on Earth, and he wasn't happy about it. He'd also objected to Krueger accepting their parole.

Clayton knew the type of man Ulysses was. He'd dealt with far too many like him over the years. The bastard would cause him trouble at every turn.

With a sigh, he pushed the toad from his thoughts and focused on the handheld monitor. "What do you suppose they're going to do, Commander?"

The officer shrugged. "Probably look around the general area.

The elevation is good for that. They're not going to find the cave, based on the route they picked, so that probably wasn't their destination in the first place."

The men on the hill made their way up to the clearing Clayton and the rest had visited yesterday. The drone was too far away to capture their facial expressions, but based on how far away they stayed from the altar, it wasn't their objective, either.

That said something good about their character, he supposed. The human bones scattered around the slab of stone indicated the owners had some bloodthirsty habits.

The primitive men ended up going to the rough platform the Special Forces troops had found. They either wanted a look at the dead alien city in the distance or something between it and the hill.

"Bring the drone in for a pass with the engine off," Krueger said to the operator.

"Aye, sir."

The officer glanced at Clayton. "The prop is quiet, but without it, the thing is almost undetectable on a close pass. Anyone seeing it will think it's a bird soaring by."

"That assumes there are birds on this world."

"Good point," Krueger said approvingly. "One that I've already verified, but still good thinking."

The operator took the drone around then dove in from the side, capturing the men and the area around them as he soared past. A few people looked over at the drone but didn't seem to pay it any undue attention.

Once the drone was safely back up and away, Krueger had the operator extract the video and pass it on to a second handheld wielded by Gunnery Sergeant Danvers.

The man found a good view of the people on the platform and paused the video. "Those are uniforms but not ones I recognize," the marine said. "I suppose there are some similarities to what was used around the time of the Revolutionary War, but I think that's more a factor of manufacturing methods than design.

"I'm more interested in their weapons, honestly. They share a lot of similarity with muskets of around the same period, too. I'm not a black-powder man, but they don't look like repeaters to me."

"Let me see," Mick Bird said. "I have some friends that are into historical reenactment."

Clayton raised an eyebrow. "New Zealand seems to be quite a stretch for Revolutionary War reenactors."

The young man grinned. "You'd be surprised how many people outside the US have interests in the time period. I'm not one of them, mind you, but I enjoyed shooting the guns. Lots of smoke and a big kick."

The New Zealander examined the image closely. "I hate to disagree with you, Gunnery Sergeant, but that is a uniform from the American Revolutionary War. At least I'm pretty sure it is. One of the State Militias, I think. Couldn't tell you which one, though. And those long guns are definitely of a similar make to the ones I fired."

Krueger frowned. "How can that possibly be? You said the war between the aliens and the humans with bases happened a thousand years ago. The Europeans hadn't even found the New World back then."

Clayton snorted. "I've stopped asking how anything is possible. I've discovered that I'll probably never find out the answer. All we can do is take in the facts and make educated guesses. I'd say that at least one gate exists in the United States and these people's ancestors came through it a few hundred years ago."

"I suppose that's as good a theory as any," the officer admitted. "Take the drone over the camp. I want to see this army. Make the pass high enough to keep the drone looking like a bird."

The drone captured the camp in enough detail to see the layout. There were a lot of tents and campfires.

"It looks as if there are a few thousand men," Krueger said after a long look. "The layout isn't as regimented as I'd have expected."

Something caught Clayton's attention. "There is something at the center of the camp. I caught a bit of the light."

The gunnery sergeant backed up the video. There was a large tent in the center of the camp, and someone was standing outside it. They seemed to be watching the drone through what looked like a long glass—one that briefly flashed in the morning sunlight when the angle was perfect.

"Oh, crap," Krueger muttered. "They've spotted the drone."

Gunnery Sergeant Danvers shrugged. "That probably doesn't matter, sir. It's not as if they know where we are. They might not even recognize what the drone means, even after seeing it."

Honestly, the fact that someone had seen the drone mattered less to Clayton than the person who'd spotted it. The figure below was a woman, based on her generous cleavage, but her clothing was out of step from what he thought he knew about the revolutionary setting.

The image was too distant to make out her features in detail, but the woman looked more like she was dressed up for an Errol Flynn movie than the Revolutionary War.

That actually matched more closely with the seaman's eyeglass she was using and the curved sword strapped onto her hip.

Who the hell were these people?

* * *

HARRY WATCHED the newcomers from his perch high on the hill over the French base. The intruders had parked their vehicle almost a mile away from the remote site and walked in on foot. Sandra had kept watch on them every step of the way via a microdrone.

They didn't look like terrorists, but he knew looks could be deceiving. He wasn't going to take any chances.

He suspected they were associated with Brenda Cabot. She was one of the few people who knew he was back on Earth. He hadn't made it easy for her to keep tabs on him, but she was a former FBI agent. That probably meant she had mad skills when it came to tracking people.

These people were probably French members of her secret organization. It had existed for a thousand years and probably stretched around the globe. He'd be astonished if they didn't have people literally everywhere.

Unbeknownst to their watchers, Rex had taken his team around to keep a close eye on them. The scout had mad skills of his own. He and his people were less than twenty meters away from the concealed men.

A second team had already secured their vehicle. As soon as Rex had them in custody, they'd bring the vehicle closer. Once again, he didn't want to chance anyone finding them with all these dead bodies. That might cause some indelicate questions.

"Rex," he said over the encrypted channel. "Are you in position?"

Two soft clicks indicated he was.

"You are go to proceed," Harry continued. "Remember, take them all alive. We don't want to kill any of our potential allies."

Seconds later, Rex and his men seemingly popped up out of the ground near the intruders with their weapons in their faces. Wisely, the invaders raised their hands. The scout team quickly secured and searched them for weapons.

"Intruders secure," Rex said. "We're on our way back in. By the way, these people aren't terrorists. They actually bathe."

Harry laughed. "Copy that. Get them and their car up here as quickly as you can. Sandra, does the area look secure now?"

"None of my people see any signs of backup," the sniper said. "We'll keep our eyes open, but I think these are our only visitors."

It took Rex half an hour to march his prisoners up to the secret base. As a precaution, he put bags over their heads to keep them from seeing precise details of the base entrance. The builders had hidden the damned thing fiendishly well, and Harry didn't want to lose that advantage.

Harry had selected an empty room on the third level to interrogate them. It had once been a storage room, he suspected.

Rex and the scouts herded the prisoners into the room and closed the door behind them. Two men stood behind each prisoner, holding their arms. Rex pulled their hoods off.

His French was crappy, but Harry had enough vocabulary to get the point across. "Who are you?"

One of the men, a tall thin fellow with a well-trimmed mustache, cleared his throat and spoke in decent English, though with a pronounced French accent. "Please do not harm us. We are associates of Brenda Cabot. She asked us to make contact with you."

That was about what he'd expected, but Harry needed to be sure. "Do you have any proof?"

The man looked at his companions and shrugged. "I'm not precisely certain what form of proof you would accept."

Harry made a mental note to work out a series of code phrases with the former FBI agent. He should've done that right up front.

Since their groups were loosely aligned, they needed to have a secure method of identifying one another's operatives.

"My concern is that you might be associated with the US government," Harry said. "They know Brenda Cabot and I are aware of one another. You need to offer me something that only she or her people would know."

The man seemed to consider that for a moment and then shrugged again. "I find myself at a loss, Mister Rogers. You see, we are not directly part of her family. Our branch is active only in France. Perhaps you could call her. She would vouch for us."

That was a possibility, but one he'd prefer to use only as a last resort. He had a number for her, but the potential for an NSA intercept was high. They'd only be able to speak in generalities, and he'd have to use one of his people as a proxy. They'd be looking for his voiceprint. Hers, too, but she undoubtedly already knew that.

"I assume your family is aware of your location," Harry said after considering his options. "What will they do if I hold on to you until I'm certain of your bona fides?"

The man smiled slightly. "The potential for conflict when we made contact was always there. I have a code phrase that I may call them with to assure them of our safety and inform them that we will be staying here for the time being. My phone was confiscated by your men."

It was always possible the code phrase would mean something entirely different, but their silence meant something, too. It was probably best to take the chance. Whoever had sent them already knew roughly where the base was located.

"I'm going to leave you with my associate so I can take care of other matters requiring my attention. He will also endeavor to verify your identity with Miss Cabot. Once we're sure whom we are negotiating with, we can settle this misunderstanding."

Once the man nodded his agreement, Harry made his way out into the corridor with a gesture for Rex to follow.

He closed the door and spoke softly enough that no one inside would overhear. "Get his phone and let him pass the code phrase along. Use one of the burner phones and call Cabot, too. Don't mention any names, but inquire whether she might have sent a friend or two to visit us. If she says yes, these people are probably legitimate."

"I'll take care of it," the scout said. "What business are you going to be looking into?"

Harry grimaced. "As much as I'd rather let him rot, I need to get to New Zealand and figure out what happened to my father. If the US has him, that's a terrible security risk. We'll have to spring him.

"If he got away, he's either somewhere in the wilderness, down in the New Zealand base, or on a world connected to it by gate. We need to secure the base and keep the government down there from seizing it."

"Good plan. I'll handle my end. We still need to move all the vehicles away from the area. When someone official finally comes looking, they're going to spark a lot of questions. There were a bunch of terrorists involved in this attack, too. Someone is going to miss them."

"We can't control that," Harry said grimly. "So long as we move the vehicles a sufficient distance away, it doesn't matter what anyone does. They won't be able to locate this base. That's the important thing.

"If the terrorists had left word of their destination, we'd have already had more company. How long do you think it's going to take you to relocate all the vehicles?"

The scout shrugged. "If we use every available body and only move the cars forty or fifty kilometers, we should be able to get all of them relocated before dawn. We'll still be on the road getting back here, but we should be safe enough."

It would have to do. "Make it happen. Gather the bodies onto pallets near the gates and move them to *Freedom Express*, too. We'll give them a quiet burial in deep space. Collect all the intelligence you can as you go. We might need to know who their friends are later."

"Copy that. Good luck on your search."

Harry headed up to the surface. He'd take the jet that had brought them to France. With the time shift during the flight, he probably arrived in New Zealand just after dusk, local time.

He had no idea what he'd tell the New Zealanders. Everyone on Earth knew he was on Mars. He couldn't just reappear with no warning. He'd need to pretend to be someone else.

Thankfully, he'd been in his suit when they'd recorded the landing on Mars. His face might not be widely known. At least he hoped it wasn't. He'd find out soon enough.

6

Queen stepped off the rolling steps and onto the hot concrete of the airfield. His hat provided some protection against the glare, but he still had to shade his eyes with his hand.

A man in a blue Air Force uniform stepped forward and extended his hand. Silver stars glittered in the blinding light. "Welcome to Area 51, Secretary Queen. I'm Lieutenant General Nick Guthrie, the base commander."

Queen shook his hand but raised an eyebrow. "Isn't that classified?"

The man smiled. "We stopped denying the place existed quite some time ago. We just keep the details of what we do here under wraps now."

He gestured toward a waiting SUV. "Let's get inside before you melt."

Queen climbed inside the air-conditioned SUV gratefully. Once he'd secured his seatbelt and the general had climbed in beside him, he inspected the man.

The Air Force officer seemed young for his rank. Of course, as

Queen got older *everyone* seemed younger. He supposed such was the nature of the universe.

"Has this vehicle been scanned for bugs?"

The officer nodded. "I had my people give it a thorough scan right before I came out to pick you up. It's clean, and the driver is cleared for anything we discuss."

"He might have the clearance, but he doesn't have the need to know. We can wait until we're in a secure facility to continue."

The building the SUV pulled up in front of was nondescript except for the hangar adjacent to it. Still, they'd originally designed the base to hide the stealth planes the US had tested here. The best way to conceal critical hangars was to have a lot of them to confuse observers.

The two Air Force military policemen guarding the door saluted the general as he escorted Queen inside.

Queen expected them to take the elevator down into some sublevel, but the general surprised him and hit the button for the top floor. He took a moment to scan the rows of buttons and quickly determined that there was no basement level to this building. None with a button, anyway.

The general raised an eyebrow. "Looking for hidden facilities concealed deep inside the earth?"

Queen allowed himself a smile. "I confess that I was. Too many old movies, I suppose."

The man shook his head. "We do have a number of underground facilities. In fact, we're converting them for project use as we speak. If you like, we can take a tour once we're done with the initial briefing."

The elevator doors slid open, and Guthrie led him to a conference room. The thickness of the doors and walls indicated it was a secure facility. No one would be able to monitor anything discussed within its confines.

Half a dozen people waited for them inside. Two were Air Force officers, and the remainder appeared to be civilians.

Queen recognized one of the latter. Ethan Wagner, the former lead scientist of BenCorp and Kathleen Bennett's scientific lapdog, sat on one side of the table.

To his credit, the man had fallen all over himself in an effort to prove useful. And Queen was willing to admit that the man *was* a valuable resource.

While he was no longer in charge of this research project, they'd continue to utilize his particular knowledge so long as he proved useful. If that ceased, the man knew he had a nice comfortable cell waiting for him at Guantánamo Bay.

General Guthrie gestured toward the chair at the head of the table. "If you'll have a seat, Mister Secretary, we'll get this briefing under way."

Queen assumed the indicated seat and waited for the general to take the remaining open chair to his right before speaking. "Good afternoon, everyone. For those of you who don't know me, I'm Josh Queen, the secretary of state, but the president has also placed me in charge of Project Prometheus and I'm here to learn what the baseline status of our investigation is."

Guthrie gestured toward the two military officers. "On your left are Majors Gregory Durant and Stephanie Mills. They fill the role of security officers for the project. Both have science backgrounds and can competently oversee all research and researchers. On the civilian side, I believe you are already familiar with Doctor Ethan Wagner."

Queen gave the scientist a cool smile. "Yes, we've met before. How are you, Doctor?"

The other man shrugged. "I suppose that depends on what we compare my situation with. Held up to a cell in Cuba, I'm doing wonderfully. Measured against the life I had before this, not so well."

"I suggest you don't use exterior yardsticks to measure how things might have been. You made the choices that led you here. You now have an opportunity to regain the freedom you once enjoyed. Don't screw it up."

Of course, both of them knew that was unlikely. With the critical knowledge the man had in his head, Queen couldn't just allow him to wander around freely. Wagner would always be subject to close monitoring and other restrictions, even if he earned his so-called freedom. Frankly, it would be a lot simpler to drop the man into solitary confinement once this project was well under way and lose the key.

Guthrie continued. "The remaining scientific researchers have all been pulled from other high-classification projects on the base. To your left is Doctor Tran Lee, center is Doctor Benedict Pender, and right is Doctor Astrid Sherrod."

"How much do they already know?" Queen asked.

"Nothing. I felt it best for you to tell them whatever you wanted them to know."

"Excellent. Everyone, I'm about to tell you a story you will have difficulty believing. Nevertheless, I assure you it's true." He glanced at his watch. "We're going to be here late into the evening, so I think it best if we send out for something to eat. Does anyone object to pizza?"

"Pizza is a favorite around here," Guthrie confided. "I know a guy that makes some amazing pie. We'll get that ordered, and it should be ready for us in an hour."

"Perfect," Queen said. "That should just about allow me to lay out the basics. It all starts in the jungles of Guatemala…"

* * *

"I TELL YOU, that cat was frozen solid," Jess insisted. "Ray can back me up."

"It was," the engineer said. "I was there when she found it."

The man blinked and turned to her. "You don't suppose any of those other people are going to come back to life, do you?"

"No. They're dead. The cat, though, appears to be a different story. Something is not as it seems."

She'd gathered her core scientific team—Emily Adams, their computer specialist; Michael and Sierra Crockett, their senior archaeologists; Rachel Powell and Paulette Young, their restoration specialists; and Debbie Callahan, the medical specialist they'd brought on board to deal with any issues in her realm—to discuss the unprecedented reanimation of the frozen cat. If anyone could figure out what the hell was going on, it was this group of people.

Debbie spoke up first. "I performed a brief physical inspection of the cat and the bodies that you brought up from the surface. I can categorically state that the cat is not a biological entity. The bodies are."

Ray Proudfoot scratched his head and leaned back in his chair. "Not a biological entity. It's some type of mechanical device. That's a hell of a thing. It looks *exactly* like a cat."

The physician nodded. "She acts like one, too. Without putting her into a scanning device, I'd never have been able to know that I wasn't dealing with a real cat. She's an amazing replica. Each and every detail is perfectly correct."

Michael Crockett shook his head. "That's crazy. Why would anyone build a mechanical cat?"

"To avoid cleaning the litter box?" his wife, Sierra, asked with a smirk. "And maybe control shedding. Trust me, nothing tastes better with cat hair as an ingredient."

The grumpy scientist laughed in spite of himself. "Those are good points. You could also program them to stop knocking every single thing you own to the floor."

Emily Adams, the third member of their poly relationship on this mission, sighed at her partners. "Context. You have to look at the context. That planet down there—that frozen, impossible Earth—is one big wall-to-wall city. I'd imagine they had enough trouble growing food for themselves, much less supporting the kind of ecosystem that we take for granted. Perhaps cats and dogs are extinct there.

"Hell, we've got enough trouble on Earth with species dropping dead. I can only imagine what it would be like in a few hundred years with the continuing population curves we're seeing now."

Jess shrugged. "That makes as much sense as anything else I can come up with. I suppose we'll have to continue our examination to be sure."

She turned in her seat to face Doctor Callahan. "If this is some type of cybernetic cat, one might assume that it has capabilities that a regular cat would not. Without disassembling it—which I am not willing to authorize—how can we know what we're dealing with?"

The woman shrugged. "Based on everything I've seen, it seems designed to behave like a cat. If it has capabilities in excess of that, it's not showing them. There's no indication that it understands anything I'm saying to it."

"It might have a command word or phrase that puts it into a different state," Ray said. "It's probably designed to be a cat unless someone intentionally places it into a different operational mode. Good luck figuring out what that is without taking it apart."

Jess scowled at him. "I'm not going to hurt that cat to satisfy your curiosity."

The engineer held up his hands in surrender. "The pedant in me wants to insist that it isn't a cat, but I know that's a losing argument. I'm simply stating a fact. Perhaps we can find out where it was made or locate one that's in a nonoperational state as we continue searching the planet."

She rubbed her face. "Talk about looking for a needle in a haystack. Searching that planet is going to be a huge pain in the butt. It's, well, Earth-sized. Obviously. Because of the temperature and vacuum conditions, I can't think of a more hostile environment."

Paulette Young leaned forward. "Rachel and I have been doing some calculations. Based on the size of the connected urban centers, which as you said take up the entire available landmass, that planet could have supported more than one hundred billion people. Perhaps many more."

Rachel Powell nodded at her partner. "With the landmasses fully occupied, all food had to have come from the only available location: the ocean. I'm certain we'll find that they had some scheme for raising and harvesting vast amounts of fish protein—"

A knock on the door interrupted the woman. John McCarthy stuck his head in. "One of the observation teams found something: a massive excavation site in what would be central China on our version of Earth.

"Based on the images I've seen, it looks as if someone was checking out what was down there on a grand scale. And by grand, I mean bigger than Manhattan. It seems they leveled a bunch of buildings and created an open space. The structures that they've raised in the center have the look and feel of Asharim technology."

Jess stood. "As interesting as the cat is, we need to focus on the Asharim presence. Emily, have you found someone we can hire to help you crack into the computers on the station and extract the destination code the ship used?"

"I have," the young woman said. "His name is Kevin McHugh. All I need to do now is convince him to help us. He's a pretty big deal in the global hacker community and can do things with computers that you wouldn't believe. That's not going to translate across to Asharim technology easily, but I suspect that he'll adapt a lot faster than many other people would."

"Make him a generous offer," Jess said. "Cash, alien computer technology, dancing girls, whatever it takes. The sky is literally the limit."

"I'll try not to break the bank. Money and Asharim computer technology will do just fine. I'll hold the dancing girls in reserve."

Jess chuckled. "The rest of you, we're mounting up to go down to the new site. Get something to eat, and meet me at the lock in an hour."

7

Nathan raced out to the room he and his men were using as a command post on the alien ship. The surviving members of his team that weren't out guarding the section of the ship they'd claimed were waiting for him. A number of them gasped and raised their weapons when his mother came into the room.

He raised a hand. "No time to explain. She's okay. We've got to go find out what those bastards have done. Focus on that, and I'll explain the rest when we're done."

With a gesture, Nathan sent the majority of them into the corridor before turning toward his mother. "Stay here. If you start wandering around, someone is going to shoot you." He didn't wait for her reply before following his fighters. Honestly, he still wasn't sure how to deal with her, either.

The strange halls of the alien ship still set his teeth on edge. There was something wrong with the geometry. The corridors were too wide and the ceilings too low. They made him feel squashed.

One of his surviving team leaders was waiting for him at a major cross corridor where they'd set up a defensive fire point. The man gestured toward the rear of the ship. "The noise came from back there."

Nathan hadn't heard a noise. He'd only felt the ship make an unusual move. "What kind of noise was it?"

"I'm not sure. Maybe a small explosion, or something big fell over. It happened right at the same time as something shook the ship. I'm wondering if they damaged the engines."

That would be a disaster. While one of the strange transport gates he and his people had used to get here from France was still intact, they couldn't go back to the abandoned base. It had been full of terrorists.

The ship had originally had three of the gates. Nathan had destroyed two of them, and he wasn't sure how to open the third. They'd used a space fighter to open the gate at the base in France.

Since his asshole brother had managed to get his people out through them, he must've discovered a portable means of controlling the gates. Nathan had collected a lot of gadgets but hadn't had time to experiment with anything. He'd mostly been concerned with finding every weapon left behind after the fight.

"It's time to finish this," Nathan said. "Either we take them out, or we die trying."

He didn't really know how large the ship was, but he understood the sections the enemy controlled. There were four corridors connecting Nathan's operational sector with the Islamic bastards. Both sides guarded them.

The two forces had settled into trench warfare like back in WWI. The two groups sat behind fortifications they'd arranged and waited for any attack by the enemy, occasionally pouring forth to try to overrun the other side.

In order to breach those lines, Nathan needed more force than he currently had available. Oh yes, he had enough men. Unfortunately, he didn't have very much ammunition for the alien weapons.

Over the course of the last few attacks, they'd killed a number of the ragheads. The jihadis' guns had been crap, but Nathan's people had enough ammunition to take care of the remaining foes. It was just going to be bloody.

"Send runners to the other checkpoints," Nathan told the man. "I want everyone except a skeleton crew to this location right now."

The man nodded and sent several people to gather the requested forces.

Ten minutes later, Nathan had the strongest force he was going to get. Together, they advanced down the corridor until they were just behind one of his leading fire points.

Rushing into the face of enemy fire would allow the enemy to kill a number of his people, but so long as he survived, Nathan didn't care. They had to breach the enemy line. Once they did that, they could run amok behind the terrorist fighting positions.

Nathan sent one man with a rocket-propelled grenade launcher to edge into the corridor. The man fired the explosive right before someone shot him in the head. When the explosion shook their position, Nathan sent his men charging forward around the corner, firing at anything that moved.

He followed, emptied his flechette weapon into the enemy position, and stepped back out of sight. Attacking a hardened position was ugly, but inside thirty seconds, they were behind the enemy barricade.

Nathan stalked forward and took the situation in with a glance. He'd lost a dozen men. Some were dead. Some were badly injured. None looked like they'd survive more than a few minutes. The enemy had only lost six. It made him angry.

"Get their weapons and ammunition," he said coldly. "We're moving on."

"What about our men?" the team leader asked quietly.

"We don't have the medical care to save any of them." Technically, he wasn't sure that was true, but he couldn't afford to divert precious resources at a time like this. As Napoleon Bonaparte had said, making omelets meant breaking eggs. Or something like that.

If they continued pushing in the direction they were going, Nathan suspected the enemy would come to them. He was not disappointed.

Filthy men screaming in Arabic came running from several cross corridors, firing wildly as they ran. Their bullets mostly missed, but with no cover or concealment, that wasn't always the case.

His trained people returned fire, killing many of the enemy fighters with their skill. This was going to be a war of attrition. Nathan just hoped they had enough bodies to make this work.

By the time they'd dealt with all the screaming jihadis, he had less than a dozen men still with him. He hadn't seen the enemy's cultured leader, the one who'd cut his mother's toe off, so he knew they still had at least one heavy fight still in front of them.

Nathan had spent enough time on regular ships to recognize that they were moving into the engineering section. The aliens hadn't designed this part of the ship for normal crew or passengers. The amount of equipment was increasing the farther aft they moved.

He hoped no one shot anything critical. If they disabled anything critical, there was nothing he could do to fix it.

One of his men came back from a scouting trip. His left arm was bloody, but the man still seemed combat effective.

"There's another barricade in the room ahead," he growled. "I couldn't see how many people were behind it, but it's going to be ugly. They've got a great field of fire."

One of the men had captured a rocket-propelled grenade launcher. He held up two fingers when Nathan raised his chin.

"Lead with the grenades, and take them down."

The man frowned. "Are you sure we're ready for this, boss?"

"Do we have a choice? If we retreat now, they're going to come after us. We have to end this while we have them off-balance."

The other man sighed and headed toward the forward position without another word.

The assault on the position kicked off with an explosion. Then there was a second one, much closer to Nathan than he liked. It seemed they had a grenade launcher of their own.

To their credit, his men didn't flinch from running into the hail of bullets and explosives. Nathan followed and picked up the grenade launcher from where his man had dropped it when he'd died. It took a moment to fit the final grenade into place, but his people kept the enemy pinned down long enough for him to fire it at the defenders.

Ironically, he hadn't needed to waste the ammunition. The enemy fighter with a grenade launcher raised himself from cover. One of the many bullets flying around struck him in the face, sending him staggering backward. He must've pulled the trigger because the grenade fired straight up.

Normally, a rocket-propelled grenade had to travel a predetermined distance before it armed, but they must've done something to their ammunition. It exploded the moment it struck the ceiling, delivering its lethal payload to each of the defending terrorists.

Nathan and his men advanced and shot anyone that still twitched. He was down to five people, counting himself.

He raised his radio to his lips. "I want every man to move forward and join me. Every single man."

Ten minutes later, his force was back up to just over a dozen men. If this wasn't enough to end the fight in his favor, he was going to die.

They probed ahead and found a large compartment ahead of them. More defenders were waiting there.

"One final chance to surrender," Nathan called out in French. Not that he intended to allow any of the enemy to live.

The cultured tones of the enemy leader came back. "We only surrender ourselves to Allah. Come and take us if you can." He punctuated his demand with a rain of bullets.

"Charge," Nathan said. "Kill everyone."

The final assault was brutal. Even though Nathan held himself to the last position, he found himself flat behind the body of one of his people and shooting at the defenders. It wasn't that he was a coward, but he preferred not to risk his own life. It was the only one he had.

With a wail in Arabic, the enemy rushed from behind their position. His people gave a good account of themselves but were overwhelmed.

Nathan emptied his rifle into the enemy, drew his pistol, and shot several more before finally finding himself with only a knife as a weapon.

In the smoke and confusion, he wasn't sure how many of the enemy remained standing. At least two, since both of them charged him. They must've been out of bullets as well, because they had curved daggers that cut toward his face and body.

A trained knife fighter, Nathan knew the odds of him coming out of this conflict with his blood still inside his body were slim. He dodged to the right, placing one of the attackers between him and the other. The man stabbed at Nathan's face before slashing down.

Nathan resisted the urge to retreat and pushed forward, accepting an intensely painful gash to his arm. The end result was worth it. He jammed his knife into the other man's throat and pulled it brutally out the side. Then he kicked the dying man into his friend, sending both of them tumbling to the deck.

While the second man was attempting to extract himself, Nathan drove his knife through the man's eye and into his brain.

A slow clap accompanied him rising to his feet and looking for new enemies. The only one he could see standing was the enemy leader. He was just walking from behind the improvised barricade. Not the kind to risk his skin, then.

"Most impressive," the other man said. "Though you are an infidel, you are not a coward. I salute you."

Nathan eyed the other man. He held a pistol, but it pointed toward the deck, and the slide had locked open.

"You're boring me," Nathan said. "Let's end this."

The other man smiled and produced a magazine for his pistol. Now that wasn't very sporting. The distance between them precluded Nathan from reaching the man before he finished reloading. A thrown knife was chancy at best. He needed another option.

One presented itself in the form of a rifle dropped during the earlier fight. Nathan had no idea if it was even loaded at this point. He'd just have to take a chance. He threw the knife at his enemy on the assumption it would force him to dodge and disrupt his reloading.

Taking advantage of that hoped-for lull, Nathan threw himself to the deck, grabbed the rifle, and rolled desperately to the side while bringing it to bear. The sights lined up with his enemy, and he pulled the trigger.

Nothing happened.

That's when Nathan noticed his throw had been better than he'd had any right to expect. The hilt of his knife protruded from the other man's throat.

To his credit, the dying man was slowly raising his now-loaded pistol toward Nathan. But it never rose high enough. With a gurgle, the man fell backward. The pistol discharged into one of the bodies just in front of Nathan.

To be safe, Nathan waited an additional thirty seconds before he rose cautiously to his feet. The bolt on the rifle he'd picked up had locked back, but he found another magazine with ammunition to recharge the weapon.

The enemy leader was still alive when Nathan stepped over to him. Barely. He tried to say something, but his ruined voice box wouldn't cooperate.

Wordlessly, Nathan raised the rifle and fired a single shot into the man's head.

Taking the dead man's pistol, he went from body to body and made sure that all his enemies were similarly dead. Unfortunately, all of his allies seem to have perished as well.

It took him more than an hour to finish searching the area for potential hostiles. None remained. The ship was his—and just about his alone. Only his mother remained.

He took the precaution of collecting enough ammunition to fight if he was wrong, but he didn't think he was. These people had fought to the death. They'd almost been good enough to take him out.

He found no signs of sabotage. What he did find was an observation chamber above the engineering compartment. It wasn't very large, but it had a view of the entire ship forward of engineering. What he saw chilled him.

The ship was now in orbit around a large planet. It was definitely not Earth, and the ship wasn't alone. Scattered across his view were other ships.

Or perhaps it would be more accurate to say parts of ships. While there were some large chunks, the ones he could see didn't seem to be whole. There had been a battle here at some point in the past.

That explained the noise and vibration. A chunk of debris had struck the ship. Obviously not disastrously, but with the amount of potential ruin he could see floating around them, that probably wouldn't last.

The victory he'd sacrificed his men for had been fleeting. This new danger was even more of a threat. He needed to get himself and his mother off this ship before something punctured the hull and left them trying to breathe vacuum.

8
_____

Clayton stared at the woman in the image. She was just another question mark in the middle of the mystery people that were dressed as if they'd come from the Revolutionary War.

Commander Krueger leaned in and gave her a close examination. "Is she a pirate?"

"Whoever she is, she's spotted your drone," Clayton said. "They know we're around here somewhere. How is that going to change what we do next?"

"It doesn't change one damn thing," Ulysses snarled. The CIA agent stalked into the chamber and gave them all a withering stare. "They're primitives. It doesn't matter one damned bit what they think or know."

Clayton shook his head and smiled sadly. "Those who do not learn from history are doomed to repeat it. I'm quite sure the British felt somewhat similarly about the Zulu nation back in the day. That didn't turn out as well as they'd hoped."

Ulysses rounded on Clayton, brandishing his fist in the older man's nose. "You shut your mouth, traitor. I've had more than enough of your crap. You're a prisoner, and you don't get a say in anything."

The other man smiled cruelly. "If I had my way, I'd chain your ass to a rock and keep you there until I got you to Guantánamo. And once I did, I'd break you."

The other man's expression changed to one of panic as Gunnery Sergeant Danvers grabbed him by the back of the neck and yanked him off his feet. The noncommissioned officer shoved the CIA agent against the wall. He grabbed Ulysses's right hand as the man tried to go for a weapon.

"I've had enough of you, cockroach," Danvers growled. "If we're going to chain a prisoner to a rock, it's going to be you."

"Call your dog off, Krueger," Ulysses sneered. "We both know who's going to win this confrontation."

"I'm not sure that we do," the Navy officer said. "Frankly, you come across like a congenital idiot and a man born outside of his time. You seem the type of man who'd be much more comfortable working for the Nazis. Probably torturing people for them."

A wave of shock traveled across the CIA agent's face only to be replaced by rage. "If there's an idiot in this room, it's you. Now call him off, or every single one of you gets a room next to Rogers in Hotel Guantánamo."

"I don't think so. Gunnery Sergeant, I'm placing Agent Ulysses under confinement. I'm afraid the situation is too much for him, and his demonstrated instability has become a threat to our mission. Secure him somewhere, and search him thoroughly for weapons."

"Yes, sir!"

"You sonofabitch!" Ulysses screamed. "I'll see you executed for this!"

Whatever else the man had been about to say was cut off when Danvers drove a fist into his gut. The gunnery sergeant threw the CIA agent flat on the ground and planted a knee in the center of his back while other members of the team helped secure their new prisoner. They then roughly hoisted the CIA agent to his feet and hustled him out of the chamber.

Clayton gave Krueger a curious look. "His superiors are not going to be pleased. Frankly, he's probably right. They'll throw you into a cell right next to mine."

The Navy officer sagged a little. "Maybe, but there's only so long I can tolerate assholes. Frankly, Ulysses is the kind of guy that ends up being shot in the back by friendly fire before he gets a chance to report."

"You'd actually kill him before we go home? That's quite a step, Commander Krueger. I didn't think you had it in you."

The other man sat on a handy rock. "I probably don't. It's just wishful thinking. Frankly, Mister Rogers, I'm not certain what I'm going to do. I'm not certain what I *can* do. The information that you've uncovered—the things we've seen on this mission—was probably already going to get me and my men locked away."

Clayton considered the other man for a moment. "I know you've heard a lot of bad things about me. Many of them are true. I've done awful things in pursuit of money and power to fulfill my goals.

"But you also know my son. He's not the kind to work with me on something that doesn't have the potential to help a great number of people. You've only seen the tip of the iceberg. There are greater threats to humanity than you can imagine and the potential to uplift us all to a new level of free society that hasn't been seen in the United States for decades. Hell, maybe a century.

"You've burned your bridges behind you. Allow me to extend a hand in friendship. Don't trust me. Trust my son."

The officer rubbed his eyes tiredly. "I don't suppose I have much of a choice."

"That's not true. You have a very stark choice. You can continue to support an authoritarian regime that Mussolini would be proud of or you could become part of an organization that is trying to secure freedom for humanity."

Krueger considered him for a moment. "At the moment, it's a moot point. We're trapped on an alien world with people seemingly plucked out of history. Until we find a way home, it doesn't matter what I decide."

Clayton smiled more widely. "That's not true, either. It matters very much. If you join my team, I can fill you in on everything we've discovered. Everything we suspect. Then we can work together to find a solution without worrying that the other is going to betray them."

"How do I know you won't betray me?" Krueger asked. "As you say, you've got quite the reputation."

"A reputation for driving a hard bargain and then abiding by it. I'm confident we can work out the verbiage in a way that satisfies you, but we can come to an agreement in principle right now. My son needs as many other trained military personnel as he can get because the alien threat is much greater than even the United States government currently understands.

"If he's agreeable, you could stand at his right hand. You have all the skills one could hope for and probably many contacts that would prove exceptionally useful. Since you have doubts about me, I'm more than willing to allow him to do the negotiation of the details. I assure you that he will confirm everything I'm telling you now."

Krueger sighed. "It seems that events have overtaken our earlier agreement. I'll pass the word to my people that we're releasing you on your own recognizance. You are no longer our prisoner. But we don't work for you. Not yet. I'll do everything I can to get us home, then we'll see. That's the best I can offer."

Clayton extended his hand. "That's more than good enough for me. Allow me to welcome you provisionally aboard. I suppose our first question is what we'll do about the people in that army out there."

The drone must've been hovering uncontrolled this entire time. The stabilized image of the woman showed that others had joined her. In particular, a distinguished-looking man in uniform. He held the spyglass now and was observing the drone.

"It does appear the cat is out of the bag," Krueger agreed. "We can get the drone away, but they'll be on their guard now. If we wish to avoid meeting them, we can huddle inside the cave, and they might miss us."

"But they might not," Clayton argued. "I think the time for concealment has passed. Besides, if we're ever going to learn the lay of the land and find a way back home, we're going to have to talk with these people. We have to convince them that we're friends, or at least potential allies."

He examined the woman in the image again. She was speaking with the man beside her. He didn't know them, but Clayton was a master of body language. The man might be the military officer, but she was his superior. Perhaps socially. In any case, she was ultimately the one he'd have to convince to help them.

He allowed himself a smile. Well, high-pressure negotiations were his specialty.

* * *

HARRY STARED out of the helicopter as it flew over the wilderness. The New Zealand landscape below was lush and untouched. "It's beautiful."

The pilot—an officer in New Zealand's air force—nodded his agreement. "Sure is. Hell to walk through, though. I feel sorry for the poor buggers wandering around down there."

"Any word on the search?"

"Some. We sent a ship out and confronted the US destroyer yesterday. They refused to let us board, so we forced them to turn back with our jets and ships. Since they weren't in our waters, this has turned into a real international incident."

Harry shook his head. "Sorry about that."

"Not your problem. Hell, it's not even your boss's concern. He came here with diplomatic immunity. America had no right to send soldiers onto our soil, much less kidnap two of our citizens and someone under our protection."

The man sounded grim. If his attitude was widespread—which Harry suspected it was—that boded ill for the US's influence in the area for a long time to come.

"They didn't turn up on the ship once we impounded it, either," the pilot continued. "No one is talking, but based on personal belongings, at least a dozen of their people are unaccounted for. That probably means they're still around here somewhere. We'll find them."

Harry suspected they wouldn't find anyone at this point. The only reason he could think of that the military people hadn't made it back to their ship was that his father had led them into the base. They were either still down there now, or they'd escaped to another world.

Yet one more headache for him to deal with.

"You've confirmed it was an American drone?"

That bit of information had been waiting for him when he'd landed. The US forces had left quite the calling card.

"Oh yeah. A number of our boys have worked with American forces before. One of them recognized the drone as a kind favored by the CIA. No weapons but great cameras. Somebody shot out the engine and it crashed. The electronics were booby-trapped, too. It was American."

"I'm sure that's going to prove awkward when you trot it out as evidence at some future point."

"I hope so," the pilot said. "I bet they cart it to the UN and make a huge stink over it. Not that the UN is good for much except generating hot air.

"We're almost to the landing zone. The search parties are centered on the area where Mister Rogers was camping. Once I drop you off, I'll join the search."

Harry nodded his thanks, even if it wasn't a prospect that filled him with joy. The man might've shown himself to be a human being, but Harry had a lifetime of dislike to overcome. Frankly, he doubted he'd ever change his opinion of his father.

That didn't mean he couldn't work with the man. So long as their goals aligned.

The landscape around where his father had set up camp was gorgeous. It seemed to be untouched by human hands before their helicopter had touched down. He could imagine living out here himself.

The headquarters for the search area consisted of several tents set up near a large flat stone suitable for landing a helicopter on. Just adjacent to that was a larger mesa that Harry immediately suspected housed the New Zealand base.

Not that he was likely to confirm that anytime soon. Several men and a tall woman stood waiting for the helicopter to idle. No doubt these were the people coordinating the search. They'd occupy his time to a much greater degree than he'd like for the foreseeable future.

At some point, though, he'd be able to slip away and examine the mesa for concealed entrances. He just had to bide his time.

Once the rotor blades had slowed, Harry shook the pilot's hand, set his headset down on the seat, and made his way out to meet the New Zealanders.

As he'd expected, the woman stepped forward. "Mister Jacobs? My name is Molly Goodwin. I'm sorry to meet you under these circumstances. We're doing everything we can to find your employer."

He hoped the false name and cover story held long enough for him to find his father. Harry shook her hand firmly. "I'm sure you are. Do you have any idea which direction they went? Were they injured?"

"I'm afraid not. They sent the rest of their party off while they created a distraction. They climbed up on that mesa over there and rappelled down the far side."

Harry looked at the mesa. "If you don't mind, I'd like to take a look up there. Alone."

She gave him an odd look before shaking her head. "That's not going to be possible. They used a large stone to take out the easiest way up."

He smiled. "I served in special operations for quite some time. I have a lot of experience climbing places you wouldn't think people could get to. I assume you've already got a rope hanging down to assist people in getting to the top?"

"We do, but it's not the safest option."

"The important things in life rarely are. I understand that sounds strange, but I need to see this for myself."

She looked unconvinced. "I'll see what we can do."

He didn't feel bad about manipulating her. If that was the last place anyone had seen his father, the odds of the entrance being up top were exceptionally good.

Not that he'd have an opportunity to explore the base right now. The very last thing he wanted to do was tip the New Zealanders off that they had an ancient installation in their backyard. If that happened, they'd seize it.

He'd locate the entrance and perhaps scout it out. Then he'd come back once everyone was asleep and check it out in more detail.

Harry hoped whatever problems his father had embroiled himself in weren't time sensitive. Otherwise, the old man would have to get himself out of them all by himself.

On second thought, he hoped the man wasn't all that safe. The bastard deserved some grief for all the hell he'd caused Harry over the years. Karma was a bitch. He'd settle for pulling the old man's ass out of the fire at the last minute.

9

J ess had to travel to the French base in order to contact Brenda
Cabot. She really needed to figure out a better way to
communicate with people on Earth.

By the time she arrived, it was dark in the United States.
Though it might be rude, she didn't have time to waste. She dialed the
burner number that Cabot had given them using a burner of
her own.

That number had changed after Harry's people had called to
verify the intruders at the base were associated with Brenda. That
made sense to her. With the global communications intercept
capability of the NSA, they would quickly tag any call in the world
that seemed suspicious. And international calls to US citizens *always*
made the US government suspicious.

The phone rang twice before Cabot answered. The woman
sounded a bit groggy. "Do you know what time it is?"

Jess considered her watch. It was still on GMT. She did a rough
calculation in her head. "Late?"

"Early," Brenda said firmly. "Is there a fire? There better be some
kind of fire."

"We need to talk face-to-face as soon as possible."

There was a moment of silence. "Give me a half hour to get set up."

"Thank you."

Jess ended the call, removed the SIM card from the phone, and crushed it under her heel. She handed the now-useless burner to Rex. The scout took it and dropped it into one of his many pockets.

In exchange, he pulled out a different phone and handed it to her. Then, to her confusion, he pulled out a third phone and handed it to her.

She glanced at them before giving him a quizzical look. "Is this some kind of social commentary about me talking on the phone too much? Seriously, I'm not a chatterbox."

He laughed. "Not at all. You're holding a piece of brand-new technology, one that can make your life a lot easier. Those are quantum phones. Apparently, Clayton Rogers had perfected the technology and then kept it secret so that the US government wouldn't get it."

Jess examined one of the phones more closely. It was a bit bulkier than her usual one, but not by much. Honestly, some of the carriers had gone ridiculously slim. At least these had enough bulk for her to hold them comfortably. She touched the screen and found that it looked very much like the phone she'd just used. "It seems pretty normal to me."

The man nodded. "And it behaves fairly normally as well. It can connect to any of the regular cellular networks. One positive is that it utilizes software embedded inside the network to generate a false identity for the phone. You don't have to pull out a SIM card once you use it.

"Every call appears to come from a different phone—one already located in the general area that you're in. Apparently it's some kind of backdoor that Clayton Rogers installed before he sold that company to the Chinese."

She had to admit that sounded useful. "Why do I have two?"

"Because it also has a quantum mode. You don't have to use any existing cellular network. You can call other quantum phones directly. I haven't tested the range, but the geek that delivered these said I should be able to call Harry directly without any issues. I figured you'd want one to give to Cabot so you could have secure communications."

"That does sound like a good idea. The last thing we want to do is bring the US government down on her people. They have the only operational gate inside the United States. Did you get one sent to Harry?"

Rex smiled wryly. "They arrived about an hour after he'd left. I paid an exorbitant amount of money to send someone after him. It'll be dark there before my guy lands, but he should be able to get a phone into Harry's hands early tomorrow morning."

"How can it call from here to New Zealand without using a cellular network?"

The ex-military man shrugged. "Damned if I know. I've never even used it."

As an engineer specializing in space projects, Jess knew a lot about science. That didn't mean she understood quantum mechanics. Frankly, she was halfway convinced the scientists that claimed they did were just making things up.

Still, the universe had proven itself stranger than she'd anticipated. She'd do more research and then some real-world testing before she formed an impression.

"Once I'm done meeting with Cabot, I'll get her to send me directly back to *Freedom Express*," she said. "If you've got one of these close at hand, let's get the number in my contact list now."

"Already done. The units are meant for Harry and Cabot, too. As far as I know, that's all there are. These are prototypes. The guy that dropped them off said it would probably be another six months before there is any kind of real production, but who knows what that means?"

"I'll need his contact information, too."

"Will do."

Jess waited until the designated time and went down to the gate. She grabbed the cat carrier that she'd left down near the gate when she'd gone upstairs. The artificial black cat stared patiently at her through the grate.

That made her feel guilty. She knew intellectually that sitting down here for half an hour hadn't hurt the mechanical device, but she should've left it somewhere more comfortable. Somewhere with food, water, and a litterbox.

Once she'd established the connection to Cabot's gate, her end filled with mist and lightning. She waited for it to clear and then walked through.

Cabot and two of her associates were waiting on the other side. Jess wasn't familiar with either of the men.

The other woman raised an eyebrow at the carrier. "Stopping by the vet after your visit?"

Jess smiled. "Something like that. I wanted to know if you have any kind of advanced scanning technology to look at the cat."

The other woman's expression became confused. "I'm not sure I understand."

"Then allow me to explain. You're going to find this fascinating."

* * *

BRENDA STARED at Jessica Cook in shock. She knew her mouth was hanging open but couldn't help herself. "Is this some kind of joke?" she asked. "An artificial cat? Why in the world would the Asharim build an artificial cat?"

"They didn't. It appears that the Asharim were investigating something amazing in the outer system, way out past the orbit of Pluto. They have a station there in orbit around a dead, frozen planet. The cat came from there."

Brenda stared into the cat carrier. The small black cat looked completely normal. Nothing struck her as off.

"Are you sure it's artificial?"

Cook nodded, her expression dark. "It was lying in the lap of a frozen body. Someone who had probably been dead for more than a thousand years. That's the minimum. We found definite signs that the Asharim were exploring the world. The cat was there when the world died, however long ago that was."

"May I? Is it safe?"

The other woman gestured toward the carrier. "It seems friendly enough."

Brenda figured out how to open the carrier and held a hand in. The small black creature delicately sniffed her fingers and then brushed her cheek against them. Brenda could hear a soft purr coming from inside the carrier.

This was unreal.

When she encountered no resistance, Brenda pulled the cat out of the carrier and set it on the table in front of her. It stood under her hand as she petted it, its tail flirting.

"This has got to be some kind of joke. I've never heard of anything like this. Even the Asharim couldn't have built such a perfect replica. You say you found a dead planet. Why would the inhabitants build a replica cat?"

The other woman extended a tablet toward her. "I think I'd best let the pictures explain for themselves. These were taken from the camera on my vacuum suit."

Brenda took the tablet and brought it to life. The first picture was already queued up. It was the exterior of some kind of building with lots of snow piled around it. She felt her hackles rise as she flipped through the images. The sight of the frozen bodies made her heart lurch. Especially the family on the couch. The little girl with the small black cat in her lap.

Her eyes shot up to meet Cook's.

"Humans?"

"Our doctor confirmed it. These people were completely human. What's more, they didn't come from anyone taken by the Asharim." The woman pulled an ID card from her pocket and slid it across the table.

Brenda saw that it was a Virginia driver's license. Then she started noticing the oddities. The birthdate was August 4, 2223.

"That's bullshit!" she said.

"I have proof, if you have some kind of scanning device."

"We have some scanning technology," Brenda admitted. "It's designed for human medical issues. I have absolutely no idea what it would return from a mechanical device. Or a real cat."

Cook smiled. "I suppose we'll find out." She took the unresisting cat and put it back into the carrier.

Brenda looked at one of her men. "Get Granger down to the medical center."

He headed out at a trot.

She led Jessica Cook down to the area they were using as a medical center in their new headquarters building. Five minutes later, Doctor Todd Granger walked briskly into the room.

He smiled at Cook. "Jessica! It's a pleasure to see you again though, I must confess, I didn't expect you to come visit me. You're not hurt, are you?"

His asian looks and deep southern accent made her smile at the discontinuity. Granger had been with Brenda when she'd led a group to meet Harry Rogers and Jessica Cook for the first time. He'd been escorting their prisoner at the time, Secretary of State Josh Queen.

The doctor had a way with people. He got along with everyone. It was all part of his bedside manner and general personality.

Cook smiled more widely as she shook Granger's hand. "It's good to see you again, Todd. Though I still can't get over your accent. It throws me for a loop every time."

That made Brenda laugh. "I've known him since we were kids. It still messes me up. How can somebody that looks like he just stepped off a flight from Japan sound like he came from Appalachia?"

"It's a gift," Granger said with a grin. "What can I do for you ladies?"

Cook hefted the cat carrier. "Agent Cabot says that you have a scanning device that might be able to take a good look at my cat."

Granger raised an eyebrow. "That may be one of the most unusual requests I've had in recent memory. Though I suppose there's some sense to it. You are one of the most wanted women in the world, after all. I'll wager dropping in on your vet might be a poor idea.

"I'm a human doctor, not a veterinarian, though. Perhaps if you tell me what the problem is, I might be able to work something out, but I wouldn't hold my breath." The man bent over and peered into the carrier. "The little thing looks healthy enough. She's a cutie by the way. At least I assume she's female from the size."

Cook set the cat carrier onto the examination table. "I'd rather not lead you down any specific trail of thought. Could you just give her a general examination and tell us what you think?"

Brenda nodded when he glanced at her. "It's actually more important than you think. Be thorough."

"Okay. She doesn't bite or scratch, does she?"

Cook shook her head. "She's one of the friendliest cats I've ever met."

Granger shrugged, took the cat out of the carrier, and began examining it. After a few minutes, he carried it to a hooded machine with a gurney that slid inside it.

"This might look like an MRI machine, but it's capable of several different modes of scanning. As I told you before, I don't know that much about cats, so I don't know if I'll be able to determine anything. Also, if she doesn't stay still, the scan will be useless."

Cook stepped up beside the gurney and squatted so that her face was just a few inches in front of the cat's. "Sit still for a minute."

To Brenda's amazement, the cat promptly sat down and curled her tail around her legs.

"It's almost as if she understood you," Granger said with a smile. "Let's see if we can take advantage of this miracle." He gently pushed the gurney under the scanning hood and stepped back to the controls. A few deft motions and a low hum emanated from the machine.

"All done. Go ahead and get her out, and we'll take a look at what the scan recorded."

To all appearances, the cat was sitting in exactly the same position it had been when they rolled the gurney into the machine. Cook picked the cat up and held her to her chest, petting her. That seemed to be precisely what the creature wanted because it snuggled against her and began purring loudly.

Granger brought up an image on the built-in screen and stared at it. "What the hell?"

To Brenda's inexperienced eye, that didn't look like a cat. She wasn't sure what it was. "What are you seeing?"

The doctor turned and squinted toward Cook. "That cat doesn't have any internal organs. Hell, it doesn't even look biological. What is going on?"

"That's what I was hoping you folks could help us figure out." Cook turned her attention to Brenda. "Is that enough evidence for you to accept what I'm telling you?"

"Provisionally," Brenda said. "I want to see this place with my own eyes. What does this have to do with the Asharim? Hell, if this planet was there before they even visited us, what has it got to do with humanity?"

"I haven't got the slightest idea. We're going to contact someone someone that might help us get into the computer systems on that station. Not only would it be useful to find their research notes, I'd like to unlock the destination that Harry's relatives used to escape in that ship. The longer they're on the loose, the greater the chances that someone we can't deal with is going to come visit us."

"I've already taken some steps in that direction," Brenda said. "I'll have a guy here in the morning who might be able to help you crack those computers. Not only is he one hell of a hacker, he's made a specialty of porting that skill over to Asharim technology. His name's Kevin McHugh."

Jess laughed. "How weird is that? He's the guy Emily Adams wanted me to contact. That's excellent new. In exchange for your help, I'm willing to share everything we find there with you and your people. That world looks like one huge city. A megalopolis spread across every single bit of land.

"We haven't even begun to scratch the surface of their technology. Everything is in a vacuum and frozen. It's going to be in amazing condition, I think. I don't know if they were more advanced than the Asharim, but just based on this cat, I would suspect that they had some areas they were ahead in."

Brenda considered the cat. "It's really damned hard to argue with that. I can already see one aspect of technology that these people had the Asharim beat in. You say this critter was frozen for over a thousand years but came back to life as soon as you thawed it. Smaller Asharim power supplies would've failed long ago."

Cook's eyes narrowed. "I hadn't thought of that. Good point. Oh, and I have another present for you." The woman dug a phone out of her pocket and handed it to Brenda.

"I've got plenty of burner phones," Brenda assured the woman.

"Not like this one. You don't have to destroy this one when you're done. It's linked into the carrier networks with an artificial SIM card. Software in the carrier will give it a different identification every time it's used. Basically, it clones a nearby phone and pretends to be it.

"But that's not the biggest thing. It also incorporates quantum technology. Something that Clayton Rogers had been working on. There are only four of these phones in existence, but when communicating between these units, the transmissions are undetectable. No way that anyone can intercept what we're saying."

"Seriously?"

"That's what I'm told. The range is also much greater. It won't use any of the equipment here on Earth or in orbit, but it should be able to call someone on the other side of the globe. I have one unit, Harry will have one in a few hours, Rex has one, and your group will have the last. The numbers are in the contact list."

Luckily, Brenda had someone who understood quantum mechanics very well. Victor Holyfield had been a doctoral candidate in particle physics. He'd be able to use words small enough to explain what this meant to her.

Even so, she already grasped the implications. They'd built a level of trust with Cook and Rogers that might allow them to become real allies. That was a hell of a lot more valuable than any toy.

She glanced at her watch. "We've got a couple of hours until your hacker arrives. Why don't we have breakfast and go over what you found in more detail? Then we can work on how my organization can do the most to help you leverage what you've found."

Cook smiled at her. "That would be perfect. Please tell me you have blueberries."

"I'm sure we can find some. Thanks for your help, Todd."

"My pleasure. If you ladies don't mind, I'm going back to bed. Somehow, I suspect tomorrow is going to be a busy day."

10

I t took Clayton twenty minutes to convince Krueger that they
had to meet with the woman and her army. He understood why
the man was reticent. Once they revealed themselves, there was
no going back.

Yet they didn't have much of a choice. Now that these people
knew someone was around, they would look hard to find them. The
simple fact that the drone hadn't completely discombobulated the
viewers indicated they'd seen its like before. Unless the Americans
wanted to be thought of as hostile, they had to create a different
impression and soon.

Even though Krueger eventually conceded the point, he'd insisted
the contact happen in stages. He'd sent scouts to keep an eye on the
army while they put together a group to meet with them.

"Honestly, I think we should send as small a party as possible,"
Clayton said. "If things go wrong, I'd prefer to leave some options on
the table. I think I should meet them alone."

The Navy commander raised an eyebrow. "That's risky as hell.
Why would you volunteer to do something like that?"

Clayton shrugged. "Do you happen to have a better negotiator in
your back pocket? While I've never dealt with this particular situation

before, I don't believe they'll see me as a threat, so they'll allow me to approach. A larger group might come under fire."

"I can see the logic in that," Krueger conceded, "but why not take one or two other people? Having a few extra bodies isn't going to raise the threat level that much. They have an army."

"If I'm going to put myself in danger, why put other people in the pot with me? If these people aren't willing to discuss things in good faith, that seems like the safest move."

The officer shook his head. "And a dangerous one to our eventual chances of getting home. You have a lot more knowledge about this alien technology than anyone else in our group does. I understand that even your insight is limited, but ours is nonexistent. We didn't even know these gates existed until after we'd walked through one. What else don't we know?"

Clayton nodded. "That's a point. Still, my computer has every bit of information I have. If things go sour, you'll be able to study the files. As long as the battery holds out, anyway.

"In any case, time is wasting. We need to send someone before they conclude the drone is hostile. Frankly, they've probably already assumed that. It's going to be difficult for me to convince them that we're harmless. Spending extra time talking with you isn't going to help me do that."

The Navy man sighed. "I'll have someone escort you down the hill. The trail is rough, and no one seems to have used it in a long time. It's not like the one their party took to the crown of the hill. That one has seen occasional traffic.

"Our scouts have been down this one several times, and we've blazed a trail that won't be obvious to any observers. We'll also send a small group with you to provide cover in case you need to retreat."

Clayton cocked his head a little. "You mean like snipers?"

"That's exactly what I mean. I'll give them orders not to interfere unless they believe your life is in danger. If you want to risk capture, I can't stop you. Well, I suppose I could, but I sort of agree with everything you've said thus far.

"Nevertheless, if it looks as if somebody is going to shoot you, one of my people will put a bullet in their head. I hope that my men will be able to give you enough covering fire to retreat if that happens. We'll turn this hill into a fortress if we have to."

Clayton stood and brushed his pants off. "It's my job to make certain we don't have to. Under the right circumstances, you can make a deal with anyone. You just have to understand what they need and come up with a way to provide that in exchange for something you want.

"They have detailed knowledge of this world that we don't. If there's something our technology can allow us to do for them, it may very well be that we can come to a straightforward solution to our problem."

The officer didn't seem convinced. "They're obviously outfitted for war. I'm not sure that anything we can provide will make much of a difference. Yes, our technology is of a higher caliber than anything we've seen them use, but there aren't that many of us, and we didn't bring a lot of ammunition. I was only supposed to make a brief foray into New Zealand and take you into custody, not fight a war."

Clayton smiled. "As you well know, fighting isn't the only thing that can be brought to the table in a combat situation. Gather your men, and let's get this going."

Krueger rose to his feet and summoned several of his men. He gave them instructions in a low voice then came back over to shake Clayton's hand. "Good luck and be careful."

Gunnery Sergeant Danvers led the small group of men that escorted Clayton to the bottom of the hill. Frankly, Clayton was glad he had the man. He didn't see the trail at all. It just looked like rough hillside to him.

Thankfully, they managed to get him to the bottom of the steep slope without him breaking his neck. Once he was on relatively level ground, Clayton felt a little bit more confident about his ability to move around.

"The army's that way," Danvers said, gesturing toward the forest in front of them. "I've got two guys out front keeping an eye on the area between here and there. As of five minutes ago, the path forward was still clear. We'll accompany you until we get to the edge of the clearing on the far side."

"Thank you, Gunnery Sergeant. I hope I won't require your services to extract me."

The man gave him a humorless smile. "Me, too."

The journey through the rough woods wasn't nearly as difficult as climbing down the hillside, but it still took longer than Clayton would've liked. He was grateful that he'd been dressed for the wilds of New Zealand when he'd come through the gate. The vegetation would've torn his regular business suit and loafers to shreds in minutes.

By the time they arrived at the edge of the clearing where the army had bivouacked, almost an hour had passed since the strangers had spotted the American drone. Just looking at them, Clayton couldn't see any indication that they were overly concerned about coming under immediate attack. Still, he wasn't a soldier. He didn't pretend to know what that type of reaction would look like.

"Be careful, sir," Danvers said. "If we have to start shooting, there's no walking that back."

He clapped the other man on the shoulder. "Then let's not be hasty. I'd prefer it if you only took action under the direst of circumstances."

"Yes, sir."

Clayton sighed, stretched his back, and stepped out into the clearing. No one noticed him immediately, so he continued walking slowly forward.

He'd made it about a third of the way to the nearest tent when some of the soldiers noted his approach. He kept his pace easy and his hands in plain sight. Hopefully, the fact that he wasn't carrying a weapon would preclude them taking any precipitous actions.

Half a dozen men came from the camp with their weapons at the ready. Clayton was no firearms expert, but it certainly looked as though these were relics from the Revolutionary War or based upon them.

When they shouted at him to stop, he did so. He was grateful that he could understand them. That had been one of his worries. If they'd spoken a different language, negotiation would've been almost impossible.

He kept his hands out to the sides at waist height, palms toward them. "I'm unarmed," he said. "I mean you no harm."

One of the men came forward after handing his rifle to one of the others and roughly searched Clayton. Undoubtedly, he was looking for weapons. Clayton's modern clothing seemed to confuse the man. Understandable.

Once the man seemed satisfied that Clayton was unarmed, he grabbed him by the arm and dragged him forward without a word. The other men formed up around them, making certain that Clayton had no avenue of escape.

The people in the camp stared at them curiously as they made their way toward the central tent. The looks weren't overtly hostile, but they weren't friendly, either.

When the group arrived at the large tent, the same group of individuals he'd observed watching the drone came out to meet him.

It would be interesting to see if the woman took a direct role in questioning him or allowed the senior military commander to do so. If these people were indeed from revolutionary times, it was entirely possible that the woman's role was constrained in some manner.

She corrected that notion immediately. "Who are you, and what do you want?"

Her English was excellent, though her accent was quite distinctive. At first blush, he was tempted to say it was Jamaican, but that didn't sound quite right, either. It was definitely something from the Caribbean. Interesting.

"My name is Clayton Rogers, and I represent the people who control the device you were observing an hour ago. We would like to talk. We mean you no harm."

The woman snorted. "Well, of course you don't. Why would you? And what is that accent? I can't quite place it."

He blinked in surprise. This was a turn of conversation he hadn't expected. He wasn't quite sure how to respond. How could a group of armed people not regard a stranger as a potential threat?

She must've found something in his expression amusing because she laughed. "You're an odd bird. Wherever you come from, you must know the fact you are a human makes you our ally. Unless, of course, you're telling me that you're a traitor."

"I'm not, but my story is somewhat more complicated than you might expect. If you don't see me as a threat, perhaps we could speak more privately."

The woman considered him for a moment then gestured for his guards to take him into the tent.

Large tapestries covered the sides of the tent, thick carpets covered the ground, and ornate wooden furniture filled much of the interior. It all looked quite opulent.

The woman sat in a padded chair with armrests. Two of the men brought out a stool at her gesture and forced him to sit. The other men that looked like military officers arrayed themselves against the side of the tent. The woman was *definitely* in command.

She lounged in her chair and considered him at length.

"I cannot say that your clothing strikes me as familiar. To my mind, that means you must come from afar. Perhaps from one of the other colonies?"

Clayton smiled a little. "I'm not familiar with the colonies to which you refer. Are you perhaps acquainted with the gates between worlds?"

"Of course. Hence the colonies to which I refer."

That was interesting information. They had operational gates. Somewhere.

"My companions and I traveled through one quite recently. We're not familiar with your world."

She frowned. "I find that most difficult to believe. Unless, of course, you claim that you have traveled through a gate under the control of our enemy."

Clayton shrugged. "I'm not even certain who your enemy is. This entire world and its peoples are new to me."

"All this dancing around the subject bores me. I refer to the Asharim, as you undoubtedly know."

That made him blink in surprise. From what he knew of the aliens, they were used to gravity significantly lighter than held sway on this world. They'd fallen a great deal if these primitive people were able to fight them.

He leaned forward on the stool. "Perhaps I might be permitted to question. From your accent, I would guess that your people originate from somewhere in the Caribbean. Would that be true?"

Her eyes narrowed. "That is a name I haven't heard in many long years. I find myself wondering how someone unfamiliar with my people would even know it."

"That's simple enough. I've been to many of the islands there."

The woman smiled widely. "Finally, you interest me."

11

———————

Chen had been expecting Secretary of State Queen's summons, so he allowed only mild interest to show on his face as the man's guards escorted him into the American's office.

"You wish to see me, Mister Secretary?"

"You're damn right I do! What the hell do you people think you're doing?"

Chen smiled blandly. "I presume you are referring to our repossessing our property on the Yucatán Peninsula. The spaceport, to be specific. Our government has nullified the sales to Kathleen Bennett. That being the case, you had no right to seize our property, and we won't allow that situation to stand."

Queen surged to his feet. "This is an act of war."

"Your *original* seizure of our property was illegal. Our retaking it is merely seeing justice done."

The other man stared at him for a moment before he apparently mastered the anger inside him. "On behalf of my government, I give you one day to withdraw your forces from the spaceport and release our people."

Chen spread his hands slightly. "I do not need such time. We refuse to relinquish our property. We will release your personnel, however. In fact, that task is already under way as we speak.

"Now it falls to you to decide how our countries proceed. Will you initiate a war to seize property in our possession? Do you believe you can win that fight? We are both aware the United States military is not what it once was. China is ascendant. You would do well to consider your next words *very* carefully."

Queen took a deep breath and let it out slowly. "If you think for one second that we'll allow this situation to stand, you're wrong. Others have misjudged how strong American will is to their sorrow. We bow to no one. That is something *you* should consider carefully.

"Send this message to your masters. We will forcibly eject whatever Chinese forces are still present inside the Yucatán Spaceport in twenty-four hours. If they resist, our soldiers will use whatever force is required to dislodge them. Any deaths will be on your hands."

Chen bowed slightly. "I will pass your message along to Beijing, however, they have already authorized me to speak to this eventuality.

"If your forces attack the Yucatán Spaceport, we will view that as an act of war and will strike at you wherever we choose across the globe. Our navy is better positioned than yours to attack any number of targets. Our ground forces outnumber yours ten to one, and they are better outfitted. Take this moment to save face, or feel our wrath."

Without waiting for a response, Chen turned and walked out of the room. His guards flanked him to the embassy car, and he was on his way back to the embassy a few minutes later.

That had proceeded just about as poorly as he'd expected. Good. He honestly wasn't sure what the United States would do in the face of his country's provocation, but it hardly mattered. Everything he'd said was true. The United States could ill afford a direct confrontation with China. It was a fight they'd lose.

More importantly, it was a fight that would distract them from the critical tasks they had before them. They could hardly exploit the technology that had come into their possession if they were busy fighting a war for survival. That gave the Dragon an opportunity to act if they played their cards correctly.

The expected courier had arrived to collect the information Chen had gathered and to give him specific instructions on how to proceed. The Dragon had its claws into the highest levels of the Chinese bureaucracy. It would dance to the Dragon's tune.

He considered his options as the limousine drove through the gates to the embassy. Once securely on Chinese soil, he felt somewhat safer. The possibility always existed that the United States would violate diplomatic norms, but he personally doubted he was personally in any danger.

His expulsion from the United States was the worst threat facing him. That was hardly something to worry over, though it would make his job more difficult.

No, it would probably be better to have his forces in place before trouble erupted.

The Americans thought they were clever using Area 51 in Nevada to house the research on the Asharim technology. He had to admit it was an isolated, well-guarded facility.

Still, its very isolation provided him an opportunity. It wouldn't do to have a direct conflict here in the United States, but the Dragon had personnel inside the secret base. In fact, one of their operatives was assigned as a senior researcher to this very project.

Doctor Tran Lee had been in place at Area 51 for several decades now. The Americans trusted her, and rightly so. Her instructions had been precise. She made obvious her distaste for the Chinese government. That wasn't difficult. There was much to dislike about it.

He climbed out of his limousine and sauntered into the embassy. His official tasks concluded, he headed for his quarters. The guards standing by outside his rooms were not only Chinese security, they were also vetted members of the Dragon.

He had no cause to worry that anyone had invaded his privacy, but he still instructed them to do a sweep in case someone had managed to place listening devices anywhere inside. He waited patiently for them to conclude their search.

Once they declared his rooms clear and departed, Chen settled down in front of his personal computer. This unit wasn't connected to any external networks. In fact, he'd paid quite a bit of money to be absolutely certain it was impossible for anyone to connect with it at all.

Everything was encrypted, and the external connections required both a fingerprint and voice recognition for a very specific phrase to activate. Once that was done, the system still logged every action. He checked the file to verify no one had attempted to access it during his absence. No one had.

He activated the external reader and plugged the chip from his pocket into it. A different courier had brought it from Nevada. The woman had met with someone who worked outside the confines of the base. Discreetly, of course.

The deep-cover agent had collected the chip from Doctor Lee in a manner designed to pass muster with the security people that undoubtedly watched her every move. She'd then waited half a day before leaving it in a specific location where Chen's courier had retrieved it.

The courier had then driven to Las Vegas and taken a flight through Texas before changing identities and flying to Washington. It was all suitably spy-like but very effective in making sure his connection to his agent was not compromised. Above all, that could not be allowed.

Once he'd accessed the chip, he'd reviewed the covert images Lee had sent to him. There was no written report, but that was to be expected. Merely taking the pictures in that facility was challenging enough.

Lee utilized an exceptionally miniaturized camera built into her glasses. The security apparatus at the base regularly checked everyone for bugs and other monitoring devices, but these were designed to be virtually undetectable. They were literally part of the frame.

The courier had to recover the glasses themselves in order to read the data from the camera. Lee had swapped her pair for an identical set at the spa.

Once Chen knew what the Americans had, he would determine what level of force would be required to infiltrate the base and destroy the equipment. If nothing was important enough to require retrieval, the task would be straightforward. If there was an item the Dragon required, that would make the task significantly more complex.

He preferred the former case. If he arranged for the destruction of all the Asharim equipment, he would not have to see it removed from the United States. All that truly mattered in that case was denying the Americans access to the forbidden technology.

Forbidden to them, anyway.

If the United States decided it wanted a military confrontation with the Chinese, Chen suspected the Dragon would use that conflict as an opportunity to destroy the Indian-built Mars craft that the Americans had purchased.

Honestly, that could be the only reason the Americans were making the Yucatán Spaceport into such a flash point. They had to have some means to access their craft if they wanted to contest Roger's ownership of whatever he'd discovered on Mars.

The Chinese government was unaware of the Asharim. The Dragon would prefer to keep it that way for as long as possible, but that wasn't likely to hold for a great deal of time.

The best the Dragon could hope for was to ensure everyone on the Chinese-built craft belonged to their organization. Then, no matter what happened on Earth, the Dragon would reap the benefits of whatever Rogers had found.

* * *

KATHLEEN BENNETT STARED out from the massive viewport over the engineering section of the ship at the debris swirling around them. It was both glorious and terrifying.

The way the ship was oriented, it seemed as if the planet was above their heads. It was obviously not Earth. The colors were similar, and the cloud-covered view of the continents delivered the same impact as seeing images taken from orbit around Earth.

This was quite the counterpoint to the death and destruction she'd witnessed on her journey from her hiding place to the rear of the ship. She'd seen a lot of blood and pain over the years, but never anything like that.

She turned to her son. "Are you sure that you got them all?"

He shrugged. "It's been hours, and no one has turned up. None of the places I checked had any indication there were holdouts. All we can do is shoot anyone who appears."

"What about this junk? Are we in any danger?"

"Probably. Again, I have no frame of reference. If something large enough comes along and smacks into us, it'll rupture the hull. Nothing we can do about that."

That was true, based on what Nathan had discovered in searching the forward part of the ship. The control room—if that was what it was—didn't even have chairs or consoles. Everything seemed to be computer controlled.

That might indicate the computer wasn't worried about the debris. She supposed she'd have to hope this turned out favorably.

"Well, now that we control the ship, we have to figure out what to do with it," she said. "If we can get it back to Earth, we can bring more of our people on board."

Nathan snorted and shook his head. "You're not thinking clearly, Mother. The only way on or off this ship is through that damned gate. Unless you know of one on Earth that I'm unaware of, that means going back to the base in France. You know that one. The one full of terrorists."

It was her turn to smile. "Actually, I do know of another one. Remember how I used the controls of the fighter to activate the gate? I took pictures with my phone. There were two others on that screen. From reviewing the records, I know one leads to the far side of the moon and another one leads to a jungle somewhere on Earth. Probably in South America."

"I hope you know which one is which," Nathan said dryly. "I'd prefer not to open the gate to the moon."

That was a concern, she admitted.

"That isn't our only possible destination," she said after a moment. "There's always that." She extended her hand and pointed. Floating just off to the side of the ship was something she'd at first dismissed as debris, but now seemed to be whole. It looked like some kind of space station.

Nathan considered it for a moment. "Since we don't know what the code is to open a gate to it, I'm not sure how that's going to help us."

"Do I have to think of everything?" Kathleen asked waspishly. "I've already seen an answer to that question, too. Look down."

Her son leaned forward and stared out the viewport. "Is that a—"

"A ship?" she asked, cutting him off. "It looks like one, doesn't it?"

Seated directly in front of the observation area and below it was the nose of what certainly appeared to be a small craft similar to the one she'd stolen from her ex-husband. Only this one seemed to be in excellent condition.

"I'll wager this ship went many places that didn't have gate access," she said. "It only stands to reason that you'd need something to land on a planet with no gate."

"I didn't see any way to access it, but I wasn't looking at every single hatch," Nathan admitted. "Even if we can get inside, what do we do then? It's not as if either of us knows how to fly these damned ships."

"One problem at a time," she said firmly. "If we can't figure something out, there's always the gate. A fifty-fifty chance is better than none."

12

C limbing up the mesa in pitch-black darkness was significantly more difficult than Harry had anticipated. That didn't mean it was impossible, though. Slipping out of the camp in the dead of night was probably the easiest part of this operation.

These people were rescuers. They weren't military guards used to keeping watch. Everyone was sound asleep by midnight. He waited an additional few hours to be sure no one would get back up before starting out.

As the woman leading the rescue operation had explained earlier, someone had tumbled a large rock down the path up the mesa. It was totally blocked. A rope trailed into the darkness above. The moon provided some illumination but hardly enough to offer any margin of safety whatsoever. He needed to go slowly and cautiously, or he was going to fall to his death.

Forty-five minutes passed before he stood on top of the mesa. It was a fairly large swath of territory to search, but this was where his father had been seen last. If there was an accessible entrance to the base, it would be up here.

As he was above the camp, he felt fairly safe in bringing out a light to assist in his search. He was only in danger if he flashed it toward the edge facing the tents. That being the case, he started his search there and moved away from it.

It took an hour, but he found what the other searchers had missed. An opening that led deeper into the mesa. Someone had used brush very astutely to conceal the cave, but once he suspected it was there, it was simple enough to move it out of the way and descend into the darkness below. He made sure to put the brush back in place. He didn't want to chance the New Zealanders finding the base.

It quickly became obvious that the depression was actually a collapsed ceiling above the first level of the base. There was no telling how long ago the roof had come down, but it had been a significant amount of time.

The corridors inside were laid out in a similar fashion to the base in France, but there was no power. The lights were completely dark. There were also signs of combat. Nothing recent, in any case.

The scattered bones and armor of long-dead fighters littered the floor. He recognized the body shape of numerous heavy-worlders. Obviously, they'd found this base and attacked.

There were signs in the dirt on the floor that led him toward the stairs. He knew the gates would be on the lowest level. Since his father hadn't reappeared, the safe bet was that he'd gone through a gate.

Even though the base seemed to be without power, he wagered the gates were still operational. He'd find out soon enough.

The door at the bottom of the stairs was wedged open and led into a corridor. That was different from what he'd seen at the French base. There must have been different floor plans. The corridor led to an intersection.

He chose to go one way and found what seemed to be a large power-generation room. He'd seen one like it at the French base. Huge machines filled with light from massive cubes. The cubes were missing from this room, and everything was dark. That explained why there was no power.

He reversed course and went the other direction. Inside another door, he found the gate room he had been expecting. It was just as dark as the other room, but much larger. It was obviously used for cargo handling, too. A small machine holding one of the blue cubes that powered the Asharim ships sat near one of the arches. Perhaps a makeshift power supply for the gates.

It had a large cable running to the arch, undoubtedly to provide power for its operation, and a second smaller cable that lay on the floor. That one was more confusing. Why did they need the second cable? He shrugged. The question would answer itself if he could figure out how to reopen the gate to its last destination.

Harry pulled out a gate controller from his backpack and brought it online. It found one gate but not the other two. As he'd suspected, this device was providing power for it.

Unfortunately, the gate was locked. Nothing he did released it to his control. He couldn't even determine the last address it had used.

He eyed the cable again. It stretched toward the gate as though someone had pulled it after them. What if they had? If the power supply was jury-rigged, perhaps they'd needed a hardwired controller as well. If so, they might've taken it with them when they left.

If that was the case, he was screwed. They hadn't figured out a way to access the gates directly yet. That was something Jess was eventually supposed to work on with Brenda Cabot. Until they worked a method out, he had no way of pulling the address from the gate's memory.

Well, he hadn't expected this to be easy. His best guess was that his father had retreated through the gate and the American military forces had followed behind him. They were probably trapped on an alien world.

He'd have to circle back to this base once the search ended. That might take days or weeks to accomplish. Harry sighed. It wasn't as if he had a choice. If Jess came up with a solution before then, he could always return here in the dead of night and follow his father. He just had to hope the old man didn't get himself killed first.

* * *

QUEEN WORKED LATE into the evening, gathering every bit of data he could about the potential operation in Mexico. After considering all options, he'd recommended to the president that they wait to take the spaceport back.

Chen was right. A war with China would be disastrous. Congress had whittled the US military to the bone over the last three decades. They were a hollow shell incapable of fighting a serious war against anyone, much less a superpower like China.

As much is it galled him, the United States no longer qualified for that title. Perhaps they would once they'd mastered the technology Rogers had found, but today was not that day.

Far better to focus his country's attention on the more serious prize: the technology on Mars. The Indian-built ship would take months to reach the Red Planet, but once the United States put marines on the ground, that fight would be over. The younger Rogers wouldn't fight other Americans.

That mission was outside the scope of his current duties anyway. His immediate goal was to assess the technology they'd already captured and locate the traitors. Brenda Cabot and her organization were a direct threat to the national security of the United States. Hell, the world.

Thankfully, they'd gotten the captured technology placed securely inside Area 51. The facility was hardened and isolated. There was no way anyone would figure out what they were doing.

The irony that all the conspiracy nuts thought the government used the place to study alien technology amused him. It was certainly true now.

Eventually, he decided that he had to get something to eat. He considered ordering delivery but decided a quiet table at a nearby restaurant would suit his needs better. The low murmur of conversation while he had a good meal and some wine would settle him. It took less than ten minutes to get his security detail in motion. They saw him down to his armored transport and off to the restaurant.

This late, the place was only half-full. That suited his mood perfectly. The maître d' found him a table in the back, away from the rest of the diners. His security detail settled around him as he ordered an appetizer.

The man had barely left his side when an odd noise made Queen look up. The member of his security detail closest to the front of the restaurant was talking to someone.

No. Not talking. Arguing.

That was unusual. Most people didn't screw with armed security in Washington. There were plenty of high government officials that warranted protection, and no one really wanted to mess with that kind of person.

Another of his guards went to back the man up while the remaining one stepped nearer to Queen's booth. No one was pulling weapons, but they were preparing for the possibility of trouble.

Queen finally got a look at the person confronting his guards and realized it was a woman. Not anyone he recognized. Her annoyed expression marked her as someone used to getting her way. Not today. With a huff, the woman turned and stalked off.

He'd barely returned his attention to the menu when a much louder noise sent adrenaline roaring through his system. A gunshot. The guard standing next to Queen's table jerked and collapsed. The other two members of his security detail whirled and went for their weapons. The shooter was somewhere in the back of the restaurant.

Queen rolled under the table and pulled his concealed pistol. He hadn't carried one before but had decided it was necessary after Cabot kidnapped him. Not that it would've helped that time, but it could certainly help now.

The crescendo of gunshots trailed off. Since he wasn't seeing his people, Queen took that as a bad sign. He'd really rather not risk his neck, but if he waited for his attacker to come to him, he'd be at a distinct disadvantage. After taking two quick breaths, he shoved himself out far enough to get a decent look while retaining the option of ducking back under cover.

That move caught the shooter out in the open. The man's attention was focused toward the front of the restaurant, so Queen had a short window to act. He snapped off three quick shots at his attacker and was rewarded by seeing the man dive for cover. Unfortunately, he was pretty sure he hadn't hit the bastard. Queen ducked back inside the booth.

"Damn, but you're hard to kill." The voice was unfamiliar, but that reduced the number of potential attackers down to one: the guy who'd shot him right after Cabot had kidnapped him.

"You'll have to forgive me, but I don't believe we've been properly introduced."

"Nor will we. I'm afraid I really must be going, but I think I'll send you on your way first."

Queen prepared himself again. "Might I inquire what I've done to offend you? I'm sure that we've never met."

"What else? Money. Though I will confess that I'm going to take some small measure of personal satisfaction in killing you. I was sure I'd hit you the last time, but somehow you managed to slip away. Not this time."

Knowing he wasn't going to get another opportunity, Queen rolled out from beneath the table and fired in the direction the assassin had gone. He didn't stop rolling—which was a good thing because the killer had been waiting.

The hail of gunshots partially deafened Queen, but anything that interfered with the other man putting a bullet into Queen's head was a good thing. Unfortunately, all the movement put Queen out into the open. Once the man drew a bead on him, this was going to be over fast.

Of course, that's when the slide on Queen's pistol locked back. He was out of ammunition.

The other man rose from his hiding place and brought his pistol to bear on Queen. "Bye-bye."

The next shot made Queen flinch, but it caused him no pain. That's because the assassin hadn't fired. The guard beside Queen's booth must not have been dead after all. He'd gotten his weapon out and proceeded to fire shot after shot into the killer, even after the man had gone down.

Queen didn't wait to see the results of the man's shots. He leapt to his feet and sprinted toward the front of the restaurant. He recalled the woman who had tried to gain entrance to the seating area and decided that she had probably been an accomplice. That convinced him to grab one of the downed guards' pistols.

It wasn't necessary though. The restaurant was pure pandemonium. Everyone was rushing to get away. No one seemed to have any interest in him at all. He considered running out with them but decided that would be the perfect time to take him down. The woman might be waiting to do just that. He'd let the police come to him.

Queen didn't believe the assassin was still alive, but he hoped he was wrong. Getting some answers about who was trying to kill him would be useful. Stopping them from sending anyone else would be even better.

13

———————

Jess stayed with Brenda Cabot and her people until Kevin McHugh arrived. The young man fit her idea of what a hacker looked like precisely: tall, gangly, and bald. He favored small round lenses on his glasses. Colored purple, of course. His clothing fell somewhere between hip and trendy.

At least she didn't need to explain Asharim technology to him. He already knew far more about it than she did.

"So let me see if I've got this straight," he said as they stepped through the gate and onto *Freedom Express*. "You found the big gate on a space station, and you want access to figure out the address it used to send a ship somewhere else. Is that right?"

Jess nodded. "Exactly. Unfortunately, while we know where the gate is, we haven't found the computers that control it."

He smiled. "That's easy. The computer is in the gate itself."

She frowned. "That doesn't sound easy. The gate is on the outside of the space station."

"Hmmm. That *does* add a layer of complication. Still, it's not impossible. I assume you have spacesuits. I'm not trained to use one, but if you can get me out to where I need to go, I could probably still make it happen."

Jess considered him for a moment. "I think that's a really bad idea. If something goes wrong, you could die in a moment. If you're going to use a spacesuit, we need to train you.

"How about this? We send someone out to examine the gate, and you watch the video feed through the helmet. We've got some expert spacewalkers. Hell, I'm an expert spacewalker."

He raised an eyebrow. "Do you have a technical background?"

"You could say that. I have several degrees in engineering, and I've messed with this technology before."

"That might work. You'll need some tools to open the panels on the gate, but I should be able to provide those. I came prepared."

"The tools need to be large enough for somebody wearing gloves to manipulate them," she warned him. "It would be better if we could attach a strap to them as well. Things tend to float off in Zero-G."

"That shouldn't be a problem, but it'll add a little time to the project. If you want to do this right, I should probably work with a machinist to copy the tools."

"We can do that, but first I want to give you a look at the big gate."

The hacker looked around them at the corridors as they walked. "So this is a spaceship."

"Sort of. It's actually a hollowed-out comet. A dormant one that your ancestors modified for their use."

He didn't ask any more questions until they arrived at the central control room. The view stopped him in his tracks as they came out of the lift. "Whoa!"

The control center had that effect on almost everyone the first time. Hell, it still affected her that way. The lift exited out onto a walkway that was in the precise center of the comet.

That meant that the spherical chamber sat all around them in every direction. The use of artificial gravity meant up and down had very little meaning in this case. Stairs led down to various parts of the control room.

She automatically selected the one that would take them to the pilot's station. "Watch your step. It would be awkward if you fell and had to explain to Miss Cabot why we had to send you back for medical treatment."

"Isn't that the damned truth?" The young man took a firm grip on the handrail, but he didn't let his eyes stop wandering. "I've heard stories, but I never really imagined it looked like this. You know how you get a picture in your head of how something is? I'm not sure what I expected, but this isn't it. This is *way* more awesome."

She gave him a suspicious glance. "Did you grow up in California? I swear you talk just like every surfer I've seen in a movie."

McHugh laughed. "You figured me out! And I'll have you know, talking that way is like a badge of honor there. Even if it does occasionally get me laughed at."

She stepped over to the pilot's console and smiled. "Morning, Lindsay. Everything still looking good?"

Lindsay Waller was nominally the command pilot on *Liberty Station* but was on long-term loan to *Freedom Express*. *Liberty Station* didn't really need a pilot while it was in Mars orbit. If trouble came calling, they'd have months to prepare, and she had very competent assistants.

"We're good," Lindsay confirmed. "Black Jack just took a team down to the new site. I expect to have some kind of report on their general status in about forty minutes."

"Excellent. Lindsay, meet Kevin McHugh. He's one of Brenda Cabot's people, and he's going to help us with the big gate. Can you give us a look at it, using one of the probes?"

The pilot nodded and turned back toward her console. "Sure. We got several of them mapping the surface of the station. It won't take long to relocate one."

The woman's hands moved confidently over the controls. They'd only been in possession of *Freedom Express* for a short while, so the pilot's competence amazed her.

"Wow. You've really got this under control."

Lindsay grinned. "I've been working hard, and I have to admit, the latest iteration of the translation software really helps. Emily has just about got this thing nailed down, I think."

The woman glanced at McHugh. "I'm betting that's because of

the help we're getting from your people on the language. That's putting this whole project way ahead of where we expected."

The young man inclined his head. "I can't take any credit for that, but you're welcome. Allow me to second what Miss Cook said. You sure look like you've got this whole thing under control."

Jess made a face. "I'd rather you just use my first name. I'm not that formal."

"Awesome. Call me Kevin."

"Okay," Lindsay said. "Here we are."

The view on the screen was far enough out to show the entirety of the massive gate. The damned thing was huge. Easily big enough to move a spaceship across the universe.

Not *Freedom Express*, though. The comet was too big. Pity.

McHugh leaned forward and examined the image. "I think the access panel we want is down and to the right. Maybe a little lower than the center."

Lindsay made a few deft adjustments, and the image of the section McHugh was pointing toward began to get larger.

He waited until the gate filled the screen to ask her to stop. "Right there. That's the access panel to the computer."

To Jess's inexperienced eye, it looked just like the rest of the gate. "How can you tell?"

"Believe it or not, color. That panel is just a bit darker than those around it. That's how the Asharim denoted access panels. As for knowing where on the gate it was, that was an educated guess. This is where I'd find one on a smaller gate. Well, the one gate that we have anyway."

Jess nodded, still a little jealous of the fact that Cabot's people had a mobile gate. One they could pick up and move wherever they wanted. She really needed to find something like that.

McHugh turned toward her. "Basically, once we open the access panel, I should be able to plug in a computer to pull the data from the controller.

"Well, it's not exactly the controller. Technically, the controller is what sends the signal to the gate, but I call the receiving equipment that activates the gate a controller, too."

"How difficult is it to get the data from the gate? Is it going to be password protected? Encrypted?"

He shook his head. "I don't think so, though I suppose it's always possible. That's not how the Asharim set up their computers. If you like, I can give you a demonstration on a different gate. One of the ones inside."

"I think that would be very helpful," Jess said with a nod. "Lindsay, thank you very much for your help."

"You're welcome, and it's a pleasure to meet you, Kevin."

Getting to the gate room took another fifteen minutes. The young computer expert grinned when he saw the gates built into the side of the cargo room.

"Now *that's* what I'm talking about! I've seen some pictures of the original tech. These are permanent gates, not like our portable one. You want me to pull a destination log out of one of these for you?"

Jess gestured toward the gates. "Actually, I'd like to get destination logs for all three. And once you do, there are a few other gates I'd like to get information from as well: the ones on Mars and the ones at the base we discovered in France."

"I heard about that one. Brenda was pissed. It's been right there all this time, and none of us ever suspected."

"I'm pretty confident we'll find a way to share. As a matter of fact, we believe we know the general locations of several other bases on Earth. If our relationship develops the way I expect, some of those can certainly go your way."

"That would be awesome! Our own secret base. Well, not that our current base isn't secret, but you know what I mean."

Amusingly, she did understand. "Go ahead and get to work. I can't wait to see how you do it."

"You betcha." The young man walked over to one of the gates and began taking tools and equipment out of his pack.

* * *

CLAYTON LEANED back on the stool and waited for the woman to continue. This was her show. He had nothing to gain by rushing her into making a hasty decision. He'd dangled the fruit. Now he'd see if she was hungry.

She seemed content to let the silence drag out for a long minute. Then she seemed to make a decision. She gestured toward the guards, and they filed out of the tent, leaving only the two of them and the officers dressed in military garb.

"Since it seems we have things to discuss, I suppose it would be prudent to introduce myself. I am Susanna Adorno, the civilian commander of this force. These men are my military adjuncts: General Norbert Norris and his assistants Colonel Brock Carver and Major Antonio Logan."

The three men inclined their heads toward him. At her gesture, they stepped away from the side of the tent and arranged seats for themselves.

Adorno leaned forward. "We only have contact with other humans intermittently. Sometimes for years at a stretch, other times only for hours. No one has ever found a way to return to the place we came from. Earth.

"My people and the Volunteers are the most recent immigrants to the stars by many centuries. It has been hundreds of years since we came to this place. I find it curious that you have come through at this particular time. And I'm somewhat confused as to how you managed it."

Clayton shrugged. "Not knowing the specifics of your circumstances, I find it difficult to comment. In the end, I can only speak for my own people and how we found our way here.

"Before I can do that, I want to be sure we don't see one another as enemies. We have no desire to fight your people or to defend ourselves from you. You said earlier that we weren't your enemy because we were human. I'm not sure how seriously to take that statement."

She considered him shrewdly. "You do not know the circumstances away from Earth, do you?"

"In large part, no. We're familiar with the Asharim, though only recently so. My son and people in my employ found discarded items belonging to them only a few months ago. That led us to the discovery of the gates. We are still exploring, but we believe the Asharim have fallen from their pinnacle of technical know-how."

"That latter is true," General Norris said. "The Asharim were no longer wizards when we came to this place, with some limited exceptions. Only the large numbers of slaves at their command prevent us from outright victory.

"Your accent is somewhat strange, but you sound as if you come from the colonies. Might I inquire as to the situation that holds sway there now?"

"Are you referring to the War of Independence? The fight against King George? If so, that ended successfully. The colonies have become a powerful nation in their own right."

The officer gave him a steady look and slowly nodded. "We knew that the fight must have ended long ago, and we took it as an article of faith that our righteous cause would be rewarded. It's good to hear it, though."

The woman shook her head. "I won't bother to ask the situation in the Caribbean. My ancestors knew quite well that their time was coming to a close, and that was probably a good thing. I might count pirates and privateers among my ancestors, but I don't think I would relish practicing their trade."

She crossed one leg over the other knee. "We have no quarrel with your people. This regiment is moving to secure the ancient city just over the horizon. Every few decades it trades hands between the Asharim and us.

"The fighting spills our blood, leaving both sides exhausted for years at a time. Once we recover, the fight begins anew. The city holds the only operational gate on this world. We use it to be part of a wider universe of human colonies. I'm unsure what the Asharim do. Nothing good, I'm sure."

"You said that your people worked with the Volunteers," Clayton said. "I'm assuming these folk were a militia during the War of Independence, so please correct me if I'm wrong. How did both of your groups find the gate that brought you here? To my sorrow, none of the gates that we have located on Earth are inside the United States."

The general leaned back in his chair. "The United States," he said slowly, seeming to savor every word. "It rings upon the ear, does it not? Oh, I've heard the name before. It was bandied about for long years before the fighting started, but it still sends a thrill up my spine."

Clayton smiled. "The United States of America came into the world as something completely new and turned all the other nations on their head. Through many of the trials and tribulations in the centuries since its founding, it has stood for truth and justice. Sadly, that has changed in recent years, though we hope to reverse the process."

The other man considered that. "I've heard it said that, from time to time, the tree of liberty must be refreshed with the blood of tyrants and patriots. Perhaps such a time has once more come.

"In any case, I cannot tell you the precise nature of how we came to this place. Our ancestors were maneuvering in the wilds of Virginia when we came across a cave. Inside this cave, they found the wonders of the Asharim. We did not know that at the time, because the place was abandoned.

"At some point, they found a way through the gate and brought a number of refugees from the fighting with them. This method is still known to us today, but I am not sure how they learned it. That story has been lost in the mists of time."

"The story of my people is much the same," Adorno said. "They were in Port Royale when a mighty earthquake leveled the city. Many of the survivors were brought to a place near the water that had a gate.

"The people that brought our ancestors there warned of a great tsunami that would likely come. I have no idea who they were. They saw the survivors of Port Royale through the gate just before the wave came. They left us on this world and went elsewhere. Since that time, they have never returned.

"The Volunteers came through many years after us. They were very lucky that my people had seized the city at the time, or the Asharim would have executed them in a grisly fashion."

Clayton considered the strangers but decided he couldn't worry about them now. He had more important and pressing worries.

Adorno pressed her lips together. "If you only recently came to this world, where is the gate? Surely not the one in the city. The Asharim would have dealt most harshly with you."

He didn't see how he could avoid talking about that, so he didn't try to lie. "There's a hidden cave in a large hill nearby. Inside is a gate. Unfortunately, we have no means of controlling it. Once we came through, we were trapped here. I know how to return to Earth, but I must have a way to control the gate to use it."

"I suspected something of the sort. If I am correct about which hill you mean, no one ever had cause to believe there was anything inside it. It's a place where the Asharim conduct unholy ceremonies.

"We have discovered that humans must stand together against the Asharim and their slaves, Clayton Rogers. I look forward to hearing more from you and your people. On behalf of my forces, I invite you and yours to come dine with us tonight in safety."

Trust had to start somewhere. It wasn't as if they had much of a choice. They needed these people's assistance to get back to Earth.

"We would be happy to join you."

14

Nathan found the entrance to the small craft easily enough now that he knew where to look. It was a hatch no different from any other he'd seen on the ship with one exception: it had something written on it in an alien script. That was new.

His mother stopped abruptly in front of the hatch, her mouth hanging open.

"That's not a very elegant look, Mother," he said snidely.

She ignored his taunt, still staring at the hatch.

"Mother? What's wrong?"

She raised an arm and pointed toward the hatch. "What does that say?"

He glanced from her to the hatch and back again. "I have no idea."

She turned slightly toward him. "I do. It says 'shuttle access.' What I don't know is how that's even possible, because it's not in English. Nathan, what's going on?"

He stared at her, dumbfounded. "How am I supposed to know? How could you possibly know what it says?"

His mother rubbed her face. "It had to be the machine I was in.

Not only did it heal and make me younger again, but also it put something in my head. The knowledge of what those words mean."

Nathan felt his eyes narrow. If it put that in her head, what else might it have done? Could she be under the influence of the alien computer? Dealing with his mother was already a frighteningly dangerous proposition, but if she was under alien control, that added an entirely new element of uncertainty.

One he couldn't deal with right now. He'd keep an eye on her and see how she behaved going forward. If she became a problem, he'd solve it.

He opened the hatch, and it led into a short corridor with another hatch at the end. He recognized the far hatch as part of an airlock. That made sense. If the shuttle were gone, you wouldn't want to open a door into vacuum.

Thankfully, the operation of these hatches was relatively simple. He turned and found his mother still standing in the main corridor.

"I realize this is unsettling, Mother, but you need to come along. Our time is limited. If something comes and smashes the ship, we don't want to be here."

She shook her head as if she were waking from a daydream. Her face scrunched into a snarl, and she stalked forward. The two of them entered the airlock and then the shuttle beyond. It was *exactly* like the ship they'd stolen from his brother. Only this one seemed to be in perfect shape.

His mother led the way to the front of the shuttle. They settled into the couches set aside for the pilots. She reached out and swiped her hand across the control console. It came to life, and so did the large screens in front of them. Those showed the view of the ship they'd captured. It was an impressively vivid image.

"The researchers showed me how to bring the systems on the other shuttle to life," she said. "Or at least to look at the controls. Beyond that, I'm not sure what I'll be able to figure out."

Nathan wasn't going to be of any help. His use of the alien technology had been extremely limited. If she couldn't figure out something, they weren't going anywhere.

She stared at the control console for a moment. "Weirdly, I seem to know what each of these symbols means. I mean as in what will happen if I touch them." Her eyes swiveled toward him. "We want to go to the station?"

He shrugged. "That seems to be the only place worth visiting, unless there's something on the planet below that would be useful. That said, I'm not sure how much I'd trust you guiding a spaceship during reentry based on information implanted in you by an alien computer. One mistake and we'd burn up."

"I can't argue with that." She reached out and tapped one of the icons, and the console reconfigured into a different layout. Hesitantly, she touched three symbols in sequence.

The shuttle shuddered and came loose from the ship. He could see them rising in the screens.

"We've separated from the ship," his mother said needlessly. "Let's see if I can guide us toward the station."

He hoped she could. They were committed now.

She tapped a few more controls, and the ship reoriented itself and began moving toward the station. Thankfully, not very quickly.

"What about the debris?" he asked. "If we get hit by a piece of wreckage, we're done."

"The shuttle seems to have taken that into account. It's marking the courses of everything that might come near us. I have it adjusting course to miss anything flying in our direction. I can't say that's going to keep us safe, but it's the best I can do."

The situation unsettled him significantly more than he'd prefer to admit. Trusting his mother's strange new knowledge and skills was against his nature.

The station slowly grew larger in front of them. Nathan had no frame of reference, but he thought it was large. Very large. It didn't seem to have taken significant damage, either. Which was odd considering how much debris still floated in the area.

That made him wonder. How could there still be debris left over from some event that must've taken place centuries ago? Perhaps even a thousand years ago. Even at the time of the event, shouldn't the debris have floated away? Something wasn't right here.

His mother brought the shuttle around, and he saw places dotted across the hull that looked as though they had massive hatches. She seemed to have one of them selected as a destination. He hoped she could get it to open.

Thankfully, it began sliding ponderously open as they approached. His mother guided the shuttle through it and into a dark cavern beyond.

Overhead lights snapped on, revealing they were in a massive hangar filled with numerous small craft similar to the one they were in and many others besides.

She brought the shuttle down onto an open area on the deck. "I've signaled the hatch to close. According to these instruments, there's air outside. We can go see what's out there."

"Forgive me if I seem confused, but how could there be air outside when we just opened the door?"

His mother shrugged. "I have no idea."

"Why would they even bother to have airlocks if they had a means of keeping air inside? Or did the air come in after we did?"

"I have no idea," his mother snapped. "Stop asking me questions I can't answer."

Nathan was tempted to keep badgering her, but he knew he had her right on the edge of outright rage. He'd rather not have her come after him.

"Sorry, Mother," he said soothingly. "What should we do now? Is it safe to leave the shuttle?"

"I suppose there's only one way to find out."

She stood, walked back into the main body of the shuttle, and tapped the control by the airlock. The inner door slid open. She turned toward him. "Are you coming?"

He'd have really rather not, but he supposed he didn't have a choice. He rose to his feet. "Let's go see what we've found."

* * *

HARRY MADE it back to camp with plenty of time. He was sitting at one of the campfires when the people tasked with cooking breakfast rose for the morning.

He hated that he needed to stay here while the searchers scoured the area. Particularly now that he knew there was no chance they'd find anything. That galled him.

The list of things he needed to do was ridiculously long. He couldn't afford to be tied up waiting for them to declare his father lost. Worse yet, if he did find a way to activate the gate, he'd need to lead the force after his father. He couldn't just sit here waiting.

Well, he supposed some "dire emergency" could call him away. It wasn't as though he didn't have enough of those on his hands. Thankfully, the locals didn't know his true identity. As an employee, he could slip away.

Molly Goodwin rose just as the sun peeked over the horizon. She got herself a cup of coffee and sat down in a folding chair beside him. "You're up early, Mister Jacobs."

"I had trouble sleeping. I must confess that I'm concerned you haven't managed to locate any of the missing people yet." He held up a hand to forestall her response. "I'm not implying that you aren't doing everything you can. It just seems as though some sign of them should've turned up already."

She sipped her coffee and nodded. "That worries me, too. The terrain around here is very rough, so that makes it hard to spot them, but it also means they can't have gotten very far. Mister Rogers should have been able to flag down a helicopter. He should've realized by now that all the aircraft in the area are friendly."

She considered him for a moment. "I wanted to bring up another issue before the day really gets started. Perhaps you could help me understand something."

"I'd be happy to try," Harry said.

"We'll see how happy you are once I've asked my question. Is your name really Jacobs? I think the answer is no because I'm almost certain I saw your face on the news. Mister Rogers."

Well, this was awkward. Did he attempt to lie his way out of it, or did he confess that he'd snuck back to Earth? He probably should've sent Rex in his place. Coming had been a mistake. He wasn't sure what he'd been thinking.

He took a long drink of his coffee to give him a moment to

consider his options. In the end, he decided that it really didn't matter. His father had bought the land in order to claim the New Zealand base. The place was a wreck. Maybe the gates could be salvaged and relocated elsewhere, but he wasn't even sure of that. The government of New Zealand would seize the place in a heartbeat.

Still, that might work to his advantage. Up until now, they'd been operating in the shadows. Only the US government had a clue what was going on. Perhaps it was time to widen the circle.

"I prefer to keep that to a limited number of people," he said softly. "I recognize that you're going to have to report my presence, but I'd rather not have it become general knowledge."

She shook her head. "I can hardly believe it. You were on Mars, weren't you? Was that all some kind of trick?"

"You mean like the conspiracy theory that the moon landing was faked? No. It was real. I was on Mars."

"That's been one of the main features of the news for the last several days. Your spaceship or space station, whatever you want to call it, is still there. How could you possibly be sitting here next to me?"

He grinned. "Aliens."

A bark of laughter escaped before she could clap a hand over her mouth. "I'd say that's not funny, but it obviously is. You're not going to be able to get away with laying this at the feet of mysterious aliens you found on Mars."

"Let me ask you a question, Miss Goodwin. Do you work for the government of New Zealand?"

"In a manner of speaking, yes," she said. "I act as coordinator in cases where people have gone missing in the wilds. I'm not a policewoman or anything. And I'm also not a government bureaucrat. I actually work for a living."

"That's good to hear. I'm going to tell you a story that you'll find very hard to believe. I can prove it, though. Once everyone is up and about their business, if you'll accompany me to the top of the mesa, I can show you how I got here. Honestly, you wouldn't believe me if I told you without proof."

She stared at the mesa in the early dawn light. "You're going to have some kind of alien ship land on the mesa? Is this going to be like a scene out of *Close Encounters of the Third Kind?*"

"Something like that. I promise there won't be any probes."

The woman laughed again, not trying to hide it this time. "I can't imagine what kind of story you're going to try to sell me, but I need to have some breakfast before I think about it.

"It seems the cooks have wrapped up their preparations, so let's get something before everyone stampedes them. You haven't seen how searchers go through food. They'll eat everything in sight and then come back for another pass. They're like locusts."

He rose with her, his stomach already grumbling from the delicious scent of the bacon. The next few hours could go very badly, so he'd eat well and hope for the best.

15

Jess floated in space outside the station using her maneuvering thrusters to stay near the access panel Kevin McHugh had identified on the big gate. She'd watched him open a number of access panels on the smaller gates, so she felt confident that she could do the same here.

"Yeah," he said over her radio. "That looks right. You remember how I showed you to open the panel?"

"I remember. It's just this one is a little larger than the others."

That was certainly true. This panel was the size of a hatch on the lifter. If it proved difficult to move, she wasn't sure how she'd gain the leverage to make this happen.

Well, no time like the present to figure this out.

She found the recessed grip that allowed for movement of the access panel. On the smaller gates, either a screwdriver or fingernail would do the trick. On this one, she needed a pry bar. Thankfully, she'd come prepared.

First, she used the special tool to unlock the panel. It was a special kind of screw, acting almost like a key. She'd worried that it would be different on the larger panel, but it was thankfully the same as the smaller gates.

With that done, she pulled the bar off her belt slowly so as not to tangle the cable keeping it attached to her. The fit of the head was a little loose when she put it in place. If she ever had to do this again, she'd bring a bigger bar.

Since she was in Zero-G and had no grip, she used her suit's maneuvering thrusters to apply pressure, and the access panel popped open. Like the ones on the smaller gates, this one was attached so that it only swung open rather than flying off into space.

Unlike the smaller gates, the larger version shielded a lot more equipment. She had no idea what most of it did.

"Wow," McHugh muttered. "That's a lot of stuff. Look around for a port like the one I showed you. There has to be one that will accept the cable."

It took about fifteen minutes of examination before she found the small port. At least it looked like the one Kevin had shown her. "Is this it?" she asked.

"I think so. If it's not, it should be no harm no foul. Just plug the comp in and see what you see."

She took the time to reattach the pry bar to her belt before she pulled the comp from its pouch. It only took a few moments to seat the plug into the port. "Here goes nothing." Jess tapped the icon on the comp just as Kevin had shown her. A new window opened, and a series of codes began scrolling by. They were the same twenty-character codes she'd seen on the smaller gates.

"You did it!" he said. "The comp will have them saved in its memory once you come back in."

Jess was relieved, but this didn't solve all her problems. Having the code that Harry's family had used was useful, but unless they knew how to activate this larger gate, it wouldn't do them any good. She'd already tried connecting to it with a standard hand controller. The device didn't even see the massive gate. There had to be something else required to link with it.

They'd try to use one of the smaller gates to link with the code Nathan and his mother had used, but she personally doubted the smaller gate would link with the larger one. There had to be some type of safety mechanism. After all, one wouldn't want a massive starship trying to come through a small gate. The reverse might work, but it seemed as if the systems would be radically different.

Once she had the codes, Jess detached the cable and put the comp away. She maneuvered herself around to the other side of the access panel and used her thrusters to push it slowly closed. She couldn't hear any noise when it sealed, but it didn't pop back open.

She gave it a good thump with her fist just to be sure. Having this come open and be at risk for micrometeor damage was unacceptable.

"I'm on my way back in," she said. "We can go over the numbers once we have everything in the lab."

"Roger that. See you in a few minutes."

Jess jetted back to the lifter that was waiting for her and closed the airlock behind her. As the pressure began rising, she considered her next move. They'd already pulled all the codes off the gates on *Freedom Express*, the Mars base, the French base, and the gate rooms they discovered on the station.

She was sure there were plenty more gate rooms on the station that they hadn't discovered, but the exploration was still in progress. The place was bigger than Manhattan. It was going to take a lot of time to look into every single compartment.

Meanwhile, she'd finally spoken with Harry. The delivery of the quantum phone right before she'd gone outside for this job had allowed her to give him an update on the situation.

To her astonishment, they were able to communicate from this great distance with no time lag or loss of signal. These new communication devices were finally going to allow them to coordinate their actions.

The next thing she wanted to do was test how far they'd really reach. Being able to communicate across the solar system was absolutely worthwhile. Yet if it worked at interstellar range, that would be even more impressive.

Once the pressure in the airlock came up and the temperature had risen to the normal range, she popped the helmet off her suit and opened the inner door.

Black Jack McCarthy grinned at her from the pilot's couch. "I was listening in over the com. Everything went well. That's awesome."

The ex-marine pilot waited until she'd strapped herself in and then turned the lifter to head back toward *Freedom Express*.

"It did, but that's only a start. There are so many other things we need to do. Including being able to get someone down to where Harry is in New Zealand. He's going to need this comp to pull the gate codes."

The man nodded. "I suppose we can send it through to France and have them fly it out to New Zealand. That's going to take a while."

"We could do that, but I have a better idea. One of the biggest issues in travel we've had is the fact that we can't get any of our lifters to the gates. There are ships down there, but we don't know where to send them.

"There must be some way to get them to the surface. Probably a gate stashed somewhere on the side of a mountain or something. If we could find one of those, we could get the ships out and use them."

He shot her a considering glance. "And you want me to fly one of them?"

"Do you think you could?"

"I've been working with Lindsay Waller quite a bit, learning how to fly the big ship. If the controls are similar, I think so. You know, you've been pulling codes out of gates, but you've missed an angle. The ships need to open gates that are useful to them. That means they've gone places that will accept a fighter flying out. We should get into one of them and see if we can access the codes *they've* used."

Jess smacked herself on the forehead. "Crap. I've been so focused on the gates that I forgot the ships probably act as controllers. If we look for codes that are the same on both the ships and the gates, we'll find the best potential places to send a ship through."

She gestured toward *Freedom Express*, which was growing larger ahead of them. "Let's get this thing landed and head down to the gate room. I want to start working on this right away."

* * *

QUEEN WASN'T able to get away from the restaurant. Even his high position in the government hadn't shielded him from having to answer to the police for the violence that had taken place.

At least there were enough people present that no one believed he'd instigated the attack. It had quickly become apparent to all that he was the victim here.

He hated playing the victim card. It made him feel weak. Nevertheless, it got things moving in a productive direction in fairly short order.

All three of his guards had died in the attack. Apparently, the one that had killed the assassin had been almost gone. Queen was genuinely sorry for that. They'd been good men.

He tried to get the police to give him information about the assassin, but they'd kept their mouths shut. He'd have to see about alternative methods of identifying the man.

There were no cameras inside the restaurant, unfortunately. It was well known for its discretion. That meant identifying the woman was going to be difficult. The police would look at cameras in the area to see if they had an image of her, so it was always possible they'd have another thread to follow.

They'd spent hours questioning him over who might want him dead. He'd laughed. With his work, there were any number of people that might want him to bleed out on some floor. Nothing he could tell the police would narrow their suspect pool. Only enlarge it.

In any case, he was fairly certain that he'd figured this out. The first attack had come during the investigation on Kathleen Bennett. If he were a betting man—and he was—then he'd wager she'd paid quite handsomely to have him eliminated. He'd proven to be quite the thorn in her side.

With her in hiding, she'd probably thought eliminating him would simplify her situation. She was probably right. Other people in government might make a deal with her. Not him. Not now.

He'd come to see her as the worst actor in this little play. Her ex-husband was no winner, but he wasn't in her league.

Her son, Nathan, was more like an evil force of nature. Harry

Rogers was mostly honorable, which was something Queen could use against him.

Jessica Cook was a mystery. He still didn't know quite what to think about her. She should've been a mousy little scientist, but she had a spine of steel. Harry Rogers deferred to her. That had to mean something.

Brenda Cabot and her group were a wildcard. Still, she'd saved his life the last time the assassin had struck. He could safely remove her from the suspect list on this one.

With the assassin dead and a description of his accomplice spreading across the city, he really needed to turn his focus to dealing with Cabot. Unfortunately, just about all the useful organizations were in disarray due to the search for moles.

Sadly, it hadn't taken long to find people who had been doing questionable things. Investigators were tugging on strings to see if they connected to Cabot's organization, but Queen wasn't sure he could trust what they found.

If he were on the other team, he'd frame people to take the fall while leaving his own operatives intact. They could still watch everything that took place and direct the investigators to people who would not harm their organization.

The investigators would find some people to question, but he doubted anything would come of it. Cabot's spies would still be in place. After all, they'd already passed every lie detector test required for their sensitive work.

That probably had something to do with the technology they had access to. Some type of alien machine that made it so they could lie their asses off about being traitors.

That annoyed the crap out of him. His only option was to continue the search for people involved with the organization. Eventually, they'd find something.

His phone rang. He brought it up to his ear. "Queen."

"Guthrie here. I need you to call me on a secure phone."

Oh, that couldn't be good. "Give me ten minutes."

He disconnected and walked over to the detective in charge of the scene. "I have to step out to my car. Something has come up, and I need to use the secure phone."

The man in the rumpled suit turned to Queen with a look of annoyance on his face. "We'll be done with you in another half hour, Secretary Queen. You'll just have to wait until then."

Queen smiled coldly. "That's where you're wrong, Detective. I'm going outside right now to take this call, then I'm leaving. We're done. If you need any further information from me, you can contact my office."

The detective scowled. "Don't try to pull that crap with me. You might be the secretary of state, but you aren't above the law."

"We've already determined that I'm the victim here," Queen said calmly. "All you're doing now is being an ass. You can do that on your own time. Push this and you'll find out how much of an ass I can be in return."

The two men glared at one another, but the detective eventually nodded brusquely. "Fine, but don't think this is over. I'm going to figure out who is behind this. If you're connected to them in any way, you're going down, too."

"I can say with a clear conscience that I had nothing to do with that man. No illegal dealings whatsoever. You're not going to find anything that worries me. Good day, Detective."

Queen stalked out toward the parking lot. He wasn't completely certain the detective would find nothing. It was entirely possible that some of the alien knowledge would seep into this investigation, in which case the federal authorities would have to quash it.

He smiled at the thought that they might have to take the detective into custody. That would serve the bastard right.

New guards surrounded him as he exited the restaurant and saw him safely into the armored limousine he was using for transport. Once he had the door closed, he picked up the secure phone and dialed the number for the general.

"Guthrie."

"Queen here. What's the problem?"

"There's been an incident at the lab. An explosion of some kind."

The words made Queen sit up abruptly. "How bad is it? What's the damage?"

"Total. It had to be sabotage. There was nothing in that lab capable of producing that kind of blast. Someone managed to sneak something past security or rigged something up with materials in the labs themselves.

"I'm afraid that either the explosion or the fire that followed has ruined every bit of technology you brought here, Mister Secretary. Worse, it killed a lot of researchers, including Doctor Wagner and the guy doing the forensic work on the bodies. They're gone, too. Everything is gone."

16

C hen leaned back in his chair, pleased at the report that had just arrived. Doctor Lee had successfully escaped Area 51 before the explosion.

One of his remaining operatives in the zone indicated the blast had been even stronger than anticipated. Odds were very good that it had destroyed everything in the lab. Frankly, based on images of the building, the lab itself was gone. The attack had undoubtedly eliminated many of the researchers as well.

His operative had manipulated the exterior security logs, so it was entirely possible the Americans wouldn't realize that Doctor Lee had escaped.

That would be the perfect outcome, but he couldn't count on that. Chen would settle for a less than optimum result so long as all the equipment was gone.

News from China itself was also good. The Dragon had successfully sunk its claws into the Mars mission. The fact that they would need to contest with armed personnel for control of the Red Planet had finally convinced the Chinese leadership to go with an all-military mission.

That had always been one of the options, so there were suitable personnel already trained. The Dragon had made certain that many of them were already loyal. In the aftermath of the events leading up to the confrontation with America, they had replaced any unaligned soldiers.

The rest of the world believed the Chinese Mars mission would leave in three weeks. He knew that date was a ruse. Much like Clayton Rogers had done with his so-called space station, the Chinese Mars mission would leave early and had engines more powerful than anyone would expect.

Not as strong as the ones that pushed the space station to Mars in a matter of days. No. It would still take them weeks to arrive, but they had a nuclear power source, too. The UN and America would undoubtedly wail. Let them.

Harry Rogers would expect the mission's arrival. There was no way to conceal the fact that they were on the way. What the man wouldn't be ready for was the level of weaponry they had outfitted the Chinese ship with.

The Chinese had always intended to arm the vessel. They would never allow any other nation to contest with them while they were unarmed. They would take those weapons with them, but the Dragon had used technology of their own—salvaged from ancient Asharim equipment—to create devices that were even more potent.

Chen wasn't cleared for the details, but those he'd spoken with seemed confident the forces of the Dragon would have no difficulty in securing the Red Planet.

Since they would control every aspect of communication from that world, they didn't need to worry about leaving evidence behind. They could destroy *Liberty Station* and every person they'd brought with impunity.

His contact had indicated the mission would depart soon, but he hadn't known the precise time due to mission security. He also hadn't been able to shed any light on what steps the Chinese government intended to take against the only other spacecraft in orbit.

If the official government decided not to directly act against the Indian-built ship owned by the Americans, the Dragon would surely arrange some suitable sabotage to remove them from the game. If that sparked a greater conflict, so be it.

The soft rap at his door caused him to frown. He'd left strict instructions not to be disturbed. He secured his computer, rose to his feet, and unlocked the door. One of his bodyguards bowed when he looked out.

"Deepest apologies, Ambassador. Your secretary indicates you have a visitor that you should see without delay."

That surprised Chen. His secretary would not interrupt this moment unless there was need.

"Send the visitor in at once," he said. He returned to his desk and resumed his seat. This should be quite interesting.

Another rap at the door a few moments later preceded the entrance of the guard and a short man with blond hair. An American by all appearances.

The man waited until the guard retreated and closed the door before he bowed deeply. "Ambassador Chen, my name is Arthur Hyde." The man then uttered a long code phrase that only an operative of the Dragon would know.

That intrigued Chen. He'd thought he knew every operative inside America. Obviously not.

Chen gestured toward one of the chairs in front of his desk. "Please sit, Mister Hyde. I'm told your news is quite urgent. Perhaps you'd care for a drink to ease your story."

The man smiled. "I wouldn't turn down some whiskey, but I believe it can wait until I'm done, sir."

"Proceed then."

"As you probably surmised, I'm embedded inside the United States government. Something has come to light that is important enough to warrant I reveal my existence to you.

"I work for the CIA at a high level. There have been meetings taking place between my superiors and others in senior leadership that I believed revolved around what was taking place with Clayton Rogers and his spaceship on Mars. That much turned out to be true, but there was more.

"The United States government is, of course, aware of the

Asharim and their technology now. The new factor is that Secretary of State Queen was kidnapped briefly by an organization familiar with Asharim technology, operating inside the United States—an organization that is not connected with the Dragon."

Chen slowly straightened in his chair. "Are you sure of that?"

The man nodded. "I've now confirmed it independently with two sources that were present at the meeting. Queen briefed the president and others on the existence of this group.

"A former FBI agent named Brenda Cabot kidnapped Secretary Queen and took him through a gate to a location where they met with Harry Rogers and Jessica Cook. I presume that location was Mars. Possibly an old resistance base there."

That was quite the revelation. Someone here on Earth had access to a gate, the Holy Grail of Asharim technology. How could the Dragon not have known about them?

"I see," Chen said coolly. "This is indeed explosive information. Have you determined anything else about her group?"

The man shook his head. "I'm afraid not, sir. It's entirely possible that more information has been shared but has not yet made its way to my ears."

"I assume that you have instructions for me," Chen said.

"That's correct. I'm to continue assisting you in every way possible. I have many assets inside the various arms of the US government. Those are now at your disposal.

"Our superiors are willing to risk anything to gain access to that gate. I feel confident that a courier with instructions to that effect is already in route."

That wouldn't surprise Chen at all. For possession of a gate, the Dragon would set China against America in a heartbeat. Millions of dead was a small price to pay for the universe.

With a smile, Chen rose to his feet. "This is indeed momentous news. Allow me to pour you one of the finest whiskeys in my bar. We shall toast to the success of the Dragon."

* * *

It took quite a bit of persuading to convince Commander Krueger to come out and meet their new friends. He was rightly concerned there would be some type of betrayal.

Clayton had to admit there was a risk. None of them truly knew the people of this world. Despite what he believed, the sacrificial altar on the top of the hill might belong to the very people they were going to dine with tonight.

It was with that in mind that Krueger decided Gunnery Sergeant Danvers and his best people would take up positions watching the camp. If there were any shenanigans, the frighteningly competent man would settle it.

Mick Bird and Penny Cash—his civilian employees trapped on this unplanned adventure—would accompany Clayton. This was an all-hands-on-deck sort of event. Those not directly involved in watching over them were going to have to socialize and learn about their new hosts. Every additional pair of ears might hear a critical piece of information.

Krueger took in the camp as they walked closer. "Perhaps it's just me, but it sure looks as if they're a little lax with their security. We have people in the woods watching them. They should have sentries out to make sure that doesn't happen."

Clayton could see the logic in that. He wasn't sure why they didn't. Perhaps he should ask.

In a very similar fashion to when he'd approached the camp the first time, soldiers came out to meet them. Thankfully, they didn't feel the need to point their weapons at him or his companions. They merely formed up around the group and escorted them into camp.

He did note that the soldiers were eyeing the modern weapons carried by his friends. They were radically different from the long rifles the Volunteers carried. The Volunteers might not even understand that the weapons were multi-shot, much less fully automatic. That would be a truly unpleasant surprise for them if things went badly.

That set him to wondering why the technology for weapons had not improved here over the last several hundred years. Had their population been so low that they had no time? Or was this some kind of ritualized behavior?

An anthropologist would have a field day here, but he didn't have time to worry about it. He made a mental note to see about sending one if he ever got home.

Once again, Adorno and her military companions waited for them outside the large tent. Unlike last time, the sides were raised and the contents had been rearranged. It seemed to be set up for a party gathering now.

Clayton bowed toward the woman as they approached. "Susanna Adorno, allow me to introduce the military leader of our expedition, Commander Karl Krueger. He's a Navy special operations officer."

Krueger mimicked Clayton's bow. "Ma'am. It's a pleasure to meet you."

The woman eyed his camouflage clothing and strange gear. "Commander. I confess that I thought Mister Rogers dressed strangely, but your adornment is even more unusual. I barely know where to begin asking questions about it."

The officer smiled. "Wherever you like, of course."

Clayton cleared his throat and introduced Mick and Penny then allowed Krueger to name his people. Adorno did the same for her senior officers.

With the introductions out of the way, she gestured for them to proceed under the tent. "Meal preparation is always a challenge in the field, but we've done what we can to provide some palatable food. I do hope it is to your taste."

"I'm certain it will be fine," Clayton said. "If I might ask: Commander Krueger was somewhat concerned that you didn't have sentries posted along our route of approach. Aren't you concerned that the Asharim will come upon you unawares?"

She smiled. "We do have sentries out but not so close to camp. They are set up some distance away along all the avenues of approach that the Asharim might use. If they detect enemy forces in any number, they'll send word back here quickly. We are in no danger."

Krueger didn't seem convinced. "With all due respect, ma'am, it's the enemy's job to do inconvenient things at the worst possible moment for you. If they know how you have your sentries set up, they might be able to slip around and surprise you."

"My military commanders disagree. I suppose the possibility exists, but we would surely hear the fighting if they tried to overrun any of our lookout posts. There is no method they can use to slip past so many observers with any force at all.

"I grant you the possibility that they may scout our position, but they won't pose any danger to it. Their strength lies in their defenses in the city. They know that. They'll wait there for us."

"The perimeter is my responsibility," Major Logan said. "I take that duty quite seriously. You may trust that we are in no danger tonight.

"If I might ask, what manner of weapon is this? As a rifle, it seems quite short. Its accuracy must be terrible at anything more than a few dozen yards."

Krueger's smile widened. "Appearances can be deceptive, Major. I can hit a man-sized target at quite a distance with this weapon. Perhaps, if circumstances permit, I might demonstrate it for you tomorrow."

"That would be very interesting," the officer agreed. "I see a particular pattern in your clothing would make it difficult to see you in the foliage. That's quite clever."

"I wish I could take credit for it, but some bureaucrat in Washington probably figured it out."

The man frowned. "Washington? Did you perhaps mean some bureaucrat with General Washington? I would have thought him long dead."

Clayton allowed himself a smile. It seemed he and his people weren't the only ones that had some adjustment to do.

"That's a very long story," he told the officer. "One that I'm convinced we can expand on at length. However, the food will be getting cold. Perhaps we should sample it before we settle in for a long night of conversation and getting to know one another."

Adorno nodded. "Quite right. Please, step this way. Our beer is perhaps not the best, but it is palatable."

Late-night parties weren't exactly Clayton's thing, but he'd spent more than enough time at such events. Tonight was important. They had to learn as much as possible about the world they were trapped on.

He'd learned one never got a second chance to make a first impression. Tonight, he would make these people his friends.

Clayton hoped Commander Krueger was wrong about the danger. He had no desire to fight anyone, much less at night. With any luck, Krueger's fears would prove unfounded.

17

K athleen stepped out into the wide bay and stared around in amazement. The damn place had easily four or five times as many vessels as she'd seen inside the base in France. The designs were different, but she wasn't sure what that meant. Honestly, she wasn't sure it really mattered. Alien ships were alien ships.

Nathan stepped up beside her. "It looks as if you score another point, Mother. We do indeed have air to breathe."

She shot him a look of annoyance. Even though his words hadn't been offensive, his tone was. "Your attitude is wearing on me. I suggest you try to be less of an ass."

He took two steps away and turned back to consider her. "You've known who I am my entire life. Hell, you've had a big part in making me the person I am. If there's any considering to be done, I suggest you consider how our circumstances have changed."

"What the hell is that supposed to mean?"

Nathan gestured around them. "Does this look like your corporate headquarters? Oh, that's right! You don't have one of those anymore. Not only that, you don't have any people, either. The government took everything. The only things we have are on our backs."

He drew his pistol and pointed it at her head. "I have nothing to lose by shooting you, and you'd best begin remembering you're not the boss of me."

The sight of the deadly weapon pointed at her did indeed frighten her, but she wasn't going to show fear to the likes of him. Once people knew someone was afraid, they'd come back again and again to take what they wanted.

She reached out, grabbed the barrel of his pistol, and pulled it to her forehead. "Pull the trigger and then figure out how you'll get off this stupid station. Can you fly the shuttle? No? Do you know the gate code for Earth? No? That's unfortunate."

Kathleen pushed the pistol away in a safe direction and planted her knee in his crotch. That was a fairly risky maneuver. There was a chance he'd shoot her for it. Still, it was a chance she had to take. Her dominance must be absolute.

The blow doubled her son over. Thankfully, he didn't shoot her. Rather than provoke him further, she strode away without looking back.

Inside, she was trembling. She'd never been in as weak a position as she was right now. Nathan was correct. Her only possessions, her only advantages, were what she carried in her mind.

She needed to find a way to turn this around. If she could find a way to get these ships back home, she was certain she could use them. Perhaps reducing the nation's capital to rubble would convince Queen to surrender.

An airlock similar to the one they'd found on the ship, only much larger, stood in front of her. It opened at her touch. In fact, both doors did. A wide corridor sat beyond it.

She frowned and looked at the deck. Everything was so clean. Shouldn't an ancient facility like this be coated in dust? Perhaps there were machines that kept everything in working order.

Right now, her only concern was determining who controlled this facility—if it was occupied at all. It seemed as though anyone here would know the shuttle had arrived. Hell, it should know the ship was sitting out there in space near it.

A glance over her shoulder showed her son hobbling along behind her, his pistol once again in its holster. Good. He'd learned his lesson. Too bad it wouldn't last.

The idiot would continue challenging her unless she acquired enough power to keep him in his place. At this moment, he had no choice but to follow her orders. That would change the moment they had a way back to Earth.

He'd always been a problem for her, but he'd had his uses. Now she thought that time was coming to an end. To keep things tidy, she needed to acquire muscle of her own and then eliminate him.

As she'd told him just a few weeks ago, she didn't need to have him to create grandchildren. She could do that in a lab. With the right amount of money, she could hire a suitable woman to bear her grandchildren. Yes, that was sounding better every day.

The wide corridor led deeper toward the center of the station. It seemed sensible to place critical facilities inside the deepest part of the station. She wasn't sure what those looked like, but until she explored the area, she couldn't be sure. The center of the station would be an excellent place to start.

What she found when she got there confounded her. The center of the station appeared to be an atrium. The wide-open space was perhaps one hundred meters across and a dozen levels tall. Based on her relative position, she seemed to be in about the middle.

Running from the top of the chamber down to the bottom was a thick cable. She couldn't tell what it was made of, but it didn't seem to be metal.

Perched on the cable was a huge cylinder that filled the atrium completely. It rested at the very top. The only reason she could tell it wasn't the roof was the gap that went around the edge. It was deep enough for her to see that the cylinder was a separate object.

She considered the strange setup for a moment but wasn't able to determine what it could be. Perhaps a massive elevator for moving things from one level to the other?

Kathleen watched her son walk around the circumference of the central area. Only when she was sure he was far enough away did she step near the railing. It would be just like Nathan to try to throw her over the edge and damn the consequences.

The floor of the atrium seemed to be made of clear material. She could see it was longitudinally split, almost as if it were a massive hatch that closed around the cable. Considering that she could see the cable continuing down toward the planet beyond the edge of the station, that didn't seem to be a stretch.

This tickled the edge of her memory. She'd read something about this kind of technology before. Was this a space elevator? A way of cheaply transporting a large amount of goods from the planet to orbit?

If it was, she wondered why the aliens used it. They obviously had spaceships. They even had small craft capable of entering an atmosphere. Why build something so radically different?

Kathleen shook her head. She wasn't going to find her answers standing here wondering.

It took her a moment to locate the stairs about a quarter turn to her left from the atrium. "I'm going to see what that is," she told her son. "Are you going to continue being difficult?"

He gave her an angry stare. "No. You've won again. For now."

That was so like him. He couldn't keep his thoughts to himself. She wasn't going to miss that at all.

Without waiting for him to respond, she turned and headed for the stairs. If that really was an elevator, she might see if it could take them down. The station was obviously unoccupied. Any answers would probably come from the planet.

It took several hours before Molly Goodwin was ready to accompany Harry up to the top of the mesa. She was leading a rescue effort, after all. He couldn't very well tell her he knew where his father had gone. Not yet.

When she finally had everyone performing their tasks, she set her assistant to keeping an eye on things and accompanied him to the path leading up to the top of the mesa.

She stared up the path at the huge rockfall. "What a mess. If there wasn't already a rope there, I wouldn't believe it was possible for anyone to get past that."

He smiled at her. "It all depends on the level of training. I went up last night."

Molly gaped at him. "Are you serious? It was as black as a pit last night. How could you possibly have climbed over that?"

"I won't say it was easy. Have you ever done any rock climbing before?"

"A little."

"Then this is going to be a piece of cake. Basically, we'll climb directly up the face until we get to the top of that big boulder. It's a lot easier on the other side."

She didn't seem convinced, but she was ready to give it a try. Moving carefully and slowly, he assisted her on the climb until they stood on top of the mesa.

When they were away from the edge, she stared back down. "I can't believe we just did that. Worse, I can't imagine going back down. Whatever you brought me up here for better be worth it."

She gave him a smile, probably to take any sting out of what she'd just said.

"I think you'll find it fascinating."

He led her to the depression and pulled the brush out of the way. "We're going down there. I brought lights for us."

"You brought me up here to go spelunking?" she asked incredulously. "I don't want to find myself wedged in some tight crevice I can't get out of."

"It only goes down a few meters and opens up almost immediately. Trust me."

With seeming reluctance, she sighed. "I hope to God you're not just a nutter."

"The jury is still out on that."

He clicked his light on and went down into the passage. Once he'd reached the bottom, he turned and shined the light back up. "See? Just come down right to here."

She made it about two-thirds of the way down before the ground slid beneath her feet. She shrieked as she came the rest of the way down.

He caught her arm to steady her as she came to a stop. "Are you okay? No twisted ankle or anything?"

She shook her head. "I'm fine. Now what is this place? A cave?"

He helped her to her feet then turned his light down the corridor.

"Bloody hell!" she said. "This is artificial! No way straight lines like this happen in nature."

"This may be hard to believe, but somebody put this here before New Zealand was colonized. I'm not joking. When I said aliens, that wasn't an exaggeration or a joke. Human beings associated with them dug this mesa out and constructed a facility inside of it."

He took a few steps and gestured for her to follow him. "Let me show you a few things I found last night. I'm afraid some of this is a little grisly."

Harry had already identified several of the skeletons as heavy-worlder. He wasn't interested in frightening her with the bones, but the dead warriors had left armor and weapons scattered about as well.

It only took a moment to find one of the latter under a thick layer of dust. "See this? You'll note that I haven't disturbed it. It's been here for a very long time."

Taking care not to scatter choking dust all around them, he raised the weapon off the floor and shook it a little. The power pack was undoubtedly dead, so there was no danger in allowing her to examine it more closely.

He put his flashlight between his teeth and extended the weapon on his palms.

Molly stepped closer and examined it. "I've never seen anything like it, and most of my family likes to shoot. So do I."

"Let me give you the nickel tour. Once I show you the bottom level of this facility, you won't doubt me any further."

"I don't need to see any more to believe you. This is tremendous. Momentous. Is that what your father was after when he came here? Is that why the United States sent military people to take him into custody?"

She wiped her face with a hand. "You know I have to report this. I can't possibly keep my mouth shut."

He nodded. "I suspected that would be the end result when you figured out my identity. Come on. If you're going to report this, you'll want to see everything I have."

Harry took her down to the very lowest level and showed her the engineering room and then the gate room.

Molly stared around in awe. "You weren't joking about aliens. Even in decrepit condition, I can tell this was high technology and it's been here a *very* long time."

She turned toward him and put her hands on her hips. "I want to hear the full story. I deserve to hear it all."

"I'll tell you everything you want to know, but I think I should mention the glowing square right there is powering the arch on the wall. I can't control it yet, but that isn't a solid wall.

"It's actually the entrance to a quantum tunnel. One that leads to other worlds. You're not going to find my father or anyone else you're searching for. They went through that. They won't be coming back unless I figure out how to go after them."

"Even having seen all this, I find that hard to believe. You mean like Mars? Did you get back here with something like that?"

"Exactly. We found a base in much better condition on Mars. Honestly, I've been to other star systems already. I'll be happy to show you once I get it working.

"The aliens that designed this technology had a civilization that spanned some unknowable distance and probably included thousands or tens of thousands of star systems. That gate right there is the key to the universe."

Molly made a slow turn, looking at everything around her. "This is going to change the world. This is what America wanted. They'll probably do anything to get this technology.

"Hell, so will my government. Do you realize you've just started a mad scramble to possess this technology? Wars have happened for far less."

Harry nodded grimly. "That's why we have to keep this quiet for as long as possible. Do you want China coming here to take it? They will. How far away are they, and what is their relative military strength?"

It was her turn to pale. "Bloody hell."

18

"We got some codes that might interest you," Kevin McHugh said to Jess.

She looked up from the screen on her desk and raised an eyebrow. "Oh?"

"I went with your friend Colonel McCarthy to the base in France and looked at the ships before he started bringing them back here. There was one open when your people got there, and it had a code that led to the ship you guys are looking for. I'm betting that's how your bad guys got in."

"We knew it had to be something like that," she said glumly.

"We found something else interesting," he said. "It seems the person who used the fighter as a controller also viewed a couple of videos of the fighter using the gate. That stood out to me, so I took a peek.

"It turns out that the fighter used two different sets of coordinates that I think you'll find very helpful. One of them opens up on the far side of the moon. I can't tell you where, but it's definitely the moon.

"The second one opens a gate on the side of a mountain over a jungle. The night sky looks familiar. Though I'm no expert, I think it might be South America."

"That's great news," she agreed. "I don't suppose you have any ideas on activating the big gate?"

He shook his head. "The people you assigned to examine it found a few more access panels, but the equipment isn't familiar to me. I'm still working on my vacuum certification, so I can go out and see for myself.

"I'm not too hopeful, though. I might not be able to figure out what it does in a short period of time. Anything that I can access, I could probably work out. Sealed components are another story."

She'd been afraid of that. Well, there was nothing she could do to speed the process along. "Do the best you can. We appreciate it."

He bowed his head. "You bet."

Once he was gone, she considered her options. The exploration of the Asharim site on the planet below was going well but slowly. It might yet prove to be a gold mine, but she was tempted to focus her attention elsewhere.

The latest update from Harry indicated he was going to discuss the situation with the government of New Zealand. No doubt that would stir up a whole bunch of new trouble.

Up to this point, their people had controlled the gates, except for the one Brenda Cabot and the Families had. Of course, no one wanted to reveal their existence to the world at large, so they wouldn't be broadcasting the knowledge.

Bringing one of the alien spaceships out into the light of day was a different story. That would prove to be a huge deal for everybody. The United States knew about the Asharim. No one else did. Not yet.

Once that became common knowledge, it would start a mad scramble to possess the technology. That would inevitably lead to war.

With the number of people learning about what was going on, that day wasn't far off, either. Would it be better to control the method in which they revealed what they'd learned? That was something to discuss with Harry.

In any case, it wasn't going to stop the government of New Zealand from taking control of the ruined base. That was a given. Based on what she'd heard about its condition, it wouldn't do them a whole hell of a lot of good. If Harry took the power cube from the gate, they wouldn't even be able to use it.

Of course, to do that, he had to get what he needed from it first. Unfortunately, the damned thing seemed to be locked up tight.

For the next few minutes, she considered the various options and made her decision. Things were about to spin out of control, so she might as well make some friends down under. They'd need allies against the United States and possibly China.

New Zealand wasn't powerful enough to deter China from invading. Its military just wasn't up to the task of defying a superpower. If she could bring Australia into the deal, and possibly Japan and South Korea, that would change the equation.

She thought about adding India to the list but rejected them. That was too risky. While they weren't as volatile as Pakistan, they had elements inside their government that would be much more problematic than she'd care to deal with.

Her mind made up, she rose to her feet and headed for the gate room. As expected, McCarthy was looking one of the ships over. The room held more than the last time she'd been there. The new ones must be the ones from the base in France. Room was limited until they figured out a way to get the ships outside, but the information Kevin had provided might be the key.

She was pleased to see the pilot working inside the same class of small craft as the crashed cargo ship. It had room for Kevin McHugh and some military types.

Jess walked through the lock and up to the front of the ship. "Everything working on this one?"

McCarthy shrugged a little. "That's what the automated systems are saying. I don't know enough to double-check anything."

"Excellent. We're taking it to New Zealand. Harry needs Kevin as soon as we can get him there, and he found a way to make that possible. He found gate codes that supposedly lead to the moon and possibly South America. The moon would be better, I think."

The ex-marine nodded slowly. "Probably. Are you sure this is the best idea? If something goes south, we'll be a long way from any kind of help."

"I think we have to. Time is growing short, and I want to make the biggest impact I can on our potential allies. We're international pariahs and need some governments in our corner."

"You're the boss," he said agreeably. "I'm ready to head out whenever you are."

"I'll get everyone together."

That took almost half an hour, but they finally had everyone in the shuttle. McHugh sat behind the pilot's couch where Jess could look back and see him. She'd taken the copilot's seat, of course.

Five of Harry's men took up the remaining seats. They were armed for bear, so to speak. All had advanced body armor and flechette rifles. She devoutly hoped they didn't need that kind of firepower today.

"We're ready," she told McCarthy. "Open one of the gates."

They'd held off testing the addresses because she couldn't be sure of the conditions on the other side. Honestly, she wasn't sure the gate would stop a vacuum from sucking all the air out of the chamber and wanted all her people away before they made the attempt.

"Here we go," Black Jack said. He tapped a control on his console, and the gate activated, filling the arch with mist and lightning that quickly cleared.

At first, she thought it had opened to another chamber, but she finally picked out the stars. She was looking through the gate at open space. Jess checked her console and found the chamber still had an atmosphere. It seemed as though the gate was somehow keeping the air from rushing out.

"At least we know we can have people in here next time," she said. "Let's see where that is."

McCarthy lifted the shuttle into the air and edged forward. Moments later, they'd slipped through the gate and into space. The sky opened up as soon as they were through, and she saw they were in a crater.

He took the shuttle up, and Jess got her first good look at their surroundings. It sure looked like the moon. That would be great news. It was a lot closer to Earth than any of the other external gates they'd found.

McCarthy pointed at part of the sky in the new screen. "I recognize that constellation. Virgo. It looks just right, so I suspect we're still in our own solar system. Let's take a trip farther up and see if we can determine where."

He brought them up high enough to see the curvature of the body they'd emerged on. That brought the planet it was orbiting into view. Earth. The gate had indeed opened on the moon.

She grinned. "This is perfect! We need to make note of where the gate is so that we can create a base there."

McCarthy glanced at her. "How do you know there isn't one there already?"

Jess blinked. "I guess I don't. We'll have to send through a search party to make sure. We still have radio contact with *Freedom Express*?"

"Sure do. The gate is still open. I'll pass word back for them to do that."

Jess looked at the Earth hanging in front of them as he murmured into his headset. Once he finished speaking, she continued. "It looks like we're in a good position for a trip to New Zealand. I can see it right there. Do you have the coordinates for the base?"

At his nod, she pointed. "Then let's get going."

"Aren't you worried they'll detect us?"

She shrugged. "If China isn't aware of what we've found yet, they will be soon enough. They have to have spies all through the American government. Still, I take your point.

"Let's not make a production out of this. Keep our speed to a reasonable level, and maybe they'll dismiss us as some type of aircraft once we get down into the atmosphere."

He seemed to consider that for a moment. "I'll take us in over the deep ocean. From there, we can come in low and fast. Radar is good, but if we're on the deck, they probably won't spot us."

"You're the pilot. Make it happen."

She spent the next half hour worrying someone was going to come after them, but they made it down to the ocean without anyone raising alarm. At least she didn't think they did. At least no one sent any jets after them.

Once he was down into the atmosphere, Black Jack McCarthy

leveled the shuttle and increased its speed until they were flying across the water at an insanely low altitude. The waves seem to be lapping just below her feet.

"Do you think you could pull up just a little?" she asked.

The ex-marine test pilot grinned at her. "Feeling a little nervous? Don't worry. We've got plenty of space. There's at least ten meters of open air between us and the water."

"Somehow, that doesn't make me feel any better."

He laughed. "I'm scanning far enough ahead to pick up any ships. Unless we have a rogue wave, we should be okay. Frankly, I should see that far enough in advance to hop over it, too."

That didn't stop her from feeling as if they were about to crash-land on the water. The only thing she could do was close her eyes and cross her fingers. And her toes.

Twenty minutes later, McCarthy cleared his throat. "We're coming up on New Zealand. I've edged around so we're coming into a relatively unpopulated area. If somebody calls the government and complains about a plane flying low and fast, they'll send someone to check it out. I'd rather avoid that."

So would she. An armed confrontation was something they could probably avoid, but she'd rather not take unnecessary chances.

It seemed to be taking longer to get to the landing area than it had taken to get to New Zealand, but she imagined Black Jack had slowed the shuttle down a little.

"We're almost to the mesa," he said half an hour later. "I'm picking up some aircraft off to the south. I think they're helicopters out in the search pattern. They don't seem to have spotted us."

Jess sat up and watched the approach on the screens in front of her. The land around the mesa was beautiful—wild and untamed.

Black Jack waited until they were almost to the mesa before he lifted the shuttle higher and brought it to a hover over the rocky top.

That's when Jess noticed the area wasn't completely empty of people. Harry and an unknown woman stood several hundred meters away. Her partner waved while the woman gawked at them with her mouth open.

"Set us down somewhere close to them," she told McCarthy. "It's time to meet the neighbors."

19

Brenda woke when someone knocked on her door.

"Just a minute," she called out groggily as she sat up. A glance at the clock on her nightstand told her it was just before dawn. She pulled her thoughts together, stood, and threw a robe on. If someone wanted her this early, she probably didn't have time to get dressed before she heard their news.

Victor Holyfield stood outside her door. The large man bobbed his head. "I'm sorry for waking you. They need you downstairs. It's urgent."

If they were sending for her at this hour, it had to be. "Do I have time to get dressed?"

He nodded. "I'll wait out here."

She closed the door, dressed quickly, and stepped out to join him. "Give me the rundown."

"It was my turn on the night shift. Cyrus just sent a runner over with information I think you'll want to hear directly."

"Is there a reason you didn't just call me down? We have these new devices called telephones."

The young man gave her a smile as they climbed into the elevator. "I suppose I could've done that, but he wanted to be discreet. The walls up here are pretty thin. If your phone rings, other people wonder what's happening."

That was one thing she didn't like about their new accommodations. The building could do with some serious renovation.

The elevator opened onto the lobby of their building. In a higher-class neighborhood, it might have a doorman. Not here. In fact, everything still seemed to be closed up for the night.

Appearances could be deceiving, however. One of the rooms just off the lobby housed the security group tasked with making sure their living arrangements remained secure. If they determined hostile forces were moving into the area, they'd see that the building began evacuation before things became too dangerous.

Not that she expected that to happen anytime soon. Every federal agency was searching for her and the Families, but she hadn't given them anything to indicate she was even in Washington, DC. Admittedly, every ordinary criminal probably thought the same of the police.

If she'd had her way, she'd have moved their headquarters to one of the states surrounding the district. The capital wasn't the safest place for them at the moment.

She made a mental note to look into that again. There had to be a better way to balance security and convenience.

Victor rejoined the other security man monitoring the cameras and left Brenda with the courier.

She recognized him as one of Cyrus's junior assistants: Danny Benoit. He rose from his seat at the table and inclined his head. "Miss Cabot."

"Morning, Danny. What have you got for me?"

He pulled the data stick out of his pocket and handed it to her. "There was some type of major sabotage at Area 51. That's where they moved all the captured Asharim technology. From what we hear, the loss was total. It's all gone."

That set her back on her mental heels. "Seriously? Are we sure it was sabotage? Maybe they had the mother of all lab accidents. The technology can be dangerous."

"We're pretty sure. Someone figured out the US government had it and decided they shouldn't. That's my read on the matter."

She took the data stick, walked over to one of the computers, and sat down to review the report. There wasn't much to it: two communications intercepts and what looked like a few long-range pictures using a telephoto lens from a great distance, so they lacked a lot of detail.

The intercepts were more interesting. They were both brief and appeared to be phone conversations. Someone had said something on an unsecure line that one of their people was monitoring—or probably one of their programs, if she was being honest.

The NSA would be horrified if they suspected the capabilities the Families possessed for intelligence gathering. Which, now that the US government was aware of them and the Asharim, was probably the case.

It only took her a minute to read the entirety of both conversations, and she saw what Danny was talking about. One of the callers was a military officer of some kind contacting a superior at the Pentagon. He never mentioned the Asharim by name or what had happened, but he stressed several times that this wasn't an accident.

The other call sounded significantly more suspicious. It mentioned the Asharim by name. Or rather, someone in the background mentioned them loudly enough to be audible on the call. The woman doing the speaking immediately instructed the other person to be silent in Chinese. That was doubly interesting.

"Do we have any idea who this person is?" she asked.

"The voiceprint isn't on file. If you think it's worth the risk, we can have one of our people at the NSA run part of the call against their databases."

Brenda immediately shook her head. "It's not worth the risk. Everything there is already under a microscope. We can't chance drawing undue attention to our people or ourselves. I'm operating on the assumption the call was made from a burner phone. Is that correct?"

"Got it in one. The destination number was also a burner, but we isolated the cell tower it used. This may come as a shock to you, but the Chinese embassy here in Washington uses that cell tower."

"So do a ton of other important people," Brenda said. "I don't want to assume anything. Did the recipient say anything?"

"Just a couple of words. Hardly enough to recognize who it was without utilizing the NSA databases."

She rubbed her face tiredly. She really needed coffee. "We have to assume the Chinese government is aware of the Asharim now. With the heightened tension between the two governments, this greatly increases the opportunity for unfortunate occurrences.

"I think the best course is to monitor every communication in the area around the Chinese embassy as closely as we can. I realize the NSA is doing the same, so keep an exceptionally low profile. Start capturing voice files for every caller that uses that cell tower. I'll also want our audio for these calls."

"You'll have it within the hour. Cyrus has already increased the monitoring of that cell tower and is capturing logs and voiceprints for everyone that uses it. If we get a hit on the guy, we'll let you know immediately."

Brenda let him go and made her way back up to her apartment. She wanted to take the time to prepare and eat breakfast alone while she pondered her next actions.

She was tempted to do something exceptionally risky. The thought made her smile. As if everything they were doing wasn't dangerous enough already.

Well, there was dangerous and then there was *dangerous*.

By the time she'd fixed herself a simple breakfast, eaten it, and fully woken up, she'd decided to proceed with her crazy plan.

The morning traffic leaving the building was in full swing when she made her way back to the security room. The majority of the residents here didn't realize they even had a security room. They just thought it was the area the building manager used.

Victor was preparing to hand responsibility over to his relief when she walked in. He raised a hand and stepped over to her. "You need me for anything?"

"Did Danny send over some audio files for me?"

The big man nodded. "We got a data stick right here."

"Pull the call to the Chinese embassy off it and see that a courier gets it into the hands of someone Secretary of State Queen trusts. Make sure the courier can't be traced back to us. I'm going to write out a note to go along with it."

Victor raised an eyebrow. "Are you sure that's the best idea? The guy kind of hates you."

She smiled coolly. "Then he's really going to love me after this."

* * *

CLAYTON ENJOYED the strange food more than he probably should have. He was used to eating the very best of everything, so even moderately decent food tasted better than usual after the military's MREs.

They'd talked late into the night about these people's situation here on this world and the Earth from which they departed centuries ago. Susanna entertained him with stories both of this world and the last.

He had to admit he was a sucker for pirate tales. He also had to admit she was a consummate storyteller. She'd obviously practiced her timing and delivery to enhance the stories she wove. Perhaps not professionally or even intentionally. It might be that she simply had style.

The amount of beer he'd consumed might also have had something to do with it. The quality of the brew had been good when he began his meal, but continued consumption hadn't hurt his appreciation of it.

She was in the middle of telling them something one of her ancestors had recounted about Port Royale when Commander Krueger leaned over and whispered into his ear. "We really need to call it a night."

Clayton slid his eyes momentarily over to the other man. He'd trained himself not to look at his watch when meeting with other people so as not to seem hurried, but realized it must be quite late.

When Susanna reached the end of her tale and they'd shared their appreciation, he cleared his throat. "As much as it pains me to say, I believe we really should be bringing our evening to an end. My companions and I are tired, and I'm sure you have important things to do tomorrow."

"Indeed," she replied. "Allow me to share my appreciation for your indulgence of my theatrics. One of my uncles was an inveterate storyteller, and he infected me early. I've never been able to resist an audience."

Commander Krueger quickly got his people into order as Clayton bowed over Susanna's hand. "If you have no objection, I'll accompany Commander Krueger back to speak with you again tomorrow. We still have many things to discuss."

"I'll send Colonel Carver and Major Logan to escort you back to your hill. It's been a pleasure hosting you and your compatriots. You've been perfect guests. I think we shall get along famously."

"I hope so. Until tomorrow, Miss Adorno, General Norris."

The buff military officer extended a hand to Clayton. "It's been a pleasure, Mister Rogers. I look forward to our continued conversation."

Major Logan preceded them out and quickly arranged for a group of soldiers to escort them into the woods.

"I must say that I've learned quite a bit about your people and perhaps even about my own ancestors," the officer said as they made their way into the open field. Several of the soldiers held lanterns up to light their way. He supposed that was so they did not fall into a burrow dug by some local creature.

"As did I," Clayton said. "I hope we have an opportunity to visit the land the Volunteers currently call home. I think that seeing how you've developed from revolutionary times will be singularly interesting."

The soldiers around them reached the tree line and proceeded under the canopy.

Clayton knew that somewhere around them Gunnery Sergeant Danvers and his people were probably watching them. He suspected the men weren't going to reveal themselves until the Volunteers had departed to maintain their security.

"I think that would be interesting as well. It saddens me that such a visit won't occur."

Clayton was just beginning to frown at the officer when the man pulled a pistol out of his belt, aimed it at Colonel Carver, and pulled the trigger.

There was a slight hitch of time between the ignition of the primer and the firearm going off. It wasn't nearly as sharp a sound as a modern pistol, but the boom of the weapon still deafened him.

It did much worse to Carver. The shot took the other officer in the side of the head, and he went down without a word, dead before he realized he was betrayed.

The soldiers all around them quickly turned their weapons to cover the Earthmen.

"I suggest you keep your hands far away from your strange weapons," Logan said with a smile. "We wouldn't want any further misunderstandings, would we?"

Even though he already knew the basic answer, Clayton felt the need to ask the question. "What the hell are you doing?"

"Your presence has vexed my original plans, but I'm staging a coup. Or perhaps betrayal would be a better word. The Asharim are certainly going to enjoy having strangers like yourselves join that bitch of a Privateer in their little ceremony on top of that hill."

The man was selling them out to the aliens. The aliens that liked ritually sacrificing human beings. That filled Clayton's blood with ice.

20

_____

Harry heard Molly Goodwin's inhalation of breath, turned, and saw the Asharim shuttle rise over the edge of the mesa several hundred meters away.

He had to admit that he was more than a bit surprised. The thing was utterly silent. Since he doubted the aliens had just dropped in, Jess must have figured out how to get one of the alien ships out of the bases. Or his brother Nathan had come to eradicate him. Not likely, but possible.

"Oh my God!" Molly gasped. "It's true!"

"Told you," he said as he raised an arm and waved at the shuttle. It slid further over the mesa and settled to the ground a few dozen meters away.

The airlock slid open a few seconds later, and Jess waved back at him as she hopped down to the ground.

"I decided to drop in for a surprise visit," she said with a grin.

"So I see. Meet Molly Goodwin. She's leading the search for my father. Molly, this is my partner Jessica Cook."

Jess extended a hand to the other woman. "Just call me Jess."

Molly hesitantly took Jess's hand. "Harry told me about the aliens, but I confess I didn't believe him. Not completely, at least until your grand entrance."

"That's how I roll." Jess focused her attention on Harry. "I decided it was time to reveal ourselves to the government here in New Zealand. I probably should've told you ahead of time."

"That's quite the reveal," he said dryly. "As it happens, I came to a similar conclusion myself. Hence me telling Molly about the base and giving her a tour."

"Great minds and all that. I brought you a present." Jess turned back toward the shuttle.

Harry's soldiers had exited the shuttle and were watching the perimeter. Black Jack McCarthy was just escorting an unknown man out of the craft.

"Harry Rogers, meet your new best friend, Kevin McHugh. Kevin is a hacker specializing in Asharim technology. He's managed to access the gates and get their destination codes.

"I thought he might be able to control the gate down in this base. If so, you can just go right on through and rescue your father."

Harry shook his head. "You used to work for my father. You know nothing is ever that simple with him. If it were, he'd have already come back through. No. Something's gone wrong on the other side. We just have to hope it's not too bad."

Black Jack escorted the young man up. "Harry."

He held his hand out to the pilot. "It's good to see you living up to your reputation, Black Jack. So you're flying alien ships now?"

The ex-colonel grinned. "You know me, always taking advantage of new learning opportunities."

Harry smiled and focused his attention on Brenda Cabot's man. The guy was young with very hip, round purple lenses on his glasses and a shaved head. "It's a pleasure to meet you, Mister McHugh. I find myself deeply needing your services. I hope you brought your equipment with you."

The man patted a satchel after he shook Harry's hand. "Got it right here, Mister Rogers. Can you tell me what I'm looking at?"

"Call me Harry. There's a gate down below, running off a

temporary power supply that seems to have a missing controller. It won't respond to the handheld I brought with me.

"I suspect whoever set it up locked it to a specific controller. One that's not here anymore. Honestly, I think my father probably took it with him. That might be why he hasn't returned."

"I've never tried to do anything like that, but I'll do my absolute best to get it unraveled for you." The man held his hand out to Molly Goodwin. "Kevin McHugh."

Molly shook his hand. "Mister McHugh."

"I think you should stay with the ship, Colonel," Harry said to Black Jack. "It might be necessary to move quickly if someone gets excited."

"Got it covered."

Harry gestured to his men and started toward the depression. "We'll go back down and see if we can open up the gate. If we can get in and find my father waiting on the other side, we'll bring them back over.

"If not, we'll make sure that the gate works then meet with the New Zealand authorities before proceeding. Do you have any objection to that, Molly?"

"I think that makes perfect sense. I'm sure some bureaucrat is going to disagree with me, but that's my judgment. They can just suck it."

Getting back down to the bottom level only took a few minutes. Jess looked around in shock. "Wow. This place is in worse shape than any of the other bases we found."

Molly blinked at her. "You've found other bases?"

The orbital engineer nodded. "Sure have. A big one on Mars and a mobile one buried in a comet. We even found an abandoned space station out beyond Pluto. All of them were in much better condition than this."

Harry noted that she didn't mention any other bases on Earth. That was good. They needed to keep some secrets to themselves.

Once they arrived in the gate room, Kevin McHugh examined the device sitting in front of the single operational gate. "Yeah, it looks as though somebody rigged up a temporary power supply. This cable right here probably went to the handheld controller. One rigged up to interface directly with the gate through the power supply. That's clever."

The young man pulled a comp out of his satchel and messed around with connectors until he was able to seat the cable to the power supply. "There we go. Yeah. It's not locked out, not in the way you mean. This isn't a security feature. More like an accidental bug. I've got the interface to the controller now.

"There are a number of destination codes in here, but it looks as if the gate accessed only one the last few times. I'll wager that's where your father went. Do you want me to activate the gate?"

"Do it."

His men gathered and raised their weapons as the gate came to life, filling with mist and lightning. It cleared to reveal a dark tunnel beyond.

"We're not going to be able to open the gate from the other side," Harry said. "Keep it open. We might be coming back in a hurry." He led the way through the gate.

* * *

NATHAN STARED at his mother as she led him into the massive chamber at the center of the atrium. What was she doing? What was this place? His eyes narrowed as he watched her begin manipulating a control panel as if she knew exactly what it did. The strange knowledge made him extremely uneasy.

If the machine she'd slept in could change her physically and manipulate her mind, it might be able to control her. In fact, this might not be his mother at all. Just because the woman resembled her didn't make it her.

After all, what was more likely? A machine capable of regenerating a human body or one that created a mechanical device that was similar? He couldn't be sure what he was dealing with.

Obviously, whatever this was, it had his mother's memories.

His eyes narrowed. Or did it? He hadn't really pushed for any specialized knowledge from her. He'd been too busy trying to save their lives.

"What are you doing, Mother?" he asked in an even tone.

She spared him an irritated glance. "There's obviously no one on this station. Any idiot can see that. If there had been, they would've come looking for us immediately. The fact that we have been unmolested means we're alone. That means we need to go where the people are."

"That's a lot of words to say nothing. What *exactly* are you doing?"

She tapped a couple of controls and swiped her hand across the screen. The floor beneath their feet shook, and it felt as though an elevator were going down. That wasn't a bad analogy. The large chamber they stood in was dropping to the bottom of the atrium. This was going to be a very short trip.

"We could've just walked down the stairs," he said dryly.

"Really? Well then, I'm so sorry to have wasted your time."

Looking through the transparent floor, he watched in awed consternation as the bottom of the atrium split apart and separated. The chamber continued through where that barrier had been and took them into space.

Now he could see the cable hadn't stopped at the bottom of the atrium. It continued on toward the planet below.

What the hell were they in? The universe's biggest elevator?

The large chamber continued along the cable at a growing pace. He wondered how long it was going to take them to reach the surface at this rate.

"That's quite clever," he finally admitted. "Climb into a large room on the surface, press the button, and go into space. Any idiot can do it."

"Apparently so," his mother said. "The only thing we don't know is what we're going to find down there. With all the wreckage in space, civilization may be gone.

"Or perhaps not. In any case, we'll undoubtedly come across people hostile to us back on Earth. We need allies."

"We didn't need allies until you started us on this harebrained trip," he said. "We could've stayed on the ship and figured out a way to get home. The ship brought us here. It could still take us back. It's by far the most valuable artifact we've found so far. One that might allow us to crush all our enemies."

When she didn't answer, he considered what to say next. How far could he push her before she snapped? Far enough to find out who she truly was?

"We haven't had time to talk since you got out of that machine. What did it do? Make you young again?"

She walked to the edge of the chamber and sat on a handy bench. "I don't know." Her voice sounded tired.

"Well, you have to know something."

"Do I? Maybe I'm just accepting that I've changed. This alien technology can do all these other wondrous things, why not regenerate an old woman's body?"

"Or create some kind of strange duplicate," he said coolly. "How do I know you're really my mother?"

The corner of her mouth quirked up in a cold smile. "Even if I answer that question, how do you know it didn't just copy my mind? That's a slippery road you want to walk down."

"Oh, I'm not the one walking," he said as he sat near her. "You are. I'm just trying to decide what to do about it."

She sat up a little. "Before you get all excited, you should remember that I have you completely in my power. Could you take this space elevator back up to the station? I doubt you can even read the language. The aliens below probably don't speak English, either. How's your Asharim?"

That was annoyingly astute of her.

He shrugged and eased his weapon over until it pointed even farther from her. "I can't know anything for sure. Perhaps you should convince me that you're really my mother."

"When you were six, you wanted a dog. I was allergic, so I said no. Anyone might guess something like that, but I'll wager you remember my exact words. 'If you want a dog, you can move out of my house and live on your own.' That's what I told you. Remember it?"

He could hardly forget. Even after all this time, it still enraged him.

The smug satisfaction in her voice also confirmed this was undoubtedly his mother. Only she would get so much pleasure from being a bitch like this.

The floor under his feet shuddered just barely enough to be noticed. He looked out through the windows and saw clouds. They were already down inside the atmosphere. Unbelievable.

He'd expected something traveling such a long distance along such a slender cable to travel slowly. Well, he supposed aliens could do what they wanted when it came to physics. They could manipulate gravity, so he supposed this was related.

Rather than goad his mother any further, he stared at the floor to see if he could discern their destination.

After a short time, the last of the clouds cleared away to reveal a wide city stretched out below them. From this height, he couldn't tell what condition it was in, but he was willing to bet it was abandoned or had fallen into ruin.

He'd find out soon enough. With their luck, the space elevator would reach the bottom to find the building collapsed and kill them both. If it didn't, they'd probably find man-eating aliens.

21

Queen was tempted to fly out to Area 51 but knew it wouldn't do him any good. All his presence would do was distract the people trying to determine what had happened.

Hell, he already knew what had happened. Someone had gotten wind of the Asharim technology and decided they couldn't afford to let the United States have it.

This was a disaster, pure and simple. They'd been on the edge of achieving something that would've changed the face of the world forever. Someone had taken that from them.

He even knew who had to be behind the attack. Very few people knew about the aliens, and fewer still had the resources to get into such a secure location. That made the suspect list incredibly short.

It was Cabot. It had to be. The bitch had figured out where they'd taken the captured equipment. As a former FBI agent that had actually seen it, the woman knew everything.

Her damned secret organization probably had people embedded in Area 51. They were probably so established it would take weeks or months to figure out who he needed to be suspicious of.

That was what was so frustrating about this damned illuminati business. Even in cases where the secret organization wasn't involved, he'd be seeing their shadowy hands in everything.

A knock at his door pulled him out of his deep funk.

His assistant cracked the door and looked inside. "A courier dropped something off for you, sir. I think you should take a look at it."

He frowned. "What is it, and who sent it?"

"The sender is listed as Brenda Cabot."

That shocked him. Then it pissed him off.

Had she sent something just to taunt him? He'd have thought somebody with FBI training was smarter than that. It would only make him more determined to bring her down.

Queen made a gesture for his assistant to bring the delivery in. The man set a manila envelope on the desk and stepped back. "Security already looked inside. There's a handwritten note and a thumb drive."

"Bring me a laptop. One that we can afford to lose if this has a virus. Make it snappy."

He emptied the contents of the envelope onto his desk. It was as described: a folded note on a regular sheet of paper and a thumb drive. He unfolded the paper and began reading.

Secretary Queen,

I rather expect this contact comes as an unexpected and unwelcome surprise. I'm not sending this message in order to gloat, as difficult as that may be for you to believe. Rather, I felt the need to give you a warning.

We heard about the attack you suffered at Area 51. I want to tender my personal regrets for any injuries or deaths. Based on the images I saw, there must've been more than a few of each.

As difficult as this will be for you to believe, neither I nor my people had anything to do with this. In fact, I believe a third party is involved. One I was previously unaware of.

The data stick I sent to you contains a call my people intercepted that we believe was made by people involved in the attack. Since it does not suit my ends to allow another group to upend the applecart, I'm forwarding this information so you can deal directly with the people who are attacking you.

As unsettling as this will undoubtedly be, if you want to talk about this I'm more than willing to do so under conditions that will assure my safety. I'm not going to be silly enough to give you a phone number that you can trace to me or the area where I'm located.

If you want to talk, all you need to do is post a note to that effect on your social media account. No need to be coy. Just say that you wish you had more of a chance to talk with an old friend from the FBI. My people will see it, and I'll contact you.

Because I know you're a man who likes to nurse grudges, I'm going to say this again. Neither I nor my people carried out this attack against you. We are not enemies of the United States, regardless of what you think. Honestly, the vast majority of my people are fervent patriots.

It's still possible we will make common cause at some point. My people only want to keep humanity safe from the Asharim. Keep that in mind.

Brenda Cabot

Unbelievable. She honestly expected him to buy that load of crap? What kind of idiot did she think he was?

He reread the note and found it just as stupid the second time through.

His assistant came in, carrying a small laptop, which he set on the desk. "This isn't connected to any of our networks and doesn't have any work-related files on it. It should be safe to use."

"Where did it come from?"

The man shrugged. "It belongs to one of the junior assistants. There's no telling what kind of crap is actually on there, but I assume you're not searching for his porn."

That forced a chuckle out of Queen. "No. I could care less what his perversions are."

He plugged a thumb drive into the laptop and looked at the folder that opened. There were two files: one audio and one text. He turned the speaker on and played the audio.

The man receiving the call had a voice he found tantalizingly familiar. He played it several times, and his certainty grew. It wouldn't stand up in a court of law, but he knew that voice belonged to Ambassador Chen.

The text file containing information about the cell towers involved with the call and the phone numbers. He could confirm much of that information with the NSA, and he would.

In fact, he'd have them thoroughly vet everything and try to get the same information without telling them one damned thing about the file.

If Brenda Cabot was telling the truth—and that was a *big* if—the United States might be in even deeper trouble than he'd imagined.

Should the Chinese be aware of the Asharim and their technology, that put a sinister twist on the military confrontation that was growing between the two nations. It also made their possession of the Yucatán Spaceport *much* more troubling.

If they'd decided this technology was connected with the rogue Mars mission that Clayton Rogers had launched, they wouldn't be sending scientists to explore the Red Planet. They'd be sending soldiers.

Not that he cared one bit about what happened to the bastards that had tricked him. His only concern was what they might have found there.

Hell, not might. Had. He'd seen more than enough to accept they had a treasure trove of advanced technology at their fingertips.

He unplugged the thumb drive and pushed the computer away from himself. "Get that scrubbed. I want to make absolutely certain there's no chance it has any information left on it. Give the guy who owns it a large bonus for his trouble. And this might happen again, so pick up a machine at some random box store for us. Just in case."

The man picked up the laptop and nodded. "Will there be anything else?"

Queen smiled coldly. "Summon Ambassador Chen. I think it's time he and I had a heart-to-heart chat. Then get me the president. I'm going to need authority to do what needs to be done."

* * *

CLAYTON OPENED his mouth to say something—he wasn't sure what—to dissuade the man, so he got a mouthful of blood when Major Logan's head virtually exploded in front of him.

Other shots rang out from close by, and the Volunteer soldiers threatening Commander Krueger and the rest staggered or collapsed. That gave an opening for the men on his side to pull their pistols and end the threat.

Clayton was still trying to spit the horrible taste out of his mouth and wipe the blood from his eyes when Krueger grabbed him by the arm and pulled him deeper into the forest.

"We need to get moving. They won't be alone."

While that might be true, Clayton dug his heels in. Literally. "No. We have to warn Adorno. She has to know they've been betrayed."

"They're going to find out soon enough," Krueger said grimly. "Logan wouldn't have acted if the trap wasn't already closing. He was in charge of the sentries. If the Asharim aren't all around us, I'll eat my boots. We need to get up the hill."

"No, dammit. They're going to be slaughtered. Being inside the hill isn't going to do us one bit of good if we're surrounded by an ocean of enemies. We have to warn them so they can fight."

Krueger took a deep breath and visibly gritted his teeth. "Shit. Danvers."

The gunnery sergeant materialized out of the darkness. "Sir?"

"Get Mister Rogers and the rest back to the hill and dig in. I'll take two men and warn the Volunteers about the ambush. Keep an eye out. We're probably going to be coming back under fire. We'll need you to clear a path for us."

"Aye, sir." The marine grabbed Clayton's arm and pulled him forward.

Clayton knew better than to argue at this point. The man had his orders, and he was going to carry them out. If Clayton didn't want to end up over the marine's shoulder, he was going to have to trust that Krueger would take care of business.

The marines all around him had extinguished the lights. It was as dark as the devil's armpit. They had to be using night-vision goggles.

He made a mental note to get something like that in his gear going forward. Hell, he was going to have to have his assistant completely update his bag. His needs and the threats he faced were significantly different than they'd been six months ago.

They reached the hill unmolested. That was actually one hell of a shock. Clayton had been sure the Asharim were going to prevent them from reaching safety.

Unfortunately, he could hear fighting in the distance. The unmistakable booms of black-powder weapons and the sharp, controlled bursts of automatic weapon fire. The Asharim had sprung their ambush, or the Volunteers had found more traitors in their ranks.

Danvers pushed Clayton, Mick, and Penny into the cave entrance. "Stay inside. We don't know what type of weapons they have. I won't have a sniper picking you off."

Clayton stopped just inside the cave. "We need to know what's happening."

"We've already got a drone in the air. We should have information in a couple of minutes. You can look at the screen. Inside. The. Cave."

Since he'd done exactly that earlier, Clayton really didn't have any room to complain. He wasn't sure why he felt the need to observe the fighting personally.

Maybe it was his innate need to control his own destiny. That was a weakness he'd realized he had years ago. Or perhaps weakness was the wrong word. He did revel in overseeing important work.

One of the marines had a tablet out and was reviewing information from the drone as he walked into the chamber. Clayton didn't know much about reading a display at night, but it didn't look as if the Volunteer army was alone.

"Tell me what I'm looking at," he told the marine firmly.

"This is an IR image, sir. The group at the center is at the camp you just came from. There are large groups to the east, northwest, and southwest. They've encircled the camp. The temperature looks a little off, so I'm not certain we're looking at human beings. I've never seen an alien in infrared."

"What do the relative numbers look like? Can they hold them off?"

The other man shrugged. "I have no idea if they can hold out, sir. I'd say the friendly forces are outnumbered at least two to one.

Perhaps three to one. The defenders are going to have an advantage, but if they don't get out of the pocket, they're probably going to get slaughtered."

Clayton cursed. "And you don't have enough ammunition to spring them. Hell, you don't even have enough ammunition for us to hold once they come for us. What are we going to do?"

"Under those circumstances, I'd call for reinforcements," a voice said from behind him.

He turned in surprise and found Harry standing at the entrance to the tunnel leading to the gate. He held a rifle and had several armed men stood behind him.

22

J ess turned to Kevin McHugh as soon as Harry was out of sight. "What's the address of this gate? Can you get me that?"

The young hacker nodded. "Sure. The address for a specific gate is locked in when it's created. That prevents any possibility of having two gates with the same address."

He tapped his comp a few times. "Got it. What do you want me to do with it? Link it to your phone?"

She raised her eyebrows. "You can do that?"

The bald man snorted derisively. "Please. I can do that in my sleep, even if you didn't give me the number first. Let's do this the easy way." He held out his hand.

She considered the security implications, shrugged, and handed him her phone. It wasn't as if Brenda Cabot didn't already have her number.

While the young man worked, Jess turned to Molly Goodwin. "This must all seem so strange to you. If it helps, you'll adjust quickly."

The other woman laughed a little. "If you say so. As I told Mister Rogers, I'm going to have to inform my superiors. I probably should do that now. Can I get someone to escort me back up to the surface so I can make that call?"

Harry had left the three of them alone. If anyone were going to escort Molly up, it would have to be her or Kevin. She wasn't sure she could trust the young hacker not to get sidetracked down some passage, so she'd have to take care of that herself.

A shout came up the passage from the other side of the gate. Jess couldn't quite make out what was said, but she recognized the urgency in the man's tone. Her hand darted down to her waist, and she pulled the pistol she'd begun carrying. Something was wrong.

One of the guards she'd brought with her from *Freedom Express* came tearing down the corridor and skidded to a halt just on the other side of the gate.

"We found them, but there's some type of military crisis involving other bad guys. I figure we have maybe twenty minutes. We need reinforcements. As many as you can get. Have them bring extra weapons and ammunition."

He didn't wait for Jess to respond before he turned and ran back the way he'd come.

"So much for having enough time to do everything nice and slow," Jess muttered. "I'll need that phone, Kevin."

He handed her phone back. "I stuck the address in a text to yourself."

"Thanks."

She called Rex. He answered after a few rings. "Jamison."

"I need the best fighting force you can gather ASAP. I'm going to call *Freedom Express* and get the troops they have on their way first. Be ready. I'll text you the gate address."

She disconnected and scrolled through her contacts until she got one of the gate addresses for *Freedom Express*.

Jess gestured for Kevin to hold up his comp so she could see it. She killed the gate, and the connection to the alien world vanished, showing nothing but a plain stone wall.

Reading from the phone, she entered the address for their mobile base. The gate reconnected, and she saw armed personnel standing in the loading bay.

"Get every single person that can fight in here right now," she shouted. "I'd prefer people that have fought together like Harry's forces, but I need everybody that can shoot.

"I'm going to disconnect the gate connection and get the forces Rex has under his command. Be ready to go as soon as I reconnect the wormhole."

Once the woman nodded, Jess killed the connection and dialed the French base.

Rex was standing just on the other side, outfitted for war. He had several dozen men standing behind him carrying backpacks and extra weapons. They rushed through as soon as the gate formed.

In as few words as possible, she filled Rex in on what she'd been told and what she suspected.

She connected the gate to *Freedom Express* as soon as she finished. Those forces boosted Rex's numbers to about five dozen.

Jess wasn't a trained warrior, but she grabbed one of the flechette rifles and checked it. She'd used one before and was trained well enough. At least she hoped she was.

She turned to Kevin. "As soon as you connect with where Harry went, I want you to take Miss Goodwin back up to the surface. Tell Colonel McCarthy he's to take her down to the camp then return to *Freedom Express*. If we run into serious trouble, we're going to go back there directly."

The hacker nodded, his face pale. "I should probably call Brenda. She'll want to know what's going on."

As soon as the hacker opened the gate back to the dark stone tunnel, Rex led their scratch fighting force forward. Jess followed them. She posted one annoyed man to stay behind and hold onto the comp controlling the gate.

The tunnel twisted and curved a little bit but quickly led them to a chamber where Harry was already directing Rex to head farther up the tunnel.

She saw Clayton Rogers standing beside his son. There were a couple of civilians and what looked to her like some marines nearby.

Her eyes narrowed, and she edged the barrel of her weapon toward what she assumed were the men that had kidnapped her boss.

The elder Rogers raised a hand. "Peace. These men aren't our enemies. We've settled our differences. Mostly.

"Jess, meet Gunnery Sergeant Danvers. He has tactical command of the American forces here. Less than a dozen men. His commanding officer, Commander Karl Krueger, is out trying to save our allies. Which is what we need to help them do."

She felt her eyes narrow. "Gunnery Sergeant *Jacob* Danvers?"

The man's eyes widened. "I'm not sure how you knew that, ma'am."

Jess lowered the barrel of her weapon a trifle. "It seems we have friends in common. I don't know if you knew, but Michael and Sierra Crockett are working for us. So is Emily Adams."

The man blinked in surprise. "I knew they had a classified project they were working on, but I didn't realize it had anything to do with Mister Rogers. Well, that's awkward."

"I couldn't agree more," she agreed.

"As unexpected as this might be, we need to focus," Clayton Rogers said. "We've got two armies just outside the cave. The Asharim—who are apparently devolved from their higher technology selves—are leading an attack against humans friendly to us with a lot of what we're told are slaves. Probably also not human. The people we're trying to save somehow got here around the time of the American Revolution."

Harry shook his head. "We've got a few dozen people. Even modern weapons won't stop thousands. Not if they're determined."

Gunnery Sergeant Danvers held a hand to his ear. Based on the way he was frowning, someone was saying something into an earbud.

"Copy that, sir. We'll be ready."

He looked at Harry Rogers. "That was Commander Krueger. The Volunteer army has broken out of the ambush. They're coming to us, and they have hostiles all over them."

"Then we better get ready," Harry said grimly. "Let's go set up a warm welcome for the Asharim."

* * *

CHEN STEPPED into Secretary of State Queen's office with a smile on his face. He felt certain he understood the true reason he'd been called here so abruptly. It had to be the attack. Somehow, the US government suspected that the Chinese were behind it.

Good luck to them in proving it.

Once the assistant had closed the door behind Chen, he bowed slightly. Somewhat less than a person of Queen's rank was entitled to, but more than enough to seem as though he wasn't slighting him.

"You wished to speak with me, Mister Secretary?" he inquired politely.

The other man glared at Chen. "You're damned right I do. I want to know what the hell you think you're doing."

Chen raised an eyebrow. "I'm afraid you're going to have to give me a little more information to go on, Mister Secretary. Precisely what do you *think* I'm doing?"

"I want to know why you attacked our facility at Area 51."

Chen spread his hands slightly. "I'm afraid that you're under a misapprehension, Mister Secretary. My government has conducted no such operation. Was there an incident?"

Queen slammed his hands down on the top of his desk and stood. "Don't play innocent with me. I heard the recording of your phone call. I heard your voice when they told you the attack had gone off just as you wanted."

That last bit sent a chill down Chen's spine, but he didn't allow his expression to change. The Chinese as a people were well-known for their ability to conceal their emotions, and he was better than most. One of the best, actually.

"Many voices sound similar to the ear, but I can assure you I did no such thing, Mister Secretary. I realize that our governments have placed us into conflict, but I urge you to seek restraint. Don't allow external events to color an already-difficult situation. Don't make accusations that you have no proof of."

"Ah, that's where you're wrong. I *do* have proof! You're probably aware that the NSA captures metadata from all calls that take place into or out of the United States. That includes calls within our boundaries.

"You probably feel fairly confident that we can't save every single scrap of audio data, and you'd be right. Unfortunately for you, I do have audio of your conversation. My government is quite capable of comparing that audio to the voice print we have on file for you."

Chen maintained a mildly curious expression when Queen paused expectantly but said nothing.

After a few moments, Queen continued. "Since you're going to make me tell the entire story, I suppose that I should just get on with it. The voice in the recording matches yours to greater than ninety-five percent. That's enough for an actual conviction in a court of law. I'd call that proof, wouldn't you?"

Chen spent a few moments considering his options and then shrugged. "I, of course, deny all of that. I don't understand why your government would forge evidence in such a fashion, but it hardly matters. I have diplomatic immunity. This farce serves no real purpose."

Queen sat back down and leaned back in his chair. "I expected you to say that. While I can't arrest you—as much as I want to—I can have you take a message back to your country for me.

"The United States hereby revokes permission for you to be here and declares you persona non grata. In fact, we're expelling the entire staff of your embassy. We consider this event to be an act of war."

Chen smiled slightly. "Don't you believe that is taking measures a little out of scale? Did someone blow up one of your cities? I have not heard of any occurrence that would constitute an act of war."

"So that's the game you're going to play? Fine. You're quite aware of what my government came into possession of. You took steps to make certain we didn't retain it. I regret to inform you that your actions were less than total, as many critical pieces are still in our possession.

"That doesn't negate the fact that you attempted to destroy them on our soil. When added together with your seizure of the Yucatán Spaceport, it's obvious that your country seeks direct conflict with us. I gave you many opportunities to step back from the abyss, but you chose to push this fight. Now you have it."

"Critical pieces of what?" Chen asked with false curiously. "If you want me to transport a message to my government, you're going to actually have to say it out loud. Use your words, Mister Secretary."

The other man snorted bitterly. "We *know* you know about the Asharim. I'm not sure how long you've been aware of them, but you're not going to be able to keep that knowledge to yourself any longer.

"Even as we speak, our ambassador to the United Nations is making a presentation to the Security Council. This is all going to be out in the open now.

"That's not going to change your fate, however. I want all Chinese diplomatic personnel out of my country within twenty-four hours. Every last one of you treacherous bastards. If you're still here by sunset tomorrow, I'll arrest you no matter what your status is. Is that clear enough?"

Chen bowed only an insulting fraction of the distance Queen would normally be entitled to, not bothering to pretend at any real respect. "As clear as spring water, Mister Secretary. I cannot wish you luck in your endeavors, but I hope that your regret is brief. Now, it seems I must go pack. Good day."

23

Kathleen felt a lot more uncertainty than she allowed her face to show as the chamber slid into a large building where the space elevator anchored to the planet. Once it stopped moving, she lost all control over events. She would be at the mercy of whoever ruled this place.

The floor vibrated as the chamber came to rest and the large hatches set along the outer walls all opened at once. Her son held his weapon at the ready and turned slowly, looking for threats.

None materialized.

She picked one of the exits at random and strode through it. The room outside was at least a hundred times the size of the chamber itself, though that was hard to see in the dim light cast through too few windows. Overhead, the domed roof soared into the darkness.

Parts of the space held what had likely been cargo at some point. It had collapsed into piles of rubbish. It was obvious that this place had not been occupied in a very, *very* long time. While that added to her safety at the moment, it was a negative in the long-term. Allies would be better.

"This place is as deserted as the ship," Nathan said, lowering his weapon.

"Perhaps," she conceded. "Perhaps not. It may just be that no one was close enough to the building to get here before we did. Or they wanted to have more numbers at their back when they did. We don't know the situation here, so we'd best not assume anything."

"What are you hoping to accomplish here, Mother? Do you really expect to find anything useful? We could've just tried one of the two gate codes that you have in your phone. Once we get back to Earth we can—"

"We can what? Scurry around like mice in the dark, hoping that no one finds us? Don't be an idiot. We need weapons and allies. It's entirely possible this place can provide both."

Nathan looked around meaningfully. "It doesn't seem that way, does it? Anyone that still lives in this place is probably a gibbering savage."

A flicker of movement to her left caught her attention. "I'd keep that opinion to yourself. It seems we have visitors."

She couldn't see where they were coming from because it was behind a large pile of debris, but she could hardly miss the people that walked brazenly into view. They didn't seem the slightest bit worried that she or Nathan posed a threat to them.

The first thing she noticed about the new people was that they were human. Built wider and a bit squatter than she would expect of a normal person, though. Each of the men looked as if he could break them both in half without any effort whatsoever.

Kathleen would hardly call their clothing modern, but it wasn't primitive like a savage's might be. They also carried Asharim weapons.

They surrounded Nathan and her at a distance of about a dozen meters and stood there silently, as if they were waiting for something.

She took a deep breath before stepping forward.

The men directly in front of her raised their weapons, but one of them held a hand out to his comrades. Perhaps he was their leader. He considered her for a moment then said something in a language that she was unfamiliar with.

No, that wasn't quite true. As she considered the noises he'd made, she was able to extract meaning from it. Perhaps it was another of those implanted memories, but she could understand what he was saying if she focused.

The real question was going to be whether or not she could answer him. "My name is Kathleen Bennett, and yes, I did come down from the sky." Astonishingly, it seemed she could speak the alien language.

From the man's expression, he hadn't been expecting her answer. Or perhaps he just hadn't believed she'd understood him.

"You do not look like any of the images of the Masters we possess," the man said, his voice a deep rumble. "You look more like us. Weaker, though."

"That is true," she admitted. "We are not the Asharim. Have you been waiting for them long? Or have you hoped they'd never return?"

The man's weapon lowered slightly, and he allowed himself a brief smile. "Depending on who you ask, some of both. I now know your name, but I do not know who you represent. The fact that you have come from the sky frightens my people. Explain yourself."

She could imagine what the unsaid "or else" might mean for her and her son. "We do not serve the Asharim."

Kathleen knew she was taking a very large risk with that pronouncement, but she was fairly good at reading body language. In her position, she had to be.

"Then who do you serve?"

"I come from a planet called Earth. The home of humans like ourselves."

The man seemed to consider that for a moment. "Humans. I don't believe that I've ever heard the word before. It's not Asharim nor is it one that the People use among themselves."

She could hear the capital letter in the word 'People.'

"That's a very long story," she said. "The short version is that I come from the place they took your ancestors from."

He nodded slowly. "How did you use the sky bridge?"

Kathleen assumed he was talking about the space elevator. "I have some knowledge of the Asharim technology. It would be helpful for me to know who you serve. Are you still loyal to the Asharim?"

The man shrugged. "That is a complex question. Some elements of the People still long for the return of the Masters. Others are pleased that we have lived on our own for so many lifetimes. If you had been the Masters, I am uncertain whether your arrival would have caused celebration or war."

He stared at her for a moment more. "I believe that we shall start with celebration. My name is Kerrick Vidar, and it is my honor to lead the People.

"I declare you our honored guest, Kathleen Bennett. We shall arrange a great celebration to herald your arrival. Meanwhile, it might be best if we meet privately to discuss the true reason for your visit and what it means for the People."

She suspected that if her answers didn't please him, there wouldn't be a celebration. At least not one where she was the guest of honor. Was the prisoner at an execution considered the guest of honor? She'd really rather not know the answer.

Kathleen inclined her head. "We have much to talk about. I assure you that I have no ill will toward your people. In fact, it may be that we can help one another."

"Perhaps. Perhaps not. In any case, we shall come to know one another shortly. Come."

She gestured for Nathan to follow her and the men formed up around them as they led them away from the space elevator. If things went badly, she knew she'd never see it again. She'd have to use her very best negotiating skills to make certain that didn't happen.

* * *

HARRY FOLLOWED the somewhat bemused Gunnery Sergeant Danvers out of the cave and onto the side of a tall hill. It was night out, but that didn't stop him from seeing or hearing the fighting. The small flickers of muzzle flash were like little lightning bolts off in the distance.

Basing his guess on the distant rumble of the shots, he suspected the fighting was at least a kilometer away. Perhaps a bit more. Most of the shots had an odd timbre.

"Do we have a better idea of the situation?" he asked Danvers. "What are the weapons in play down there?"

"The natives use low-technology weapons. Black powder. Though I suppose 'native' might not be the right word. There are apparently Asharim on this planet. At least that's what your father called the aliens. This might be their world."

Harry shook his head. "The Asharim favor low gravity, maybe sixty percent of what we have on Earth. Of course, if they lost their technology, they might not have much of a choice.

"That's actually a lucky break for us. Reloading black powder is a lot slower than our modern firearms. Once they come into range, we should be able to force them back without too much trouble."

"It depends on how fanatical they are. A dozen men with clubs can take down a man with a gun. We're low on ammunition, so if they want to take this hill, they're going to be able to do it. They just have to be willing to pay the price."

"I assume you're using standard NATO ammunition. My guys brought as much of it as we could carry. That'll help."

"Your numbers are going to help more. Trying to fight off an army with less than a dozen men was a losing proposition. Particularly if we're covering the retreat for thousands of others."

Harry stared out into the darkness. It looked as if the fighting was coming closer. At this rate, they might have visitors inside half an hour. Sooner, if they'd send out scouts to secure the way, which is what he'd have done.

"I want you to pair one of your people with each of my teams," he told the marine. "You know who the friendlies are, we don't. We absolutely don't need any blue on blue casualties."

"Roger that," the man said with feeling.

Harry watched as the marine spoke softly into his microphone. It was hard for him to accept that he had to be careful of the man beside him and his comrades. He'd fought beside many people just like them for a third of his life.

Yet these folks had come to take his father into custody and drag him back to the United States for what was probably going to be a secret trial and incarceration at Guantánamo Bay.

Clayton Rogers didn't seem perturbed, but Harry wasn't going to allow Queen to get his hands on any of them. He hoped that didn't mean he had to fight these men, but he'd do it if necessary.

"I've got men assigned to each of your teams," Danvers said. "We're spreading out around the side of the hill to get good fields of fire to cover the retreat. We'll be able to shoot at the enemy before they start climbing, if they're packed together tightly enough. One of my snipers might be able to cause a little chaos at longer range, but this is going to be a brutal, ugly affair."

Unfortunately, Harry agreed with that assessment. A team of snipers might've been able to make a difference fighting during the daylight. At night, there just wasn't sufficient time to locate and eliminate the right kinds of targets.

Danvers reached up and touched his ear. "Copy that."

He glanced over at Harry. "The lead elements of the Volunteer forces have arrived at the base of the hill. There's a path up. I had one of my folks mark it with luminescent sticks so they could find their way without being escorted.

"We've got thousands of people headed our way. There's no way we can fit them all into the cave, so they'll have to go up to the crown of the hill. Once we start spreading our forces thin trying to cover every approach, the enemy is going to be able to breach our lines."

Harry smiled. "Then we have to make sure that's not a possibility. Send them through the gate. The base might be a dead pile of shit, but that beats getting shot. Once we have everybody on the other side, we can figure out how and where we're going to relocate them."

"Thank God that's above my pay grade," the marine noncom said. "I suppose you have a way of using that gate to go other places."

"Indeed we do. We'll let my partner handle the relocation while we take care of slowing the enemy down. Once we're certain we've gotten as many people through as possible, we'll retreat into the cave and bring down the entrance with explosives. I'd like to deny them the gate."

"Considering the fact that they might come after us, I think that's an excellent idea."

When he finally saw some of the humans from this planet, it was hard for him not to shake his head in amazement. They looked as if they'd just come from a Revolutionary War reenactment.

The trickle quickly became a flood. Even as their numbers increased, Harry heard his men opening fire. The enemy must be in range. That's when he spotted several men in the flow of people dressed in modern combat gear. He recognized the man in the lead.

He smiled at Karl Krueger and extended a hand. "It's been a while, Commander."

"Let's not stand on ceremony, Harry," the officer said as he took it. "I'm damned glad to see you."

The man gestured toward a woman standing beside him dressed in what appeared to be pirate garb. "Harry Rogers, meet Susanna Adorno. She's the leader of our allies. Susanna, Harry is Clayton's son and a very skilled warrior. He leads the people who have come to rescue us."

Considering the timeframe that these people had come from, Harry had to fight to keep the surprise off his face. While he expected to see women in leadership positions in the modern day, that didn't hold true several hundred years in the past.

He wasn't sure whether he should extend his hand to shake hers or attempt to kiss it.

She solved his conundrum by reaching out and taking his firmly. "I am most pleased to make your acquaintance, Harry. Your timing is excellent.

"Without your help, we would never have been able to hold the enemy at bay until dawn. I am still uncertain as to how long we can hold out against them, but your assistance is greatly appreciated."

Harry cleared his throat. "Actually, I've decided that the simplest way to solve our mutual problem is to send everyone through the gate inside this cave. It will take us all back to Earth. We'll use explosives to bring down the entrance.

"I realize that might seem to be a major setback, but I didn't bring enough force to take on an army, even with my superiority in weapons. We can come back at a future point in time, but if we want to live, we're going to have to go."

The woman's expression was similar to that of someone who'd

bitten into something sour. "I cannot say that your assessment surprises me, but I greatly dislike being forced to retreat, much less abandon our world. We all have family and friends here. I must insist that steps be taken to see we are able to regain our footing here quickly."

Thankfully, those kind of negotiations were outside his realm of authority. "I'll leave the details of that between my father and you. In the short term, if we want to survive, we have no choice."

Susanna sighed. "No, I don't suppose that we do. Well, I've always dreamed of seeing Earth. The stories told by those who saw it with their own eyes have been passed down from generation to generation."

The ruined base in New Zealand was going to be a terrible disappointment, Harry was sure. He hoped that he could make it up to her later.

24

Brenda knew every trip into the city was a risk, but she was going stir-crazy. She was one of those people who had to be out doing things. She couldn't just sit on her butt and let other people do all the work.

Not that she was working at the moment. She was off to the deli, getting food for those who were. Which was an adventure in and of itself.

She'd never been to this particular place before, and there were a number of dishes that caught her eye. Trying new food was always a high point in her week.

Her preference was to have a meal herself and then take her friend's food to go. She loved to eat hers hot and fresh while people watching.

Today was shaping up to be a decent day. The sun was out, and the temperature was actually bearable. Some low clouds on the horizon threatened rain, but it was still a ways off.

The neighborhood they'd picked for their hiding place was a little south of middle-class. It wasn't a poor area by any means, but it was dedicated to working-class folk.

That kind of homogenization was useful in spotting people that didn't belong. The men and women they had watching the cameras were looking for people that didn't fit in, either in dress or action.

As a trained FBI agent, she noticed anything that was out of place. It was almost a subconscious process at this point. She was even better at it when she focused on a particular subject.

For example, she'd been watching the crowds as they made their way along the street in front of the deli. To one degree or another, most people fit in to the area in which they lived or worked.

Oh, there was the occasional person that stood out. The woman in the high-class outfit stalking along on stiletto heels was a good example.

Brenda considered the woman as she walked by and wondered what her story was. She didn't think the woman was suspicious. Just being dressed differently wasn't enough to set off her Spidey Sense.

The woman could be anything from a business owner coming down to check on something to a highly paid escort on the way to work. Hell, in Washington she might be a diplomat. There was no telling.

What Brenda could see of her as she waved down a cab was that the woman had no interest in anyone around her. Not even the guy who was angling to steal her purse.

Part of Brenda wanted to get involved and stop the crime that was about to occur right in front of her, but that would draw undue attention. The woman was about to learn a painful lesson in situational awareness.

Better a snatch and grab than something darker. Perhaps this would save her from walking blithely into a much worse assault some night.

The thief timed his attack perfectly. He waited until the woman was reaching for the handle on the cab door to make his move. His hand lashed out and snagged the woman's expensive-looking handbag as he sprinted away down the street toward Brenda.

The woman screamed at him to stop and took off after him. She was surprisingly fast on those tall heels. She'd never catch the man, but she was making a credible effort.

Brenda watched the thief run with interest. Was he going to duck into another vehicle or run down an alley? There was always the possibility that one of the bystanders would attempt to stop him, but the odds of that were actually much lower than most people thought.

It was all in the reaction time. It took seconds for people to realize what was going on and even more to decide if they should act or steer clear. By then the thief would be past them.

Unless, of course, someone in front of the thief figured it out and decided to intervene. Such as the large Asian man in the dark coat who stepped from a business just as the thief reached it.

The man extended one bulky arm directly in front of the sprinting criminal and clotheslined him. The runner somersaulted into the air and slammed facedown into the concrete.

Brenda winced. That was going to leave a mark. The Good Samaritan planted one large foot in the center of the man's back, pinning him to the ground just as effectively as a pin held an insect for study.

She watched the large man and felt a warning run down her spine. Something wasn't right about him.

The woman ran up and retrieved her purse, kicking the thief hard in the ribs and profusely thanking the man. Brenda couldn't hear his response, but it seemed low-key.

By now, other bystanders had gathered around and were restraining the thief. Someone had undoubtedly called the police, so it was time for Brenda to go.

Still, she couldn't dismiss the large man. She considered what it was about him that made her feel he was different while she waved down the waiter and asked for her to-go order and a box for her excellent food.

The answer occurred to her as the waiter returned with everything. It was the man's build. He looked just like Victor Holyfield. The proportions were *exactly* right. That man was a descendant of heavy-worlders.

The realization set her to looking for any possible companions. If he was an operative, he probably wasn't working alone.

While it was conceivable that the man had absolutely nothing to do with her and perhaps didn't even realize his own heritage, there weren't that many people with heavy-worlder genes on Earth.

Her ancestors had rescued four heavy-worlders after the fighting a thousand years ago. They'd kept excellent records of their genealogy since. They'd had to.

Victor might look like a bodybuilder, but his strength exceeded anyone's wildest expectations. He was designed to live on a world with three times the gravity anyone here faced.

The young man declared himself out of shape every chance he got, but there were limits on his lower-end body strength. She was sure he could flip a car. That kind of physical prowess stood out.

The Families had decided long ago that they couldn't allow those genes into the wild. They would raise all the wrong kinds of questions. So who was this fellow?

Brenda pulled her phone out and made a show of taking pictures of the ruckus. That brought her no extra attention because *everyone* was doing it. Social media consumed everything these days. Videos of this scene would be all over the Internet by now.

The man had finally disentangled himself from the grateful woman and was looking for a way out of the spotlight. That gave Brenda the perfect opportunity to snap a close-up of his face.

He turned and went back into the business he'd come from moments later.

Following a hunch, Brenda picked up the bag with her takeout and made her way around the block to the alley behind the row of buildings. Without seeming overly curious, she walked briskly past the alley and glanced down it.

As she'd suspected, the man had exited the rear of the business and was getting into a car. Three additional men with similar builds were joining him.

So much for coincidence. While she didn't know every person in the Families, there wouldn't be four people with heavy-worlder genes in one place like this accidentally. The fact that all four men were of Asian descent also struck her as odd.

She paused as soon as she passed the alley and stuck her phone out just enough to snap a few more pictures. At the very least, she'd get a license plate to run.

Moments later, the car came out and sped past her. She'd resumed walking and turned her head down to stare at her phone like everyone else around her. The car never even slowed down.

The events at Area 51, the call to someone at the Chinese embassy, and these men had to be connected in some way. The good news was that she now knew about the threat. The bad news was that they suspected she was in the area. That was the only answer that made any sense. Someone was onto them.

* * *

ONCE THE VOLUNTEER soldiers had begun making their way into the cave, Clayton made the decision to return to Earth with them. Someone had to be there to decide their eventual settlement.

He made certain that Mick Bird and Penny Cash were right there with him. They were his responsibility, and he'd see them safely home.

Clayton had to admit that even the destroyed base looked good after the situation they'd found themselves in. Part of him hadn't expected to make it home.

Jess followed him to a handy corner of the large room. "This isn't going to hold everyone, is it?"

He shook his head. "No. We're going to have to see them taken to other floors while the gate is open. Once everyone is here, we can move them to the surface. This is only temporary."

"I have a better plan. We've got full control of the gate now, so perhaps the base in France would be a better choice."

He had to agree, but if they had access to any of the other gates, there were better choices.

"I'm not sure that's the best choice in the long run," he said. "France is a very unstable country. If anyone discovers the base, there will be a lot of awkward questions or hostile actors making moves to seize it."

Jess seemed to consider that for a moment. "Perhaps we could use France as a staging base while we prepare *Freedom Express* for housing more people? Hell, the station in orbit around the frozen planet has more than enough space to hold everyone."

He raised an eyebrow. "The what? What frozen planet? Which station?"

She smiled. "That's right. You missed out on that. It's a long story, but we found something big out past the orbit of Pluto. Maybe even the reason the Asharim came to our system in the first place.

"But we don't have time to get into that yet. There's also the base on Mars. We have life support working there. It's probably big enough for this kind of influx, too."

Her expression took on a hint of unease. "We'll need to get them out of here as soon as possible, though. I made the decision to notify New Zealand's government that this place existed."

He frowned. "Why in the world would you do any such fool thing? That's going to greatly complicate our lives."

"Because it needed to be done," she said firmly. "It's only a matter of time before someone other than the United States learns we have this kind of technology. We need allies with clout in the international community."

"Such as New Zealand? It's a beautiful place but a little small, don't you think?"

"Yet it's very close to the Republic of Nauru. And let's not discount Australia and Japan. With China being so close to us, we need friends in our back pocket."

Clayton sighed. The island he'd literally bought control of was very close indeed. "Well, I suppose it's a little late for me to complain if you've already begun the process. Have you?"

Jess nodded. "I explained the basic situation to the leader of the team searching for you. She's seen the inside the base and is aware of the gates. She's up top right now, probably calling her bosses. We can expect company before too much longer."

"Then I suppose I should join her and begin making some calls."

She pulled the phone out of her pocket and handed it to him. "This is one of your quantum devices. Apparently it doesn't need cell towers."

He smiled. "Ah, I'd wondered when these would become available.

If you'd be so kind, please make certain someone escorts our new friends as they go to the other floors. I don't want anyone becoming lost. If they wander away before we leave, they might become trapped."

"The buddy system. Got it. I'll make sure everyone stays in sight of everyone else."

Clayton watched her walk back over to the growing crowd and begin calling for their attention. He didn't pay specific attention to what she was telling them, though. His mind was racing with other thoughts. Trying to consider what options made the best sense.

Obviously, he'd have to stay here in New Zealand. He had to be here in order for the surrounding governments to trust him. He'd rather not have revealed the existence of this base, even in its ruined condition, but he supposed that would play out better in the long run.

The sad thing was that the government of New Zealand would probably invalidate the sale of the sheep station he'd bought here. That was a real pity. He truly loved the land around this base and wished it could remain among his holdings.

Well, there was no use crying over spilt milk. The first person he needed to call was his assistant. Clayton was going to need a lot of help to make sure the situation didn't spin out of control. The man could send as many bodies as he needed to talk to the various bureaucrats and elected officials.

In fact, he made a mental note to snag Penny to assist him before they arrived—and after. She was very astute and knew many of the local players.

He'd take her with him to the top of the mesa as soon as he finished this call. It was now their job to delay anyone from going below until Harry had seen everyone into the base and sealed that damned cave from the Asharim.

Jess would then take them all to the base in France. They'd go elsewhere after that, but Clayton wasn't in a position to make decisions relating to that. Not until he'd been briefed on everything he'd missed.

With any luck, the authorities would get this wrecked base but none of the people inside it. If Jess took the controller he saw attached to the gate with her, the entire thing would be useless.

But was that what he really wanted?

Perhaps Jess was right. If they went out of their way to show the surrounding governments what they had access to, those people would strongly defend this area. If he made a deal to share some of the technology, they would protect his interests in the region as well.

Yes, that was probably the best course of action.

The call he'd just dialed went through, and his assistant picked up. Clayton immediately launched into a list of what he needed and where he needed it. Time was critically short.

25

Kathleen Bennett stared curiously at the ruined city around them as their party exited the massive building that anchored the space elevator. The lines of the surrounding structures were distinctly different from what she was used to on Earth. Much like the inhabitants she had met, the buildings were tall and wide.

Even though they were standing, the buildings were no longer being maintained. That much was obvious. Some had huge cracks along their faces, and others were missing windows that made their sides look like empty skulls. Still, the fact that all the buildings hadn't collapsed spoke to the technical capabilities of the builders.

Their hosts—or perhaps their captors, depending on how one viewed their circumstances—led her son and her through wide boulevards that did not seem designed for ground traffic.

Even though long overgrown, it was obvious the spaces between buildings had been meant for growing things. Perhaps the entire city had once sported wide parks between the skyscrapers. She imagined it had been quite beautiful in its heyday.

Kerrick Vidar noted her gaze. "Do you not have cities such as this on your world?"

She shrugged. "Yes and no. We have large cities, but the buildings are not as tall and strong. On the other hand, ours aren't empty, either."

The man seemed to consider that for a moment as they walked. "Our people once lived in the city, or perhaps I should say near it. The Masters and their favored servants were the true occupants. My people either served in ships in orbit or lived and trained at military bases in the surrounding lands."

"And that changed when something befell the Asharim?"

"War. The Masters found themselves in a conflict with another species. The time between the discovery of these others and the war that followed was short. The Masters tried to prepare and use the forces they had available, but they suffered greatly."

Kathleen didn't need to look around to see that was true. "Did they win?"

"I assume not, since they have never returned. Neither do I believe they lost. Surely those who sought to replace them would not have left us unmolested. The priests insist the Masters will one day return."

She tried to imagine what must've happened in the city around them and failed. "If the Masters and their trusted servants lived here, where did they go?"

"They used their gates to depart when things began turning against them. They left others to command us. Then they locked their gates and trapped us all here."

"Why haven't your people used the elevator to go to the station in orbit around your planet? You do know there is one up there, don't you?"

He shrugged. "Our ancestors did, hoping to find a way back to our home. Some great battle had taken place around this world, and all the ships were gone. Only wreckage remained. Once that was known, there was little need to return."

"Forgive me, but this world seems more like my home world than one where someone of your strength would be from. Did you come from here before the war?"

He shook his head. "The stories tell of a world with much more gravity. One that held us to her bosom so that only the strong thrived. The People likely still live there, but we have no way to return. This world is now our home."

Rather than engage him in further conversation, she let some time pass in silence. They quickly exited the center of the city and found an area cleared of buildings. It didn't appear there had ever been buildings here.

"What was this originally used for?" she asked.

"A large park, I believe. The city had many."

"I thought the areas between buildings were parks."

He shook his head. "Not precisely, but the vegetation in the parks expanded to fill that space as well."

Part of the area ahead of them was being used to raise crops, Kathleen noted. Other sections held relatively primitive buildings, like rustic villages back on Earth.

Men, women, and children waved cheerfully at the group as they passed. The men were built much like her new friends. The women, oddly enough, were more slender, though still stocky.

"Why are your men so much larger than your women?"

He laughed. "Because we were designed that way. As warriors, the men had to be very, very strong and imposing. Intimidation of our foes before the fighting began was one method to win. The Masters understood that.

"The strength of our women is quiet, subtle. Do not mistake that for weakness, though. They are as strong as the men, in their own way."

He let that sink in for a moment before he continued. "Tell me how you came to our world. Obviously, you came from the station above. You have a ship, then?"

Unsure of how much to tell the man, she glanced at her son. As he couldn't understand any of the conversation, he seemed just to be watching the area around them as they walked. His expression told her he was very unhappy at their current circumstances. She couldn't blame him.

Rather than consult him, she made the decision to be honest with their host. Not completely honest, of course. Only a fool did that. Yet, the best lies were ones planted in beds of truth.

"Yes. We arrived in a ship that is still in orbit around this world. We've come seeking allies in a war to control the home world. The place the Masters took you from."

The news didn't seem to disturb him, but it didn't seem he was very interested it, either. He walked in silence beside her for the next few minutes, and she let him stew.

Finally, he spoke. "While it is not my place to make that kind of decision for the People, I would still know more of the enemy you face. You have just arrived, and the People do not know you."

She gave him her most practiced open smile. "I'll tell you everything when the time is right. Who makes decisions like those for the People? Your priests?"

He nodded. "Anything involving the Masters must be decided by the priests. While you are not the Masters, you come from off world. They will see your presence as a sign. All that remains is for them to determine if it is for good or ill.

"When the time for fighting comes, I lead. Thankfully, the art of conducting war is one we still practice. The priests insist it remain so, since one day we may have to serve the Masters again."

"Tell me about the priests. What kind of people are they?"

Vidar shrugged. "The ways of priests are not for common folk like me. They spend their lives in contemplation of the Masters. I warn you that they do not have much in the way of humor about them. They are very single-minded in their goal to see the Masters returned to rule over us."

She could tell he didn't feel very enthused about that prospect. He was giving lip service to the Asharim, but Vidar would probably be pleased if they'd been exterminated. Personally, she shared his opinion.

So, the key to gaining allies on this world were the priests. If she could convince them that helping her take Earth would be a step toward returning the Masters—their gods, she imagined—to power, then she might be able to get them to provide military force that no one back home could resist.

Inside, she smiled. Finally, something she could manipulate to her benefit. These rubes should be a piece of cake.

* * *

Jᴇss's sᴛᴏᴍᴀᴄʜ was rumbling by the time Harry ushered the last of the refugees through the gate and onto Earth. There'd been a lot more of them than she'd expected. She wasn't certain how much of the abandoned base was occupied now, but it had to be a lot.

There'd been a loud explosion and then the unmistakable rumble of falling stone just before he and the Navy officer came through. She'd known his intent to collapse the cave entrance, but the noise was far too similar to the cave-in at the Mayan pyramid for her taste. That still gave her nightmares.

He shut the gate down and entered the code for the French base as she held up her phone for him to read the address. Once the wormhole stabilized, he turned to the woman dressed like a pirate.

"The base on the other side of this is in our hands. We still haven't finished cleaning it up or exploring it. My brother—who is not a nice person, by the way—fought some other bad people there recently, so be warned: there's still blood on the floor."

Jess suspected the warning had been meant for her, too. It must still be pretty bad.

"I have seen battle before," the woman said. "What remains of the dead and dying is never a pretty sight, but we shall persevere. When will we be able to return to our homes?"

Harry shrugged. "We've got to give them time to back off. It'll also take a little while for me to gather enough men with modern weapons to take and hold the terrain around the hill. Once we can do that safely, we'll bring your people back through."

"I note you do not give the estimate I requested. I understand your uncertainty, but are we speaking of days, weeks, or months? I have my people to consider. If we are gone too long, the Asharim will strike at our homes. They are well defended, but without this army, our families are in unnecessary peril."

"Days," Harry said firmly. "A week at most. I can't imagine it being any longer than that."

"And I accept that circumstances may alter your intentions. Man plans, and God laughs."

Jess understood that sentiment. She stepped over to the gate and motioned for them to follow. "Let's get you set up inside the other base. Once we have everyone across, I'll see about getting food and supplies. We'll have medics come in to help the injured."

She knew for certain they had many of those. The fighting to get to the hill must've been ugly. Some of the humans from the other world had been shot.

A glance at the makeshift sick area told her that not everyone was going to make it. Some had already died. Standing around thinking about it wasn't going to help them, though. She needed to get this in motion.

Getting everyone moved through the gate they'd just come through took longer than Jess would've liked. She supposed the lack of people shooting at them sapped some of the urgency this time.

In the end, it took almost an hour to get everyone into the French base. Thankfully, it was much easier to move people around here with the power on. Though the concept of elevators seemed like sorcery to the newcomers.

Sandra Dean and her sniper team had come inside the base to assist with triage for the wounded. They'd used one of the other gates to connect with *Freedom Express* and bring in every doctor and medic they had there. As soon as the triage was complete, they'd move the wounded to *Freedom Express* to expedite their treatment.

The floor and walls of the large gate room had splashes and dried pools of blood. The bodies had been removed, but the evidence of carnage was everywhere. The smell was terrible.

She added cleaning supplies and hands—willing or not—to her list of things to bring in.

The Volunteer military officer, General Norris, stepped over to her as soon as things were well in hand. "Someone called this place 'the French base.' Does it in fact belong to our old allies?"

Unlike far too many Americans these days, Jess had studied her history lessons hard. The French had been allies in the American rebellion against King George.

"Not precisely," she said softly. "The base is inside France, but the people here are unaware of it. Hardly anyone on Earth knows about the Asharim.

"That's going to change in the relatively near future, but for now, we're keeping the location of this base a secret. And unfortunately, the France you've heard about in your stories is a much different place these days. Do you know about Islam?"

The man shrugged. "I've seen it mentioned in our writings. None of its practitioners came across with the Volunteers."

That surprised her a little, but she really didn't know how many Muslims had been in revolutionary America.

"Like many religions, most Muslims are good people. Unfortunately, in the world we live in today, there are far too many using Islam—or rather its perversion—as an excuse to commit mass atrocities and murder. France has a large Muslim community.

"Again, mostly good people that just want to live their lives in peace. Yet the nonbelievers have been targeted by radicalized militants intent on overthrowing the French government and forming a caliphate.

"They, of course, want to take over the entire world in the process and murder anyone who doesn't agree with their ideas. The French people—Muslim and non—are fighting back against them, but I'm not sure how this is going to turn out."

The man looked crestfallen. "Oh, how I wish our people could lend them the same help that they offered us in our hour of need. Yet if you, with your own powerful weapons, are unable to stem the tide, I'm uncertain what we can do.

"I shall speak of this with Susanna. We must consider our options carefully. If there is some way that we can return the great boon the French people once gave America, then we must work diligently to discover it."

That was a lot more help than modern America seemed willing to give. They'd become isolationists, turning their backs on the world.

That would probably change once the mad scramble for the

Asharim technology began in earnest, but she wouldn't hold her breath that things worked out well for the French people. That was something far beyond her control.

"Let's get everybody settled in and start bringing food for them," she said. "It's probably been a long time since you last ate. It probably won't be long before Harry comes looking for you, either. There's someone he wants you to meet."

26

It was after dinnertime when Brenda's people located the unknown heavy-worlders again. They'd moved to a restaurant on the other side of the neighborhood. Or perhaps they were just having something to eat and not using the place as a base of operations. Until they watched the men for a while, it would be hard to tell.

The heavy-worlders had no reason to suspect that anyone would recognize their genealogy on sight. Hell, they probably had never even suspected there were others of their kind on Earth.

Their kind. That wasn't exactly fair. They were as human as the people around them. Just enhanced.

She still wasn't sure what the men were looking for. Did they have a description of her? She wasn't sure how they'd have gotten it, unless they'd stolen it from the US government. She was at the top of the most wanted list, after all.

That made the most sense. If they knew about the Asharim technology—which they did—then they knew about her. Worse, they knew about the Families.

Maybe not by name, but the US government understood there

was an organization of some kind associated with her. They'd almost certainly underestimated her people's numbers and reach, even after everything she'd told them.

If these men were descendants of the heavy-worlders that had been present in this system a thousand years ago, they had fully integrated into society. Most likely in China, based on where the clues were pointing and their own appearances.

The Families had never been active in China—not until recently—and their reach was still very limited there. Until a hundred years ago, the damned place had been closed off from the outside world in every way that mattered.

She wondered how much of that had been the doing of these people and their ancestors.

Now that she had eyes on them, she wanted to be absolutely certain they didn't realize they'd been made. They still thought they were operating in complete secrecy. Even the information she'd passed on to Secretary of State Queen didn't mention them, since she hadn't known what she was facing at the time.

She wondered whether or not she should tell Queen about them and their ancestry but decided against it. He was smart enough to figure that out on his own. Her speaking slowly and clearly, as if to a five-year-old, wouldn't be helpful, though it might be satisfying.

The sight of the four men on the monitor mesmerized Victor. With the number of heavy-worlders being limited inside the Families, he'd probably thought he'd known every one of them on the planet. This had to be a great shock.

"What are you thinking?" she asked him.

He shrugged. "I'm not sure what to think. These people are like bogeymen from the past. If they're the descendants of heavy-worlder fighters that never converted to supporting humanity, they're probably enemies. That's a whole new level of screwed up."

She clapped the young man on the shoulder, feeling his tense thick muscles under the skin. It was like slapping a brick wall. "At least you'll have somebody to arm wrestle with now."

He laughed. "I suggest you keep your day job. Comedy isn't in your future."

The phone Jessica Cook had given her rang. She stared at it for a moment, certain that this couldn't be good. Then she answered it. "Talk to me."

"I'd like to see you in person," Harry Rogers said. "Events are in progress that you need to be aware of, and I've got some interesting people for you to meet."

His idea of 'interesting' was probably a lot different than hers. Still, based on everything she'd seen, it wouldn't be boring.

"Give me ten minutes to get down to the gate room and power it up."

She disconnected the call and pocketed the phone. "Victor, keep an eye on those guys, and let me know if anything changes. If they lead you back to their hiding place, I want to know about it before you make a move."

"You got it, Boss."

Brenda sauntered out into the lobby and waited for the elevator to be clear. Once she could get into it alone, she hit the button for the basement. The button blinked three times and she knew it was reading her fingerprint.

That was a security measure to keep any of the curious residents from going to take a peek for themselves. Anyone not cleared for the knowledge would just think the button was broken.

Once she made it to the makeshift gate room, she gestured for the man at the table to power it on. They'd started keeping the power cube disconnected so that no one could open a connection without letting them know ahead of time.

Not that she expected Rogers to betray them. It was just common sense. That's also why she had four heavily armed men on duty here at all times.

A few minutes later, the wormhole formed, and Harry Rogers walked through with two of the most outlandishly dressed people Brenda had ever seen at his side.

The woman to his right was dressed like someone out of *Pirates of the Caribbean*. All that was missing was a gold hoop earring and a parrot.

The distinguished gentleman on the other side of her ally had seemingly stepped out of the painting of George Washington crossing the Delaware. In fact, he bore a striking resemblance to the first president.

Brenda spent a moment assessing everyone before she focused her attention on Harry Rogers. "When you say interesting, you mean it. Who are your friends?"

"Brenda Cabot, meet Susanna Adorno and General Norbert Norris. I found them on the planet my father recently visited. He's safely home, by the way.

"I thought you might be interested in how they made their way off Earth. They left from our side of the pond either before or during the Revolutionary War."

That surprised her. Her people hadn't had access to a power supply for the gate, and while she knew that Harry Rogers and his people had located several bases on Earth, the Families hadn't been aware of any them, and none of the ones he'd mentioned had been inside the United States.

"You have my attention now," Brenda said. "Miss Adorno, General Norris, it's a pleasure to meet you."

She extended her hand to the woman first. Rogers had introduced her before the general, so she was making the assumption the woman was the man's superior.

Susanna Adorno's grip was firm. "Mistress Cabot. Mister Rogers has spoken very highly of you. The allies of my allies are my own as well."

The woman's accent was like what Brenda imagined someone from the Caribbean would sound like.

General Norris shook Brenda's hand a little less forcefully, for which she was grateful. It was never a good thing when a man wanted to get into a hand-crushing contest to show how big his balls were. As an FBI agent, she'd met all too many men who wanted to do that.

"Mistress Cabot," the supposed military officer said.

"The current form of address favors Miss rather than Mistress," she said with a smile. "General, if I might say so, you look rather like paintings I've seen of George Washington."

The man nodded. "I've been told my family and his are connected in some way. It's a great honor to be a distant cousin of the great general, of course. I've never seen a painting of him. If the opportunity presents, I would be deeply appreciative of the chance to do so."

"I'll see what I can do. Perhaps the three of you would care for something to drink while Harry fills me in on what's going on."

Ten minutes later, they were seated around the table in her small kitchen. The homey room made the two people from off planet seem even more out of place, if that was possible.

She'd brewed them all some tea. As she might've expected, the strangers wanted theirs hot while Rogers and she took theirs iced.

After taking a sip, Brenda focused her attention on Susanna. "If you don't mind, I'd rather let you tell me your story in your own words, without asking questions. There's plenty of time for me to do so when you're finished."

"A sensible plan," the other woman said.

Brenda listened to what she'd have considered a tall tale under other circumstances. Yet the woman's very existence argued it was true. There had once been a gate in the Caribbean, just outside of the infamous Port Royale.

More amazingly, it had been under the control of humans that both knew how to use it and were unknown to the Families. That was shocking, really. Who had these people been? Why hadn't they sought out others here on Earth?

The mysteries just kept rolling in.

The general's story about the Volunteers was even more interesting. A gate hidden deep in a cave somewhere in Virginia. How the hell had it gotten there and why? Who'd activated it and sent them through to this other world?

Since her instructors at the Academy had verbally beaten the concept of coincidence out of her, she was certain they must be the same people. Why else send both groups to the same location?

The fact that the two events had taken place almost a century apart argued that these individuals were still present on Earth today.

The Families hadn't seen or heard of them in the intervening centuries, but she couldn't take the chance that they'd just vanished somewhere.

Odds were now good there was another player in the games afoot. One that none of them had considered before and one with aims that no one could guess at. Still, she'd best make sure before they assumed that these newcomers hadn't met the Chinese players.

"Tell me, do the old stories of your journey indicate the people running these gates were from the Orient?" Orient wasn't commonly used today, but she hoped it was recognizable to these folks.

"No," Adorno said. "The tales don't mention someone of exotic appearance. My assumption is that the men in the Caribbean look like everyone else around them. I have always seen them as dark-skinned in my mind."

General Norris seemingly agreed with her thoughts. "The volunteers believed the people running the gate were very much like themselves. There were colonists with dark skin—some brought unwillingly, to my personal distaste—but the people of the stories were of the same skin tone as myself, I believe."

The man leaned forward. "I am making an assumption, based on my limited observation, that you are not a slave. The Volunteers made the choice when we founded our society that that institution had no place in decent human company. Is that also true here?"

She nodded. "It wasn't as cleanly done here, and the repercussions of slavery are still felt in America today. No, I'm not a slave and no one in America has been for almost two centuries. Sadly, that still doesn't mean everyone is seen as equal."

The man shook his head and sighed. "It is always a great disappointment when the icons of one's youth have feet of clay. On behalf of my ancestors, I apologize."

"We all have our burdens to bear," she said philosophically. "Thank you for your concern."

Brenda suspected that the people running the two gates hadn't looked like one another. The ones in the Caribbean had probably been much darker than the ones in Virginia. That spoke of a somewhat larger organization, since she refused to believe there were two separate groups using the same destination code.

"By any chance, do you happen to know in which part of Virginia this cave is located?" she asked the man.

"That's actually what we're hoping you can assist us with," Rogers said. "If we can locate this base or gate, if it's just stashed somewhere deep inside a cave, it would give my people a way to access locations here in the United States that doesn't rely on traipsing through your hidden base."

Brenda shook her head firmly. "If there's a base inside the United States, my people want it. You already have more than enough. We can provide you with the portable gate in exchange, but if there's a permanent facility, we deserve it. So long as it's in good shape."

The man smiled. "Somehow I suspected you'd say something like that. I'm willing to be reasonable. I don't particularly care how this works out. If we find a fully operational base—or anything close to it —that you can take over, you're welcome to it in exchange for your portable gate."

She nodded decisively and extended her hand to him. "Then you've provisionally got a deal."

If they could locate an old base like he'd already found, the amount of equipment inside could be a game changer. The Families had been operating without the kind of technology their ancestors had once had. They'd be willing to deal if they could regain it.

Assuming the previous owners weren't still in charge of it, but that was an entirely different situation.

"Let me bring up some maps on my tablet, and we'll see if we can narrow down the location," she said. "I can also show you a picture of General Washington.

"Actually, I should say President Washington. I'm not sure you know, but he was elected the first leader of our country. This is the United States of America, by the way."

General Norris smiled. "I did not know of his election, but it cheers my heart. I've heard the name of our parent country before, but we were still fighting for it when the Volunteers left this world.

There is so much history that my people do not know about this nation. What a wonderful time in which to live."

Brenda couldn't argue with that. She retrieved her tablet and began searching for maps from the Revolutionary War. Those would look more familiar to the man, she suspected. With any luck, they might be able to put a search party in motion tonight. Things were starting to look up.

27

Nathan was getting tired of listening to his mother and the stranger jabber on in the alien language. He wanted to know what the hell they were saying to one another. Yet he could hardly complain about the muscular bastard not being able to speak English.

Which did absolutely nothing to improve his mood.

The group was arriving in a large village on the far edge of the wilderness zone inside the ruined city. The wilds seemed to stretch out in a radial fashion from the center where the space-elevator building was located. Perhaps there were others villages like it spread out through the damned thing.

They'd passed through several clusters of dwellings, but this one seemed larger than the rest. Not any better constructed than the previous ones, but this one had more people living inside it. And there was a building that seemed more important than the rest. Or perhaps more *self-important*.

This one was at least four stories tall—two more than the buildings around it—and was covered with what appeared to be religious carvings. Something related to the aliens, he believed.

The beings shown in bas-relief were as tall and willowy as the ones they'd heard about in relation to the aliens. Ugly bastards. Why anyone would want to show any reverence at all for them made him shake his head.

A number of men dressed differently than the ones who'd captured them came out of the building. They weren't dressed for doing everyday tasks in those long obstructive robes. Just considering how unwieldy their hats were, this had to be some type of ceremonial regalia.

These had to be priests or something. Great. Religion never improved a situation, it just made things worse. With his luck, human sacrifice was next on the schedule.

The leader of the group who'd captured them led his mother up the wide steps to stand before this group of self-important bastards. He spoke in that same indecipherable language that he and Nathan's mother had been using.

The man standing in the center of the group at the top of the stairs—the one with the tallest, stupidest looking hat—stared down haughtily and responded sharply.

That didn't seem to disturb the man who'd brought them here, but he bowed slightly from the waist and took two steps back. That left Nathan's mother standing alone.

Nathan took the opportunity to head up the stairs and stand beside his mother. It almost made him laugh when they both shot him mirrored looks of irritation. It seemed he could offend family and aliens at the same time. It was a gift.

The Grand Pooh-Bah said something to Nathan. When he shrugged back, the man repeated the words more slowly and in a louder tone. Yeah, that was going to make him understand an alien language more easily. Idiot.

Nathan made a show of smirking at the man and then shrugged elaborately. "Sorry, asshole. I don't speak your idiotic language."

"God dammit, Nathan!" his mother said sharply. "Shut your stupid mouth."

"Why? It's not as if he can understand me. I can say anything I want, like how retarded his hat looks. Like a giant penis on his head. Maybe I should call him the Grand Dickhead. That's perfect!"

Apparently, comprehension wasn't strictly required to determine when someone was being insulting. The man in front of Nathan grabbed him by the throat and lifted him off his feet with one hand.

Nathan kicked him while he used his hands to beat at the man's arm, but it was like hitting a concrete wall and a steel bar. None of Nathan's efforts even made the man wince. This wasn't good.

His mother said something in the alien language using an imploring tone.

The man stared coldly into Nathan's eyes for a moment then tossed him to the men standing nearest the entrance to the building.

Even as Nathan sucked in great drafts of air, the other men gripped his arms and legs roughly and carried him inside.

He'd been kidding about the human sacrifice part. Seriously.

Nathan shouted for his mother to stop them, but she didn't answer. She was leaving him to his fate. Bitch.

If anything, the inside of the building was even more garishly decorated than the outside. Certain sections of it were well lit, highlighting works of what looked like precious metals and sculptured stone.

His captors' rough handling prevented Nathan from seeing anything clearly, but he thought many of the objects were shaped like the aliens. That was just screwed up.

The men quickly carried him to a room in the rear of the building and down some narrow steps. Unlike the rest of the building, the room at the bottom had advanced equipment in it. Just based on the layout and shape of the consoles and machines, this was Asharim technology.

There was a wide chair sitting in the middle of the room with an extensive headset perched above it. The men slammed him into the chair and held his arms and legs in place while others secured thick straps around them. No amount of struggle did him the least bit of good.

Someone strapped a band around his forehead, brutally yanking his neck back as they tightened it. When they were done, Nathan couldn't move at all. Then they lowered the complex-looking headset down over his head.

No, this wasn't menacing at all.

The Grand Dickhead walked slowly down the stairs and into the room. He set his giant penis hat on a handy console and said something low and menacing to Nathan.

Nathan would have shot him the finger, but part of him was afraid the bastard would chop his hand off. There were limits to his insolence after all.

Another man ran down the steps with some kind of book in his hands. It was large, with gold inlay on the dark leather cover. He held it up so that the Grand Dickhead could flip to a specific page and see it clearly without having to bend over.

After consulting the displayed page for a few moments, the Grand Dickhead walked to one of the consoles and brought it to life. The book carrier followed him faithfully.

The Grand Dickhead manipulated the display and then stared at Nathan. With a cold toothy grin, he pressed something, and intense agony shot through Nathan's skull.

Nathan heard someone screaming and only belatedly realized that it had to be himself. He wanted the pain to stop, but there was nothing he could do about it. He was completely within their power.

It might have lasted five minutes or five hundred, for all he knew, but the pain eventually ceased. Nathan sagged, panting hoarsely. Based on the stench, he'd soiled himself. Oh, the bastard was going to pay for that.

The Grand Dickhead was standing in front of him with his hands planted firmly on his hips. His smile, if anything, was even wider than before.

"I'm going to kill you," Nathan muttered roughly. "When you least expect it, I'll plant a knife in the center of your back and leave you to bleed out."

"You're not the first to want me dead, and you'll hardly be the last," the man responded with a laugh.

Nathan gaped. "How did you learn English?"

The sonofabitch laughed harder. "Fool. It is below my dignity to use any language other than that of the Masters, which is what you are now soiling with your impudent mouth."

What? That couldn't be right. "How is that possible?"

When Nathan focused on the syllables coming out of his mouth, they were definitely not English. "Who the hell are you?"

"My name is Jedan Louvan, and I am High Priest of the Masters." He slapped Nathan so hard his head rang. "That is for your earlier insolence. Prepare him."

Nathan spat blood and tried to slow the spinning room. "Prepare me? For what?"

"What would be the fun in telling you that?"

* * *

HARRY LOOKED at the map on his phone then squinted into the early morning sun. He hadn't wanted to wait to start looking, but darkness had been too close yesterday. Now they had time to search. They'd pulled over to the side of the road in an attempt to reconcile the rough—very rough—map they'd settled on to the actual terrain.

Automobiles had shocked Susanna Adorno and General Norris. They both sat in the back of the SUV, where the tinted windows helped conceal their terror from the general public.

Harry and Brenda had talked the two into changing clothes so they didn't stand out like sore thumbs. Not that they looked comfortable in the modern garments, but at least they weren't drawing the eye of every single person they came across.

Their fear didn't spring from the strange technology so much as the speed with which it traveled. It seemed horses hadn't made the trip to the new world, so foot power was the fastest mode of transport they'd ever seen before.

He had to admit they were being good sports about it, though. They'd swallowed their unease and clenched their handrests until he feared for the plastic but had still taken it all in stride.

"It's hard to believe this is the Virginia out of legend," Norris said after they'd driven a ways. "Even here, far from the bustling metropolis that is our nation's capital, there are so many people. It is difficult for me to imagine how you can farm enough land to feed them all."

"Technology helps with that," Harry said. "Some of the best farmland in the US hadn't been discovered when you left Earth. Now it grows enough food for our nation and also provides a surplus that feeds the hungry around the world."

Susanna gestured out the window. "And all of it is covered by roads such as this? Each person has a vehicle such as this one?"

"Pretty much," Brenda Cabot said from the driver's seat. "Oh, the vehicles differ from person to person, but most people have one. Only the very poorest in our society get by without one.

"We couldn't travel across the country, or even the city we live in, without one. Though they have buses, like the one I showed you as we drove out of Washington. Buses help those without automobiles get from place to place inside major cities. Out here in rural areas, though, things are a lot different."

"It is difficult to believe that so many people can live in a single location," Susanna said. "While it is not the same as the ruined city of the Asharim, it is still immense in scope."

"You should see New York," Harry said with a grin. "It's starting to come into the same scale as the Asharim city. And the residents are even ruder."

That left the two newcomers sitting in silence trying to process what that might look like.

Harry used the opportunity to bring up a map of the area on the SUV's console. After a few minutes of study, he gave up trying to reconcile the old map with reality as it existed today.

He turned in his seat and gazed at the rest of them. "I think we're about as close as we're going to get without actually walking into the woods. Frankly, it's amazing that there's even a road this close to the general area where you think this cave is located.

"I think you're right that the line of hills just off the road is probably where the cave sits. The terrain is suited to something like that. The problem is going to be locating it. If it was in plain sight, someone would've stumbled across it by now."

"I may be able to assist with getting past that stumbling block," Susanna said. "Over the years, I've heard many different versions of this story. A few speak of a specific outcropping that resembles the rising sun. Surely such a unique feature will aid in finding a concealed entrance."

Harry did a quick search of the web and came up empty. If such an outcropping existed, it wasn't public knowledge.

"Do we have any idea who owns this property?" Brenda asked. "I'd like to avoid getting shot for trespassing or having the police come ask us some very awkward questions."

"This is actually public land, believe it or not," Harry said. "I have no idea what they intend to use it for—or even if they intend to use it at all—but we have as much right to be here hiking as anyone else."

Brenda stared out at the rough brambles on the side of the road. "I don't think we'll find many people hiking through here."

"Maybe not," he admitted. "It's a good thing we put on good boots and jeans."

"These boots are exceptional," Norris agreed. "I should like to keep them, if you have no objection. They are more comfortable than any I have ever owned and seem most sturdy."

"Feel free," Brenda said. "Does the map show a place we can park?"

He considered the map and nodded. "There's a side road about a quarter mile ahead. We can leave a note on the dash that says we broke down and will be back for the car. It's not as likely to get stolen out here."

"It's a long walk back if it is," Brenda said with a note of resignation in her voice. "Still, that's better than anything I can think of. Let's go find a hidden cave."

28

C layton stood with Molly Goodwin on top of the mesa and waited for their incoming visitors. Thankfully, due to the isolation of the area, it had taken quite a while to convince anyone he was serious about needing to speak with someone with real authority.

That had allowed plenty of time for the people displaced from the Volunteers' world to make it to the French base. Now there was no one below to be caught up in any trouble.

In fact, the only people here that were in potential trouble were the American military group. That was particularly true now that the CIA weasel they'd imprisoned was free.

The entire time they'd been in the Volunteers' world, they'd stashed Agent Ulysses in a side cave. Clayton suspected Gunnery Sergeant Danvers had gagged the man. Two of the military personnel still held the idiot with his hands secured behind him. Only now, his mouth was free to rave.

"You're all going to prison," Ulysses said, his mouth actually frothing. "Starting with you, Rogers. You're going straight to Guantánamo Bay. The rest of you have Fort Leavenworth in your future."

Molly shook her head as she stared at the disagreeable man. "What makes you think you're not in trouble? You came to New Zealand and kidnapped our citizens as well as those under our protection. It's you that's going to jail."

Ulysses laughed harshly. "Don't be naïve. You're not going to lock up a representative of the United States government. We'd squash you like bugs. In fact, by the time this is all over, we'll be in possession of this facility, and you'll be thankful for it. Only we can protect you from the aliens."

"It's almost as if he's a caricature," Clayton said, still not really believing the man's performance. "All he needs is a mustache to twirl and some railroad tracks to tie someone to."

The woman chuckled. "He seems more like one of those people suited to a goatee. One that he strokes while revealing his wicked plan."

"Laugh while you can," Ulysses sneered. "Once our ambassador becomes aware of what you're doing, this all comes to an end. Enjoy it while you can."

Clayton pulled Molly a little farther to the side. "I've spoken with Mick and Penny. We truly don't hold anything against the military personnel. I'd prefer to see them released to their ship. None of these unfortunate circumstances was of their doing.

"I realize the whole 'I was just following orders' bit doesn't excuse everything. Still, I would like to see everyone's wrath focused on someone actually calling the shots, such as the CIA agent in charge of the operation.

"If your government could find it in their hearts to slap these gentlemen's wrists and send them back to their ship, I will cheerfully pay for any damages they have inflicted. I'm also certain that I have other information and equipment to offer as a sweetener."

Molly shrugged. "That's outside my purview, but I'll pass everything along when the authorities get here. It won't be long now. I'm more concerned about you."

"Me?"

"You were looking for a hidden alien base when you bought this property. I haven't got the slightest idea what laws you might've broken, but I suspect there's something they're going to hold against you."

Clayton smiled. "Then I suppose it's a good thing I have diplomatic immunity. Personally, I'm going to miss this place. It's very beautiful."

"It sure is," she agreed. "This mesa would've made an excellent spot for a grand home to look out over the wilderness."

About that time, he heard the low thrum of a helicopter in the distance. It sounded as though they were about to have company. Time to put on his game face.

"No matter how this turns out, I'd like to thank you and your people for coming out to search for me. Very few people recognize what good folks like yourself do for those in dire straits.

"I've already made an arrangement with my assistant to make a large donation to all of the groups involved to show my deep appreciation. In addition, I'd like you to accept a personal gratuity."

"I can't," Molly said. "I'm a government employee. That bars me from accepting anything that might look like a bribe."

He chuckled. "I've given far more bribes in my life than you could possibly believe. Trust me when I say that I can come up with a gift that is not a bribe but one that you will appreciate."

Off in the distance, he saw the approaching black dot of the helicopter. It rapidly covered the distance and began circling the mesa. Probably to make sure everything seemed safe to land.

A minute later, it settled to the rock about fifty meters off. Clayton could now see it was a military aircraft and that it was full of armed troops. They'd come expecting trouble. Good.

The helicopter doors opened, and all those soldiers came fanning out to cover everyone. The US military personnel had already taken the precaution of stacking their weapons off to the side. There was no need to invite trouble, after all.

The next person to exit the helicopter was a distinguished-looking gentleman with wavy gray hair and a suit that was both well styled and extremely out of place in the wilderness.

The man looked everyone over before he walked to Clayton and extended his hand. "Mister Rogers. I'm Isaiah Vaughn, assistant to the prime minister. I'm glad to see that our searchers located you. I confess that all too many folk who wander off into the wilderness back here don't have such a happy outcome."

Clayton shook the man's hand firmly. "I'm pleased to have come out of this intact, Mister Vaughn. I'd like to thank you, your government, and all of the searchers for the efforts you put out to ensure my safety. They are greatly appreciated, and I will, of course, reimburse all costs related to it."

"You're very welcome."

The official turned his attention to the US soldiers. His expression grew grim. "You gentlemen are far less welcome. You are illegally operating on the soil of New Zealand, and there are going to be grave consequences for each and every one of you."

Ulysses laughed coldly. "Please. Blah blah blah. You're not going to do anything to us, so let's not even pretend. Get on with your speech so we can get back to our ship.

"And if you know what's good for you, you'll send that traitor with us with the little show of resistance you no doubt have planned. The consequences if you don't are going to be extreme."

"I don't believe you know what extreme consequences are," the New Zealander said coldly. "I can think of a number of very serious crimes you've committed on our soil. If you see the outside of a cell in the next two decades, I'll be astonished."

Clayton cleared his throat. "I believe it would be in our mutual interest if you secured Agent Ulysses somewhere we don't have to listen to him rant. It become less pleasant by the minute."

Vaughn gestured toward Ulysses. Several of his men roughly secured the CIA agent and shuffled him off toward the helicopter. He resisted and shouted dire threats, but that did him absolutely no good.

"Take the rest of them as well," Vaughn said.

Clayton smiled and held up a hand. "If I might have a few words first, I think that action might be a bit precipitous."

The other man gave him a quizzical look and gestured for his soldiers to pause. "I'm not sure I understand. Aren't these the men who tried to kidnap you? Unless I miss my guess, they were going to take you to some black site where no one would ever see you again."

"Indeed. Still, we've come to an arrangement."

"That may be, but you're not the one to make those decisions."

"I was under the impression that Miss Goodwin told you what we found here."

"All I've heard are a lot of tall tales and frankly unbelievable stories that I'm inclined to blame on the great stress you've been under. Why she felt the need to tell anyone something like that on your behalf, I have no idea."

Clayton pulled his phone out and dialed a number. "Come get us."

The Asharim shuttle rose from the forest about a kilometer away and flew quickly to the mesa. It hovered silently above them.

He watched with a smile as the government official and the soldiers with him gaped at the impossible ship over their heads.

"Some versions of insanity come with props. Mister Vaughn, everything you've heard is completely true. More, it's only the tip of the iceberg. These soldiers are the very least of your concerns. Trust me on that."

* * *

CHEN ARRIVED at his new office with mixed emotions. Being thrown out of the country in which he'd resided for so long had an emotional impact, after all.

To balance that out, he was only just south of America's border. The Yucatán Spaceport would serve his needs quite well.

There was also some pleasure in being able to sit in something his enemies desired more than anything else. Something he'd taken from them.

Oh, not directly. Rogers had sold the Yucatán Spaceport to the Chinese government. Yet Chen had urged them to use force to take it back when the Americans seized it.

Without a spaceport, the Americans wouldn't be using that pretty little ship they'd forced the Indian government to sell them. Well, they weren't going to be able to use it due to other actions, but this was just icing on the cake, so to speak.

The loss of the Asharim artifacts was only the first of the Americans' setbacks and not the most painful. Now that the Dragon knew there was a base inside the caldera of Olympus Mons, they couldn't allow even the potential for any other group to travel to Mars.

Today was the day they made certain the Americans never left the surface of the Earth again. That single move would cement the future in the Dragon's favor forever.

The office that Chen had taken over was well appointed and had probably belonged to Clayton Rogers at some point. That was fitting, too.

He didn't know where the old man was at this point, but Chen suspected he'd turn up eventually. Dealing with Rogers and his son was going to be significantly more complicated than stopping the Americans from reaching Mars. The man's company was already in orbit around the Red Planet, after all.

Worse, those forces would know the Chinese spaceship was coming weeks before it arrived. The only saving grace was that the Dragon would make sure the Mars mission they sent was more than capable of eliminating any threats they might meet.

Chen settled himself at the desk, picked up the phone, and dialed his superior's number.

"Wu."

"Minister Wu. I have arrived at the Yucatán Spaceport. Might I inquire as to the status of my suggestion?"

Coming with the backing he'd had, his "suggestion" that the Chinese government use military force to seize or disable the Indian-built Mars ship was actually an order. All that remained was to discover which choice of options they'd taken.

"Ah, Chen. It's good to hear your voice. I'm pleased you've relocated successfully. Indeed, they have decided upon a course of action. One that will have permanent reverberations across the globe.

"Even as we speak, we are preparing one of our concealed satellite weapons. Very soon, the only other ship capable of reaching Mars will no longer exist."

Chen smiled. "That is indeed good news, Minister. I take it that

that also means our ship is prepared to depart. I fear the Americans will retaliate in kind if it does not."

"Then lay your fears to rest. Our ship will depart before we take action."

"Am I to communicate our intentions to the Americans before our strike takes place?"

"No. The decision was made to allow the strike to speak for itself. So far as we are concerned, the Americans initiated this war by seizing the spaceport in which you sit. All we are doing is making certain our assets are in no further danger and repaying their temerity."

That wasn't quite the smartest play, Chen thought, but it wasn't his call to make. Indeed, it hardly mattered what the Americans did in response to the Chinese provocation. The world order was about to change, and change favored the Dragon.

"I understand, Minister. I will await your instructions."

Once the call was done, Chen leaned back in his comfortable new chair and considered the future. Oh yes, things were about to get very interesting indeed. All he had to do now was wait.

29

J ess didn't think the French base was going to be a good place to
house the Volunteers over the long-term. Even having worked
for years in space, the artificial corridors would drive her nuts
over time. She could only imagine how someone used to living
out in a nature setting would react to that kind of confinement.

Still, this didn't have to be a permanent thing. Once Harry
managed to gather enough force, he could return to their world and
clear out the zone around the hill. Once he did that, all of these
people could go home.

Meanwhile, they were making themselves useful. The battle
between Harry's brother and the Islamic extremists at the base had
made quite a mess. The bodies were gone, but the bloodstains
remained. Extra hands for cleaning duty were most welcome.

As soon as she found time, she pigeonholed Kevin McHugh. As
expected, he was examining one of the gates when she cornered him.
He'd gotten a comp to replace the one he'd left with Clayton Rogers
and had plugged it into a gate.

"I thought you'd already checked these out," she said as she
stepped up beside him.

"I did. I'm looking at something else now. There has to be a way to restrict outside access. I mean, the Asharim had these things in their homes. Surely you don't want to have a door that anyone can open from the outside in a place like that."

"I can help with that. I found it on *Freedom Express*."

She found and showed him the screen with the orange knot that locked the gate.

"This part is easy," she said. "What might be more useful would be the ability to authorize only certain gates to connect or restrict them to certain times of the day. It seems like that would make sense."

"Exactly what I was thinking. If I can locate the subroutines that authorize that kind of behavior in the computer, I can lock these gates down so that only friendly people can connect rather than completely sealing them off."

He gestured meaningfully around at the people cleaning the room. "I'd sure like to avoid having the people that caused all this mess come back for a repeat performance."

Jess couldn't argue with that kind of logic. "You look for that while I do something else. We had two addresses that looked like somewhere a small ship could go. We figured out which one was the moon. I'd like to know where the other one lets out."

She walked over to the next gate and brought out a handheld controller. After consulting her phone, she entered the address that led to the mountain range she'd seen in the video they'd recovered from the fighter.

The gate cycled through and opened onto a late-night view of what looked like the same mountainous area. The full moon bathed everything in silver.

Being careful to only extend her upper body through the gate, Jess checked that this wasn't a sheer cliff. It wasn't, but that didn't mean she had a lot of room to maneuver. The gate sat on the side of a mountain, all right. It was inside a relatively enclosed space, but she wouldn't call it a cave. It was more like a massive divot.

The floor of the area seemed natural enough and extended out from the gate about ten meters. Being careful of her footing, she stepped through the gate and edged up to the opening.

There was a breathtakingly sheer drop into the dark jungle below.

The light from the French base gave her enough illumination to see the entire area around the gate.

There was no base here. This was just an exit for small ships. Pity. With a sigh, she went back through the gate and killed the connection.

She was just working herself up to helping clean up the bloody mess when Sandra Dean came into the room. The sniper immediately altered course and headed right for her.

"Good," the other woman said. "I was hoping to find you."

"Why is that? Nothing good I'm sure."

"My, haven't you turned into a pessimist? I wouldn't call this good news, but at least it's not overtly bad."

Jess smiled wryly. "Lay it on me."

"One of my people is monitoring the local police bands. They found the cars we moved away from the base. That's got them buzzing."

After the fight between Nathan and the Islamic militants, there had been no survivors left at the French base. Thankfully, it was isolated enough that no one had noticed all the vehicles they'd left behind.

It had taken Rex and his people all night and several trips to move the vehicles fifty kilometers away. That was still a bit close for her comfort, but they'd only had one night to make it happen.

"You're right. That's not good news. What do you think the odds are they're going to trace any of the activity back here?"

Sandra shrugged. "I have no idea. Rex and I have worked out an evacuation plan to get everyone to *Freedom Express* if someone comes sniffing around. They're not going to come in guns blazing. We'll have plenty of warning."

Jess supposed that was true, but she'd hate to lose this facility. Of all the bases they'd found on Earth, this was the only one in operational condition.

"If trouble comes knocking, we're not going to be able to move our refugees in a timely fashion," she said after a moment. "We need to start relocating them if we even suspect we're going to have company.

"And on the flip side, since we don't have a means of locking the gates so only we can use them yet, if bad guys come calling, we need to be able to get everyone up to the surface and away from danger. We have to keep them unlocked for Clayton to execute his plan."

Sandra considered that and nodded slowly. "If Nathan Bennett and his thugs come back, we'll give them a hot reception, but that means innocent bystanders stand a very good chance of being hurt."

Jess turned toward the gates. "He hasn't come back yet. After the ship he and his mother were on went through that massive gate, we haven't heard a word from them. Maybe they didn't make it."

"Last we saw, they were trapped on that ship with a bunch of hostiles," Sandra said. "It's always possible they lost that fight, but we can't take that for granted. That's why Rex has those men over in the corner. They'll give any hostiles an extremely warm welcome."

Jess sighed. "Christ. I hate not knowing what they're doing. I'd rather they'd just make their move and be done."

* * *

KATHLEEN PUT her best face on as she sat waiting for the high priest to return. She was more nervous about Nathan's fate than she cared to admit to herself.

Yes, the little weasel had gotten himself into this trouble. And yes, she'd made the decision that her life would be a lot simpler without him. That still didn't make this process easy. She was a mother, for God's sake.

She'd rather not be the one *directly* responsible for his death. It would be a lot better for all concerned if he managed to go out in a blaze of glory because of his own idiocy. Perhaps that could be arranged if she played her cards right.

About an hour after he'd departed, Jedan Louvan returned. He stalked into the room where she waited without bothering to knock.

Kathleen rose to her feet, hiding the irritation she felt at his rudeness. "Were you able to teach my son how to speak the language of the Masters?"

The man grunted. "Yes, but that does not make him any less of a savage. He is rude, insulting, and uncouth. Blasphemous, too, though

I must overlook some aspects of his behavior, as he is not aware of the full scope of the Masters."

"That's true of everyone on Earth. A year ago, we had no idea the Masters even existed. You're the first person we've met that could explain them to us. We have a lot to learn."

He sat, waving to one of his acolytes. "Bring us drinks and cakes. Veristar juice."

Kathleen noted he didn't ask what her preferences were. Apparently, she was getting what he wanted.

The high priest of the Masters considered her for a moment. "You claim to come from a world filled with people like ourselves. Rather, like the beings we were before the Masters changed us. Do I understand that correctly?"

"You do. For example, you saw how my son was unable to resist as you took him to educate him in your language."

The man held up a warning finger. "Not my language. The language of the Masters. Never forget that."

"The Masters," she agreed. "As I said, we know virtually nothing of the Masters. No one on Earth does. And there are people there who, now that they know the Masters exist, are working hard to make certain they can never return."

The man sat up abruptly. "What blasphemy is this? Explain yourself swiftly or face my wrath."

Kathleen made a show of shrugging. "Sadly, the leaders of the forces arrayed against the Masters on Earth are my ex-husband and other son. I can't begin to tell you what great disappointments they are to me. I'm fighting against them, but at the moment, they have the upper hand."

The high priest's eyes narrowed. "Tell me the story from the very beginning. Leave nothing out."

She gave thanks to the gods that she was a skilled liar. It took her almost no effort to morph the truth of recent events into a story that suited her ends.

Clayton and Harry became the enemies of the piece. She became the hero. Nathan was an inconvenient sidekick and fool.

The tale she told twisted everything into seeming as though she'd left the home world searching for the Masters. Looking for their aid in reestablishing their rule on Earth. By the time she'd finished, Kathleen was almost ready to cheer herself on.

Louvan seemed less than convinced. He sat there staring at her with one of the most skeptical expressions she'd ever seen.

"As High Priest of the Masters, it is my unfortunate duty to correct the faithful when they stray. I've heard many lies in my life. Some crude and others as smooth as a child's skin. I've gained some skill at sensing deception.

"I sense great deception in you, Kathleen Bennett. Oh, some aspects of your story are undoubtedly true. Perhaps even most of it. The part I doubt is your motive. That is always the place where a liar conceals the harshest of truths."

Kathleen was impressed, but she didn't let that emotion make it to her face. Instead, she showed him a gentle sadness.

"I understand your skepticism. In your place, I would feel much the same. Yet, I can prove all of these things. Whether I am telling the truth or lying, you would still stand to gain from working with me."

An acolyte walked into the room with a tray holding a pitcher of liquid, two glasses filled with ice, and some kind of small snack cakes. The man set it on a low table between the high priest and Kathleen before departing.

Louvan poured them both glasses before sipping from his and nibbling on a cake. "The juice is from a local fruit you might find interesting. It is sweet but comes with an almost shockingly sour aftertaste. It is quite good. The cakes serve to clean the palate and are also quite tasty."

Kathleen worried for a moment that he intended to poison or drug her but set it aside. A certain level of trust would serve her cause well here. Besides, they'd have to eat sooner or later.

She sipped the drink and found it was indeed just like he described it. An initial rush of sweetness like apple juice gave way to an almost lemonade flavor. It was refreshing. The cakes were sweet and light. She set herself to trying more as her stomach grumbled.

"If I were to work with you, what goals do you see us sharing?" he asked.

Kathleen smiled. The hook was set.

"If you want to bring the Masters back, then you need to suppress any who do not accept them. The forces of my ex-husband are already hard at work to make certain humanity never kneels to the Masters.

"I saw warriors among your flock. You could take some of them back to Earth where you could fight our shared enemies and establish new homes to use as bases for converting the rest of humanity to serve the Masters."

The man grudgingly nodded. "Fighting the enemies of the Masters is always worthwhile, and I agree that bringing servants who have lost their way back into the service of the Masters is also a desirable thing.

"What I do not understand is how that will benefit you? You do not know the Masters, Kathleen Bennett. They have not touched and shaped your life down to the very genes inside your body. What do you hope to gain?"

"Nothing too much," she assured the man. "Unless you have greater numbers than I am aware of, you will need the willing assistance of unmodified humans on Earth.

"I intend to enter this agreement as your partner. One can serve the Masters and still rule the land on which they live to some degree. Much as you do here. I want the same on Earth."

He considered her a moment without saying a word. Then he inclined his head.

"I cannot argue with the logic of your statement. While the People are great warriors, our numbers are not what they once were. Food was more difficult to produce after the Masters departed, so it served our needs to allow our numbers to fall.

"Yet when we fight, we still have the technology of the Masters and are unbeatable. Do not think yourself capable of betraying us. Once you enter the service of the Masters, you cannot change your mind."

Kathleen could see the fire of belief in the man's eyes. He was a fanatic. He meant every word he said.

She wasn't sure she could finesse this situation completely, but she still had faith she would win in the end. All that mattered now was securing the best outcome for her. If she ended up being a servant of the so-called Masters, so be it. They probably didn't even exist anymore.

"I'm in agreement," Kathleen said. "All that remains is getting us back to Earth. I assume you have gates here."

The high priest scowled. "We do, but they have not worked since the Masters departed. That is what causes me the most shock about your arrival."

Kathleen smiled. Her mind had promptly provided information on how the Asharim would have locked the gates. With access to a controller, she could undo it from this end. Physical access was key.

"How long will it take you to gather a strong raiding party?" she asked. "There is a base on Earth that should be easy to secure if we strike quickly."

The man seemed to consider her words for a moment before nodding. "We can gather enough men before dark. I agree that we should strike as soon as possible."

She was almost certain the man intended to betray her, but she knew that, once she reached Earth, she could turn things around. She had knowledge from the Asharim computers that this man didn't.

If things truly went badly, she could lock the gates down on that side and deal with the people that came with her. As long as they captured the base in France, this was going to work out in her favor. One way or the other.

"We have a deal."

30

It had taken far longer to gather officials from New Zealand, Australia, South Korea, and Japan than Clayton had wanted. Not that he'd allow them to see his impatience. That would never have done.

Still, he'd finally convinced people with sufficient authority that he was telling the truth. Or at least something important enough to require sending someone to report back.

The prime minister of New Zealand was put out that Clayton had contacted the other three governments. He'd much rather have kept it a close secret, no doubt.

The senior government officials from Japan, South Korea, and Australia had only just arrived at the ruined base. The Asharim shuttle had wowed them, but now they were all staring at the gates with skepticism.

Yoshida Sato, an extremely powerful ally of the Japanese prime minister, walked boldly up to the center gate, staring down at the blue cube powering it. He spoke briefly with the translator he'd brought with him, and the woman turned to face Clayton.

"Minister Sato asks what form of power is resident inside this device. Is it dangerous?"

Uncertain if this was somehow related to the man's possible feelings about nuclear power, Clayton shook his head. "The specifics of how it generates energy are something of a mystery. I can say that it isn't based on nuclear energy."

Reginald Baker, the Australian prime minister's brother, walked past the small group and into the gate depression itself. "I'm not seeing the big deal," he said bluntly. "Just a glowing cube that probably has something painted on the inside and a hole in the rock."

Clayton smiled. "If you'll step back out and away from the gate, I believe I can demonstrate what the big deal is."

Once the man had rejoined them, Clayton picked up the comp Kevin McHugh had left attached to the power device. A few taps on the screen brought up the address for the French base. He activated the gate.

Everyone stared at the roiling mist shot through with lightning that suddenly appeared inside the gate. Once it cleared, they could all see the interior of the French base.

The room on the other side was very much like the one they stood in, but it was well lit and filled with people. First and foremost among those was Jessica Cook. The engineer had known Clayton would be opening the wormhole and had been standing by.

She smiled and walked into the ruined base. "Hello, everyone. My name is Jess Cook. As you can see, this gate linked to another place.

"In this case, it's a base we have at a secret location. Basically, matter transportation via a wormhole. These gates can link to one another across the planet, across the solar system, and across the galaxy.

"They were seeded by an alien race called the Asharim. Not nice people, but they seem to have gone down in a war about a thousand years ago. Earth has a lot of catching up to do, and we can't allow any one government to do it alone. That's why we summoned you here."

"Even seeing it with my own eyes, I can't believe it," Isaiah Vaughn said slowly. "This is just too crazy."

Jess's expression turned sympathetic. "Imagine how difficult it was for those of us that actually located the equipment and made it work."

"Did you find something on Mars?" Park Sung-min, the South

Korean minister of Science and ICT—information and communications technology—asked in almost unaccented English, asked. "I remember seeing something in the news about your people landing on some big volcano there. Is that what you found?"

She smiled at the man. "That's exactly what we found. A fully operational base filled with technology beyond our dreams."

"I do not understand why you are telling us this," Sato said through his interpreter. "You are Americans. Surely the American government will be angry that you revealed it to us. Why are they not your partners in this endeavor?"

Clayton took that verbal slow ball and swung for the fences. "The government of the United States isn't what it used to be. It's become more closed-minded, more corrupt.

"The name of the company we formed to exploit the technology is called Humanity Unlimited for a reason. These discoveries need to belong to humanity as a whole, not to one government bent on using it as a club against its enemies—or even its allies."

Kevin McHugh picked that moment to walk through the gate from the French base. He edged over to Jess Cook and spoke softly in her ear. Jess excused herself and headed back through the gate while Kevin remained standing beside the power supply.

Clayton hoped there wasn't some kind of serious trouble brewing. Even if there was, however, he needed to get on with the demonstration.

He cleared his throat. "I have one other location I'd like to show you. My son inadvertently discovered this place by transposing two characters while exploring the gate system. Pure chance, you understand."

He disconnected the connection the French base and used his phone to look up the address to the world Harry had discovered. The gate connected once he'd entered the correct code and revealed a sparkling beach with plants very similar to palm trees underneath a sky with two suns.

That got their attention.

"From everything we've been able to discover, it's perfectly safe. The island is relatively small and located in the tropical zone of a world thousands of light-years away. No dangerous creatures have been identified."

Vaughn stared through the gate. "Are those palm trees?"

Clayton shrugged. "I don't believe so, but I can't rule out them being related in some way. The similarity is striking."

He stepped through the gate and into the bright sunlight. "As far as we've been able to determine, this was a resort at some point. There are no buildings on the island, just serving areas. Old tables and chairs that are just about to come apart.

"The kitchen and serving areas must've been at a different gate address. Frankly, we're told that that was a common practice for the Asharim. The wealthiest in their society would have homes with separate rooms in different locations connected by gates that were never turned off. Basically, their homes were distributed across the galaxy."

Vaughn shook his head as he stepped through and stared out over the waves. The rest of the dignitaries followed suit. Clayton said nothing, content to allow them to take it in at their own speed.

Five minutes later, even though no one had said a single word that indicated they were ready to finalize a deal, Clayton knew the inevitable outcome. They couldn't shield their body language well enough to pretend they hadn't already come to a decision.

The Republic of Nauru, New Zealand, Australia, South Korea, and Japan would have a pact for mutual protection and exploitation of the technology by the day's end.

* * *

NATHAN BURNED INSIDE. The bastard had raped him. He'd quite literally restrained him and forced something into his mind. Then, after compelling him to learn their language, the bastard hadn't asked him a single question.

And his mother had let it happen. Hell, she'd thrown her own son to the wolves. Oh yes, she was going to pay for that. Only right now wasn't the time.

His mother and the Grand Dickhead had been strategizing for the last hour on the specifics of an attack plan for the base in France. They intended to seize it from the Islamic assholes.

Nathan didn't have any objection to that. Those sorry bastards deserved to die. He just didn't want to risk his own neck to make that happen. Not when he was certain he'd never see any reward for his efforts.

The only problem was that he didn't imagine he could opt out. He needed an exit plan from this fiasco, but he'd have to execute it once he got back to Earth.

If he could arrange to separate himself from the attacking force, he could make his way to Paris and use the resources his mother and he had around the globe to set himself up.

His mother wouldn't be pleased with that. Teach her to make him do all the work. He knew where everything was.

It was at that point the conversation between the Grand Dickhead and his mother turned to him. The three of them were seated at a long table in the temple, along with the buttmunch that had captured them at the space elevator.

His first inkling that they finally wanted his input in their stupid plan was his mother's imperious instruction to tell them everything he knew about the base in France. She'd seen enough of it that he couldn't outright lie about the layout. Pity. That would've been amusing.

He sketched a verbal picture of how the gate room was at the bottom of the base, the number of floors that sat above it, and the landscape surrounding the facility. He then described in rough detail the capabilities of the jihadis.

The Grand Dickhead dismissed that last with a wave. "These savages barely qualify as combatants. Our forces will sweep them aside."

The man who'd captured them didn't look as convinced, but he seemed disinclined to argue with his leader.

"So how do we do it?" Nathan asked. "Find a local gate and push through enough force to seize the other end?"

His mother's expression became irritated. "It seems the Masters did something to the gates here that I can't figure out how to undo.

They won't turn activate from this side. We'll either have to use the gates on the station, if there are any functional, or transport people to the ship and use the one there.

"Once we get to the other side, I'll use a gate there to connect with one of the gates on the planet here. I'll lock it open, and they can bring through as many reinforcements as they want to take the base."

That was going to restrict the number of people they could send through for the initial assault, particularly if they had to transport them to the ship on that little boat.

He allowed himself to nod. "That sounds fine. When do we go? Tomorrow?"

The warrior shook his head. "We cannot allow the enemy to consolidate the gains they have made. Even now, they might be bringing reinforcements to this base.

"We leave as soon as this council is complete. I've already gathered a large force. Most will wait here while we strike, but I'll take my best men with us."

And that's what they did. The level of general planning horrified the professional inside Nathan. They were just going to take a gamble that they had enough force, push it, and hope they had what it took to open a gate back.

They'd gathered about a hundred fighters armed with alien rifles. He'd seen how potent such weapons could be and knew the men were devilishly strong, so maybe this wasn't as weak as he'd feared.

As the group marched back to the space elevator, Nathan edged close to his mother. Thankfully, the Grand Dickhead was leading the way, giving them a little bit of privacy.

"Are you sure this is the right thing to do, Mother? Once we get to Earth and open the gate back, these people are going to be in control."

She gave him a withering look. "I don't see where we have much of a choice. The entire damned planet is arrayed against us back home. We need allies."

"I can't imagine how you see these people as allies. They're going to be our masters."

"You never could see the long game, boy. Sometimes you have to do things you don't want to in order to position yourself for future success. Just trust that I know what I'm talking about."

So much for forcing her to see reason.

The force they'd gathered barely fit inside the space elevator, and the trip up seemed to take forever. The view of the approaching space station through the clear ceiling was spectacular.

As he'd expected, the gates on the space station proved to be unresponsive. Why would they be any different from the ones on the planet? That meant they had to do this the hard way. It took forever to ferry the men across to the ship. More wasted time.

The warriors they'd brought dutifully lined up in an attack formation in front of the operational gate, ignoring the ripe bodies scattered around the gate compartment after the fight with the Islamists.

Nathan set himself at the rear of the column. It appeared that the Grand Dickhead and his mother were going to wait on the ship.

The religious nut had several of his acolytes guarding them. In that particular, they didn't look much different than the warriors. They were armed and tough.

When the gate finally formed, the fighters rushed through and began shooting people. To Nathan's surprise, the people shooting back were not Islamic nut jobs. They looked like Harry's people.

Even better.

He raised his rifle and charged in, shooting as he went.

31

Jess gaped at the heavy-worlders rushing through the gate for a moment before dropping behind the closest cover—in this case, a pile of crates holding supplies from *Freedom Express* for the refugees.

Christ, the refugees. She pulled her phone out as she huddled there and called Rex. He was somewhere upstairs with Sandra.

"Go," he said moments later.

"We're under heavy-worlder attack through the gate. Get the refugees out and bring help."

"Crap. On it."

She set her phone beside the nearest crate and drew the pistol she carried at the small of her back. With the number of enemies pouring into the base, she didn't have nearly enough ammunition to stop them. Not even to delay them.

What she could do was take one down and upgrade her weapon. The downside of that plan was that she'd draw an immediate hostile response when she opened fire, and those flechettes would be deadly.

Well, it wasn't as if she had much of a choice.

Jess raised herself just enough to see what the situation in the gate room was like. It wasn't good. The heavy-worlders' attack had caught everyone by surprise, even the people who were there to defend against just such an incursion.

The defenders had taken significant casualties and fallen back to the reinforced positions. They were taking a toll on the enemy, but they hadn't escaped unscathed. The bodies of far too many of her people littered the floor.

Thankfully, they'd done a real number on the heavy-worlders, too. That left several flechette rifles lying tantalizingly close to her hiding place, and the enemy was focused on the forces arrayed in front of them.

She'd have one chance to strike from the rear. She'd better make it count.

Jess raced from cover toward the nearest of the fallen. She'd made it almost halfway to the weapon she'd had her eye on when Nathan Bennett stepped through the open gate and spotted her.

She snapped several shots at the man as she threw herself down beside the dead heavy-worlder. Harry's brother had seen her and ducked behind one of the fighters. She was pretty sure she'd missed the rat.

Apparently, her shots hadn't missed everyone, though. She saw another group of about half a dozen heavy-worlders on the other side of the gate. These were dressed in robes and wore odd headgear. Half of them were clustered around a sagging man at their center, and the remainder were looking at her with blood in their eyes.

Perfect.

She emptied her pistol at the new threat before dropping it and snatching up the fallen flechette rifle. Thankfully, she'd had the opportunity to practice with weapons just like this one.

Bennett hadn't shown himself, so she exchanged fire with the heavy-worlders on the other side of the gate.

They weren't idle or cowardly, though. Some of them charged toward her while the remainder opened fire. Their dead comrade was not going to prove much of a barricade against the flechettes coming her way.

Her initial burst took down the three heavy-worlders charging toward her. Unfortunately, that gave the three on the other side of the gate time to zero in on her.

She flattened herself behind the bulk of the dead man as flechettes ripped his body to shreds. The man's bulk miraculously stopped most of them but not all. She felt a sharp pain in her gut then another in her left leg. She'd been hit.

Jess didn't let that stop her. She exposed herself just enough to empty her flechette rifle at the enemy. Several of them went down. Not all of them, though. One was still on his feet and heading her way.

She ejected the spent magazine and tried to pull a fresh one from the dead guy's belt. Her hands felt so clumsy. She couldn't seem to focus. Her vision was narrow, and she felt so cold. That probably wasn't good.

Before she could fit the new magazine into the rifle, the heavy-worlder kicked the weapon out of her hands. He shouted something at her in an alien language and raised his weapon to finish her.

His head exploded, and he dropped like a stone. That meant he fell right on top of her, driving the air out of her lungs.

Jess struggled to roll him off, but he barely moved. The irony of being suffocated before the gunshots could kill her would have made her laugh, if she had the air.

The weight vanished as someone rolled the body off her. She sucked in blessed air and saw Nathan Bennett grinning down at her.

"Well, well, well," he purred. "We meet again."

She did laugh then. It sounded wet and horrible. She could taste blood in her mouth. A lot of it. "I think you're a little late to do anything to me now."

He scowled at her body. "No! You're mine, dammit! You can't die now!"

Then he grinned. "I have a brilliant idea. You'll hate it."

She didn't imagine the dead hated much of anything, so she wasn't going to worry about it. She'd focus on the regrets flooding over her. She'd never explore the universe and never see her friends again. That was almost worse than the physical pain.

Nathan snatched her up off the ground, threw her into a fireman's carry, and raced through the open gate.

Jess wanted to fight him, but her dying body didn't have the strength or coordination. She had no idea what he thought he could do to save her, but she knew it was doomed to fail.

She'd caught a glimpse of her body as he picked her up. Her torso was covered in blood, and she actually saw her intestines through the rip in her flesh. Her left leg had been opened to the bone, too.

She'd bleed out long before he could do anything to her, and that was just fine. Better death than being his prisoner.

The dizziness had almost overwhelmed her when Nathan carried her past the dead heavy-worlders on the other side of the gate. She saw something she'd missed in all the excitement. Harry's mother had been standing off to the side.

Somehow, she'd survived where they'd died. No, it wasn't her. It was a young woman that looked something like her. Odd. The blood loss was affecting her in some really strange ways.

Jess saw the unknown woman manipulate a gate controller, and the gate to the French base closed.

Nathan didn't slow down as he raced through the corridors. She recognized the layout and realized they were on the ship that had once been in the Sol system. The one Nathan and his mother had escaped in.

Her world had shrunk to almost nothing when he set her down on a cold metal surface and grinned down at her. "Still with me, I see. Good. We'll talk again real soon."

She wanted to spit in his face, but she couldn't focus well enough to make it happen. She was barely alive enough to see some kind of metal lid slide across above her.

She had just enough time to realize that she was in a sarcophagus before her world went dark and she died. That seemed appropriate, somehow.

The last of the light vanished and she knew nothing more.

* * *

HARRY TIREDLY OPENED the passenger door to the SUV. As he'd more than half expected, they hadn't found anything. If there was a cave out here that held one of the quantum gates, it was exceptionally well hidden.

Or perhaps it had just collapsed over the intervening years. There were enough rockfalls that could've concealed it out here. Without bringing in equipment and doing a search that would undoubtedly draw the wrong kind of attention, there was no way to know for sure.

If anything, Brenda was even more annoyed than he was. Understandable. After all, she considered this her backyard.

"What do we do now?" he asked as he handed bottles of water to the other three. The two from off planet examined theirs curiously. He showed them how to twist the plastic caps off. They made faces at the taste of the water.

"We go back into town," Brenda said. "This was a good reconnaissance, but we're going to need a lot more bodies to do this right."

They'd almost made it back to Washington when his phone rang and he saw Rex's number. "Go, Rex."

"Heavy-worlders just opened a gate into the base, and they're pouring through," he said. "We're pushing back, but Jess is down in the gate room. We're moving the Volunteers up to the surface."

"Crap. Do the best you can, and I'll be there as soon as possible." He disconnected. "We need to get back to the gate as quickly as possible. The bad guys found the French base. We're moving all your people up to the surface, Susanna."

The ex-FBI agent accelerated the SUV and turned on flashing lights and a siren.

"Won't this draw a little too much attention?" he asked dryly, trying to keep from worrying about Jess.

She grinned. "Have you ever seen a cop stop another cop? No. Does it sound bad?"

He nodded, his stomach roiling. "Real bad. I'd better call my father so he doesn't accidentally walk back into the firefight."

Harry dialed his father's number.

"I'm a little busy right now," the old man said quietly. "Can this wait?"

"That depends on how much you value your skin," Harry said bluntly. "The heavy-worlders are attacking the French base. Don't open a gate to it."

The other man swore. "Jess is there. Is she okay?"

"I don't know. Now doesn't seem like the right time to call and ask, either. We're going to have to force our way back into the gate room. Rex has virtually all of my security forces at the base, thank God."

"Is that going to be enough?"

"I hope so. I'll call you back when I know anything else."

He checked his watch. It would take them a while to get to the building holding Brenda's gate. Everything would probably be settled by the time he got there. He felt incredibly helpless. Things had gone wrong so quickly.

* * *

CLAYTON QUICKLY EXPLAINED the situation to the dignitaries. Needless to say, his news put a damper on their enthusiasm for the pact they'd just agreed to.

"That's bad," Vaughn said roughly. "Will you be able to contain them?"

"Probably. The real trick will be stopping them from bringing in too many people to overwhelm before we get more people in place. To do anything about that, we need to get soldiers there as soon as possible."

"I have an idea," Kevin McHugh said.

"Trot it out, young man," Clayton said when the boy paused. "You have my complete attention."

"Did you ever see the original *Stargate* movie? It has gates similar to the Asharim ones. The fictional US government in the franchise sent a nuke through the stargate to make sure no one could overwhelm the people protecting it if things went bad."

Clayton hadn't seen the movie, but his assistant had explained it in a general way. "That does sound like a capital idea, but I'm a little short on nuclear devices. I suspect our friends are in similar circumstances."

"True, but you have a US warship impounded here in New Zealand. Tell me they don't have portable nukes locked up on board."

That gave Clayton pause. He had no idea if they did or not, but it sounded like a reasonable possibility. They also had trained soldiers.

By now, Commander Krueger and his people were back aboard their ship. Clayton had convinced the New Zealanders to only make an example of Ulysses and let the rest go.

If anyone could save their bacon now, it was Krueger and his people. Unfortunately, they wouldn't be able to lift a finger to save them without orders.

"I'll try to get their assistance, but I'm not hopeful," he said after a moment. "To do that, I need to convince Secretary of State Queen to assist us. That seems... unlikely."

Well, unlikely wasn't impossible. He'd give it his best shot. Jess's life might depend on getting more people into the French base fast. Hell, all their lives might rest on stopping the invasion in progress.

He pulled out his phone and dialed information. "I need the main number for the State Department," he told the operator.

32

Queen rubbed his tired eyes. He'd thought things couldn't get any worse, but he'd been wrong. The damned Chinese were mobilizing all around the globe.

Not only had they blown up the lab full of alien technology, they seemed intent on making an issue out of the Yucatán Spaceport. They wanted war. That wasn't a big shock, he supposed. This day had been coming for years. Their timing sucked, though.

It had to be the damned Mars mission. They assumed—as did he —that Rogers had found the mother lode on Mars. They wanted all the marbles for themselves, and they were willing to kill as many people as needed to make that happen.

That made the next call he received inevitable but infuriating. He took it as soon as his assistant told him who was calling.

"You have a lot of nerve calling me," he snarled into the phone.

"I'm sure," Ambassador Chen said cordially. "My superiors didn't want me to do so, but I feel that we shouldn't make the same mistakes as our neighbors a century ago.

"China views your actions against us as an act of war, and we are responding to them as such. You will no doubt receive word of military action in the very near future. Regrettable as that is, you precipitated this action yourselves."

"Liar," Queen said bluntly. "You already knew about the alien technology, so don't try to spin this as anything other than a power grab. You want what Rogers found on Mars."

Chen chuckled. "Of course we do. How could we not? We shall have it, too."

"We'll see about that."

His assistant stuck his head in and started making frantic gestures.

Queen muted the call. "What?"

"Something just blew up the Mars ship we bought from the Indians. It's gone."

He sat there, stunned for a moment. "Damned Chinese. Did they fire a missile at it?"

The man shrugged. "Our national defense assets would've seen something like that. Maybe something from their ship?"

"Or a satellite already in orbit. Can we strike their ship?"

The man shook his head. "It must've already boosted from orbit. I got word of that just before they blew our ship up. It happened on the other side of the planet, so we only just got the notice."

Even if Queen called the president for authority to fire a ballistic missile at the Chinese ship, it was going to be too far away to do any good.

"Crap."

Chen had been blathering in his ear all this time, but Queen hadn't been paying attention. He cut the man off. "You bastard. You blew up our Mars ship. We had people up there."

"Casualties happen during war," the other man said urbanely. "The loss of life is, of course, regrettable. You will recall I did deliver our declaration of war before hostilities began, however. It is all as required by international law."

"Screw you, and screw your declaration. We'll burn you to the ground." He slammed the phone down hard.

Now all he needed was a way to hurt them. He had to call the president and tell him what was happening. The military needed to get into a more aggressive posture and make the bastards pay for this.

His frazzled assistant stuck his head back in. "There's another call you need to take. Line two."

"Dammit, what now? Are the Russians shooting at us, too?"

"It's Clayton Rodgers."

Perfect. The bastard had probably called to gloat.

He snatched up his handset and pressed the button for the active line. "I'd say you have a lot of nerve calling me like this, but I'm busy. What do you want?"

"The situation has changed and not in a good way," the old man said. "The Earth is in danger."

"No shit. If this goes nuclear, millions could die."

There was a long pause from the other end of the connection. "Do you have me bugged? How could you possibly know I was calling because I need one of your nuclear devices?"

Queen opened his mouth to say something offensive then realized he had no idea what the man was talking about. Obviously not the Chinese.

"You need to start over," he told Rodgers slowly. "I'm talking about the Chinese declaring war on the US and destroying our Mars ship. What crisis are you talking about, and why would you possibly need a nuke?"

"Someone activated a gate to Earth and is attacking Harry's people. They're the best, but he doesn't have many of them. If these heavy-worlders get a hold on Earth, they might pour millions of soldiers through with advanced weapons. Hell, they might have the Asharim right behind them."

Queen buried his head in his hands. "Christ. You led them right to us."

"I seriously doubt that. If anything, Kathleen and Nathan did. We never had control over them. They were on the ship that the Asharim left watching our system that jumped out through the gate in the outer system. They had the address to the base in France."

"What gate in the outer system and what base in France? How many gates and bases do you have?"

"That hardly matters, and we don't have time for me to explain in detail. I'm in New Zealand, where you tried to kidnap me, standing in the remains of another base.

"I'm sure Commander Krueger is briefing his commanding officer about the gate here as we speak. He's on his ship. The one the New Zealanders impounded.

"I want to get them back here with every man they have available, and I want them to bring one of the portable nuclear devices I suspect all US ships carry nowadays.

"They can turn the tide in France and secure that gate before it becomes a beachhead. If we don't act soon, it might be too late. The Chinese are not the biggest threat on the board right now."

This was absolutely the worst time for this kind of distraction, but Rogers was right. An alien invasion trumped a conventional war. The Chinese could be dealt with. Hordes of high-tech aliens were a completely different story.

Queen rubbed his face. "I can't just send them in. The New Zealanders would never allow them off the ship, particularly with a nuke.

"Even if I could, you don't get my help for free. Your monopoly of the alien tech is over. The Chinese ship is on its way to Mars. You have to cut America in, or there is no deal."

He had absolutely no idea if any deal he struck—even if Rogers agreed to it—would make it past the president and Senate. Still, the bastard needed help, and this was the best time to make him give up control. Besides, if what the man said was true, time was running out for all of them.

"I agree in principle. Humanity Unlimited doesn't have the forces or the knowledge to deal with the aliens. As to the latter, you need to make your peace with Brenda Cabot and her group. They know far more about the Asharim than either of us."

Perfect. One more enemy he had to bring to the table. Yet, now that push came to shove, he knew he had to do that, too. He couldn't afford a world war with an enemy like that buried in his government.

"I also agree, in principle," he said tiredly. "I can probably get hold of her in a few hours."

"Would having her call you right now help?"

He snorted bitter amusement. "I suppose that shouldn't surprise me. Yes. Give me fifteen minutes to call the ship and give them orders. Rather, to call the admiral in charge and have her make that call. I'll have to get the New Zealanders to buy in, too."

"Make your call. I have an assistant to New Zealand's prime minister standing right beside me. He's already gotten the go ahead to let your people off the ship with the weapon so long as they don't detonate the bomb on their soil."

"This changes everything, Rogers," Queen said slowly. "We've been acting like kids pushing each other around in the schoolyard. As much as it pains me to say, the United States is going to have to step back in time and become the leader it once was. You and your people can help us or hinder us. I hope we can find the right path forward to save us all."

"So do I, Mister Secretary. So do I."

Queen disconnected the call without a word of goodbye. He had a lot of calls to make and some serious convincing to do.

* * *

HARRY ORDERED every man and woman who could handle a weapon to move to the base in New Zealand. The only break in his nonstop planning sessions was while Brenda Cabot negotiated a ceasefire with Queen.

He couldn't believe they had to work with the damned stuffed shirt, but he saw the logic, as much as he hated it. They just couldn't turn back an invasion with the forces he had at hand.

If they survived, everything was going to change. He wasn't sure how yet, but that was inevitable. The American government was going to try to take over, and he'd have to work with Jess to stop them or at least slow them down.

That started another round of worrying about the engineer. Rex hadn't heard from her since the fighting had started. That meant she was hidden somewhere in the base, captured, or dead.

He hoped for the best, but deep down he knew the chances of her still being a free agent were low. He prayed she was still alive. Losing her would be devastating both personally and professionally.

Listening to Brenda fill Queen in on what she suspected about a separate group of people from the Asharim conflict a thousand years ago was educational and distracting, too.

He immediately connected the Chinese conflict with that group. Brenda's certainty that they were heavy-worlders made the likelihood of them being loyal to the Asharim—even after all this time—too great to simply dismiss. There might even be a possibility they had some connection to the attack in France, though he didn't see how.

If they were as deeply embedded in society there as Brenda claimed her people were in the US, these people were probably manipulating their government. Or they'd placed their own in charge over the intervening centuries.

It made him wonder about the Communist takeover a century ago. Had the heavy-worlder secret society been behind that?

If they were in control, the conflict wouldn't end easily. These people probably thought they had a lot to gain and very little to lose. It also meant that the Chinese ship probably had a crew of their choosing. One that likely had some kind of Asharim tech along to even the odds.

Thankfully, he had a few weeks to worry about that problem. Assuming he survived the next few hours, of course.

Rex had done the best he could, but the enemy had forced him into withdrawing from the gate room. They were steadily forcing their way up, and it wouldn't be long before he had to abandon the base entirely. At least the Volunteers had finished evacuating.

Harry couldn't imagine what the French authorities would do once they figured out they had fighting on their territory. It probably wouldn't be good. Yet another thing to worry about.

They made it back to Brenda's building a few hours after dark and raced down to the gate room. Her people had already opened a connection to the ruined New Zealand base, and he stalked through it while she finished gathering those of her people who might be able to help.

His father was talking with Karl Krueger. They both turned to face him as soon as he stepped into the room.

"Perfect timing," the commander said. "I've been going over the basic situation with your father. It doesn't sound good."

Harry looked around the room at all the people they had gathered. His people made up about a quarter of the hundred or so people in the chamber. The US forces were of a similar number. The remainder wore camouflage uniforms of an unfamiliar make.

"It's looking better than I expected. Where did you come up with so many people, and who are they?"

"A quarter of them are mine. Not all Special Forces, but they have some combat training. The rest are the best New Zealand could gather on short notice. We have enough to secure a bridgehead on the far side, so long as we can do it quickly. My team will form the point.

"The basic plan is to open a gate and launch a heavy weapon to clear the floor on the other side. If the chamber is the same size as this one, it won't do the job completely, but it will cause enough shock and awe to get our people through.

"Then we hold while we take the package through the gate to the hostiles' home base. If it seems appropriately bad there, I have the green light to set the thing on a short timer and leave it while we withdraw. It's nice that cutting off the gate means we go from having a backpack nuke in our laps to being a long way away in a few seconds."

Harry nodded. "Damned straight. What about our people on the other side? I don't want to lose a single person, but I'm concerned about one in specific. Jess Cook isn't just my partner. She has irreplaceable knowledge of everything we're doing. We need to get her out alive if we can."

Krueger sighed. "We'll do what we can, but we have to protect our forces first."

That wasn't what Harry wanted to hear, but he knew it was a hard truth. This was going to be difficult no matter how they sliced it.

"What if they've closed the gate down?" he asked.

"That's where I come in," Kevin McHugh said from nearby. He

must've slipped up while they'd been talking. Brenda stood beside the bald man.

"How so?"

"I can access the gates to read their most recent incoming and outgoing addresses. It'll take a few seconds, but I'll be able to recreate the connection. It would be useful to guess which gate up front, though. I don't want to waste time on the wrong one."

"When will we be ready?" Harry asked the navy commander.

"We're ready now," Krueger said. "Give us a minute to get into final positions and we can kick this party off."

The fighting forces were gathered on either side of the gate. That made sense. If someone shot through it at them, they'd be out of the direct line of fire.

They'd set up some kind of portable missile launcher a bit back from the gate with its tubes angled to fire into the small area. Harry hoped none of them missed, or they'd destroy the gate and probably kill a lot of people in an ugly blue on blue incident.

His people were closest to the gate and held satchel charges. They'd throw them through as soon as the gate stabilized. That would clear the immediate area of threats as they charged in.

As soon as everyone was ready, Harry gave the signal, and the gate came to life. The fight to protect the Earth began now.

33

To say the battle began with a bang was insufficient, Clayton thought. Even covering his ears, the explosive charges Harry's people threw into the French base deafened him.

Then the missiles fired, roaring through the gate and detonating so strongly that he feared the ceiling would collapse. The pressure wave actually made him stumble.

The soldiers seemed unperturbed and rushed through the active gate. There must've still been an active threat on the other side because they immediately opened fire.

He stuck close to Kevin McHugh as the young hacker raced into the other chamber and was momentarily stunned at the devastation.

Rows of Asharim ships had become blasted, burning wrecks in seconds. Bodies littered the floor, and someone at the far side of the huge chamber was actively shooting at the friendly forces. Neither of the other gates was open.

The hacker had his comp out and was tapping the screen as he huddled behind what was left of some crates. Oddly, the thing that stood out to Clayton was the phone lying just out in the open. It was the duplicate of the one in his own pocket. It had to be Jess's.

He resisted the impulse to reach for it when flechettes slammed into the crates.

"Got it!" McHugh shouted. "Dialing now!"

The gate to their left rear came to life, and men began pouring through it from their side. There were a lot of bodies in the room on the other side but no active resistance. The stench was incredible. No way those were from this fight.

Harry's people led the way in, their weapons up. The SEAL team followed closely behind. Commander Krueger held a large case that Clayton assumed had the nuclear weapon.

"Are you sure this is the right place?" Harry asked McHugh. "I'd have expected resistance."

"This is the only gate to open since the attack started. It has to be the right place. Hell, the dead guys kind of point that way."

"I suppose so. Wait a second."

Harry turned and frowned at the gates. "I know this place. This is the ship Nathan stole. He blew up the gate and cut that one guy in half."

"So what do we do?" Krueger asked.

"We make sure this area is clear while Mister McHugh checks the gate for a different destination. If they aren't here, they used the ship as a waypoint. Maybe my mother and brother didn't want to reveal Earth's address directly to these people."

The armed men spread out, setting up at the entrances to the room. One of them called back. "I have fresh blood here."

Clayton stayed back from the front, content to let Harry and Krueger lead the way. If they found anyone looking for trouble, they'd be the ones to give it to them.

The blood drops were numerous and frequent. If they were Jess's, the young woman was in a bad spot.

Krueger sent men out at cross corridors to search. That cut their numbers down, but they needed to make sure no one came at them from the sides or from behind.

Harry stopped when they reached a closed hatch where the blood ended. "Get ready," his son said before opening the hatch and heading in with his weapon up. Others followed him in.

Once they called out that the room was secure, Clayton went inside. The compartment was fairly nondescript. The only odd thing about it was what looked like a large piece of equipment that resembled a technological sarcophagus. The blood drops led up to it, and there was some smeared across one side.

"What is that thing?" he asked Brenda.

"I think that's some kind of healing unit," she muttered as she walked around it. "Some of the oldest stories talked about how the Asharim could miraculously heal themselves and their most trusted allies. Kevin, can we see what's inside it?"

"Maybe. Let me find a port and check."

He opened panels until he found something that made him grunt. "Here we go." It took the man a few minutes to plug his comp in and tap into something. Then he swore.

"What?" Brenda asked.

Kevin turned the comp and showed them the video feed he'd tapped into. Jess Cook lay there, pale as death.

Clayton opened his mouth to curse, but automatic weapon fire from outside the room cut him off.

* * *

THE SHOTS MADE Brenda almost jump out of her skin. She'd been in fights before, but this was a whole new level of pressure. The FBI hadn't trained her for war, and her Glock felt a little underpowered.

"See if you can get her out of the thing," Harry said. "We need to get the hell out of here." He ran out the door before she could argue.

What if they couldn't? What if Cook was too badly injured to move? "Talk to me," she ordered Kevin.

"Hang on. Accessing medical telemetry now."

The man's face went pale. "I'm no doctor, but even I can tell we won't be able to move her. It looks like something ripped her intestines apart, and she's lost a lot of blood.

"It says she's alive but in what amounts to extremely critical condition. If we pop her out, she'll die before we even get back to the gate."

Brenda rubbed her forehead. "Is this portable or connected to the ship's power supply?"

"It's connected to the ship, but it might have some contingency for emergency power. Let me look." The man gestured for the other techs to come help, and they started pulling panels.

Brenda stood near the door with her weapon out. Two men guarded the hatch from the corridor, but she wanted to be sure no one came in while she wasn't looking.

Clayton stepped up beside her. "This isn't going to have a happy ending, is it?"

"Most likely not," she admitted. "I'm sorry."

The older man shook his head. "What a tragedy. She was the brightest, best person I've met in far more years than I can count. She was the hope for humanity."

Part of her wanted to tell him things might still work out, but she couldn't make herself mouth the pat phrase. His partner was almost certainly already dead. She just hadn't finished dying yet.

"There's a slot for a power cube," Kevin called out.

"Too bad we don't have one," she sighed.

The man's eyes darted toward his backpack. "Well, I happened to find one in a partially disassembled ship at the French base. I hope you don't mind that I borrowed it, Mister Rogers."

The old man barked out a laugh. "If you save Jess, I'll give you a whole damn ship. Thank God for sticky fingered hackers."

The man pulled out a glowing cube about ten centimeters across and slid it inside the device. He checked his comp. "It's on backup power now. We can disconnect the unit from the ship."

"Work fast," Brenda ordered. "We might have to pull out at any moment and I don't want to leave her behind."

The sounds of fighting outside were getting louder. Someone was pushing the friendly forces back toward them. Time was running out.

* * *

HARRY SENT a burst into the heavy-worlder in front of him. The man stumbled and went down. The man behind him fired a storm of flechettes that turned the two New Zealanders in front of him into hamburger.

They were outgunned here. They'd lost almost all of their people and were still getting pushed back. They needed to get off this ship.

"Slow them down as much as you can," he told the remaining soldiers. "We need a fighting retreat to the gate room."

A Marine Corps gunnery sergeant threw a grenade up the corridor to give them time to break contact. "I'll stay here and make sure no one gets by. Good luck."

"Don't be a hero, Jacob," Krueger said. "You have a family waiting for you."

"Aye, sir."

Harry and Krueger retreated back down the corridor.

"Realistically, they won't be able to give us more than a few minutes," Harry said.

"Gunnery Sergeant Danvers will give us the time we need. I only hope you get good news on your partner."

They arrived back at the room just as the techs were pushing the sarcophagus out into the hall.

"We're good," Brenda said. "Let's go!"

They'd almost made it back to the gate room when someone ahead of them opened fire. They all hit the deck, but none of the shots seemed to be aimed at them.

To his amazement, someone in the gate room laughed. "I'd stop resisting if I were you. We found something important." It was Nathan's voice.

"Oh, crap," Brenda said from where she crouched beside the box with Jess inside. "We sent the noncombatants ahead with the other two soldiers. Everyone except Kevin."

Harry edged forward until he could peek around the corner. Sure enough, his brother Nathan stood grinning beside the gate. He had a pistol to his father's head.

Kathleen Bennett stood beside her son. The techs were gathered into a small knot off to the side, and the two soldiers lay sprawled in pools of their own blood.

"You can come out now," Harry's mother said. "This fight is over."

Harry came out slowly, his weapon aimed at the three. Nathan only seemed to have a pistol, and his mother was unarmed. Still, they didn't need much when they had his father.

That's when he noticed how young his mother seemed. Unnaturally so. She could pass for someone in her twenties. "You're looking good, Mother. New skin cream?"

She smiled coldly. "It's been a long time, Harry. You never call or come to visit. Don't you love me?"

"Let him go, and I'll let you go," he said, aiming his rifle at his brother's head. The shot was tricky, and he'd be almost as likely to kill his father, but he might have to take the shot.

"Don't be ridiculous," she scoffed. "We have the trump card now. Lay down your weapons."

His father laughed. "Now who's being ridiculous? We all know you and Nathan can't be trusted to keep your bargains. Nathan would ignore you and kill Harry for sport even if you *did* mean it."

His mother cocked an eyebrow and slowly nodded. "I suppose you have a point. That poses a bit of a problem since we have no intention of releasing you."

"Then don't. Let them go and keep me."

"Screw that," Harry said. "I might not like you that much, but that's a death sentence."

His father shrugged. "Making a deal is all about the art of the possible. Right now, I don't see a way where you get out without me staying.

"Take Jess, and go back to Earth. You might figure out a new angle and turn this around."

Nathan bristled. "You can't have her. The woman belongs to me."

His mother held her hand up. "I wish I could tell you all to screw off, but your father is right. My options are limited. That means I'm willing to make a onetime deal.

"Leave with the woman. I couldn't care less about her. I'll keep Clayton as a consolation prize. We have so much to talk about."

"Done," his father said before Harry could reject the offer.

He lined up the shot only to have his brother duck even farther behind his father. He really, really wanted to take the shot.

His mother and brother seemed to realize that and started edging toward the other exit from the gate room. With no clean options, he had to let them out of sight.

"Crap," he said. "McHugh, take my phone, look up the address for *Freedom Express*, and open the gate. I'll keep you covered."

Commander Krueger and Gunnery Sergeant Danvers used their weapons to cover the corridor behind them as Brenda and the rest pushed the sarcophagus with Jess inside into the gate room.

As unsavory as it was, the others had to drag bodies out of the way to get to the gate. The machine had almost no clearance.

Reinforcements poured through as soon as he opened the gate. Harry was tempted to go after his father, but he knew these people were not trained soldiers. If they ran into more heavy-worlders, it would end in disaster.

With a sigh, he stepped through the gate last and made the gesture for McHugh to close the gate.

His mother and brother had won.

* * *

CLAYTON HEARD the gate shut off and knew he was alone with his ex-wife and murderous son. This wasn't going to be pleasant, but it gave Harry a chance to prepare.

Nathan shoved him back into the gate room after he peered in to make sure it was clear. "I can't believe you let him go, Mother. Worse, you gave him my woman."

"Grow up, Nathan," Kathleen said. "You can always get her back when we take over the Earth. I'll have to go back to the base in France and open a gate directly to the planet. Thank God I got the address. We can throw assets at your brother until we win."

"At least the Grand Dickhead is dead," his son grumbled. "They know the ship's address. Can you disable the gate until we get some more bodies?"

She pulled out a controller and did something to it. "Done. I also have the address they just went to. We can visit Harry and pay our respects very soon. Take dear Clayton back to where you had me locked up. We'll leave him there while I take the shuttle to the station."

Nathan shoved Clayton roughly up the hall but stopped when he saw something up ahead. "What is that?"

Clayton smiled as he recognized the open case. Commander Krueger had left the nuclear bomb behind.

Oh, this was absolutely perfect. Hollywood couldn't have come up with a better ending. The only thing that could improve on it was timing.

Nathan pushed Clayton forward, and he saw a digital counter. Nine... Eight...

"It's a nuclear bomb," Clayton said.

His son raised his weapon to shoot it, but Clayton planted a fist in the brat's groin and sent him to the floor.

He hurled Nathan's gun down the corridor and turned toward his ex-wife with a grin. "Looks like we get a karmic ending after all. I'll *literally* see you in Hell."

Her mouth was only starting to open when the counter hit zero.

* * *

JESS SAT BOLT UPRIGHT. Fear flashed through her as she looked around for Nathan. She was sitting in the same box he'd put her in, but the room had changed.

This looked more like a basement with a bare concrete floor, cinder block walls, and a decrepit-looking elevator off to the side. A portable gate sat nearby. Brenda's gate?

"She's awake!" a voice said from behind her.

She turned her head and saw Kevin rising from a folding chair beside a table filled with equipment. He dropped the phone receiver and raced over to her.

"You're safe," he said. "You're okay."

She looked down at the ripped, blood-soaked blouse she wore and doubted that. Yet her questing hands found only healthy skin. The pain was gone. It was as if it had never happened.

A black cat—probably the mechanical one—rose from where she'd been curled nearby and walked up the bed to be petted.

"What's going on?" she asked as she stroked the purring device. "What happened? They're trying to capture the French base."

"Slow down," he said with exaggerated softness. "It's been two days. We poured people into the base, and they finally surrendered."

She blinked at that. "Two *days*? How? What about Nathan and his mother? We need to stop them, too."

Even as she said it, she knew they must've already done something. They had her, and Nathan didn't.

"Harry got you out. His brother and mother aren't a problem anymore."

His sad expression filled her with dread. "Something else happened."

Kevin nodded. "It's a long story, and I know Harry will be pissed if I tell it before he gets down here. He's almost been living here when he hasn't been negotiating with about a billion other people.

"He just went upstairs to grab a bite to eat and take a shower a few hours ago. Give him and Brenda a few minutes, and they'll tell you everything."

She heard the missing part of his statement. "Where is Clayton Rogers?"

The bald man sighed. "I'm sorry, but he didn't make it. If it's any consolation, he got the most *spectacular* Viking funeral in history. Harry said he went out exactly the way he'd have wanted.

"Harry buried an empty casket for him yesterday. He put a quote from Thomas Jefferson on his tombstone. 'The tree of liberty must be refreshed from time to time with the blood of patriots and tyrants.' He said his father was a bit of both, so it felt right."

Her eyes teared up, and her throat tightened. Clayton would have liked that his son had embraced him at last.

"Now lay back until Doctor Granger gets down here," Kevin said. "If I let you hurt yourself, he'll have Victor hold me over the edge of the roof again."

Jess lay back in a state of shock. She had so many things she'd never have the chance to say to the cantankerous old man now. How could he be gone? He'd been such a force of nature, how could they go on without him?

This must be eating at Harry. He'd never liked his father, but no one lost a parent and just shrugged it off. What could she say to him? How could she help him?

She had no idea. Her mind was swirling with loss, and she couldn't seem to swim out of it. It was like a whirlpool trying to suck her down.

Well, she'd deal with it like any other problem. One moment at a time.

The elevator dinged, and she knew that process was about to start in earnest, whether she was ready or not.

She'd get her answers and do what she had to do. The Earth was depending on her.

* * *

WANT to get updates from Terry about new books and other general nonsense going on in his life? He promises there will be cats. Go to TerryMixon.com/Mailing-List and sign up.

DID YOU ENJOY THIS BOOK? Please leave a review on Amazon. It only takes a minute to dash off a few words and that kind of thing helps Terry make a living as a writer and gets you new books faster.

WANT the next book in this series? Grab *Blood of Patriots* today or buy any of Terry's other books, which are listed on the next page.

VISIT TERRY'S Patreon page to find out how to get cool rewards and an early look at what he's working on at Patreon.com/TerryMixon.

ALSO BY TERRY MIXON

You can always find the most up to date listing of Terry's titles on his Amazon Author Page.

Note: the links below (ebook only, obviously) redirect you to my website where you can click a button to go to Amazon. This allows me to participate in Amazon's associates program and earn a little more. Sorry for any inconvenience.

The Last Hunter

The Last Hunter

Bonds of Blood

Alpha Strike

The Enemy Revealed

Command Authority

The Grand Conspiracy

Shield of Humanity

Fog of War

Ships of the Line

Operation Liberty

The Empire of Bones Saga

Empire of Bones

Veil of Shadows

Command Decisions

Ghosts of Empire

Paying the Price

Recon in Force

Behind Enemy Lines

The Terra Gambit

Hidden Enemies

Race to Terra

Ruined Terra

Victory on Terra

When Luck Runs Out

Gunboat Diplomacy

The Imperial Marines Saga

Spoils of War

Imperial Recruit

Enemy Action

The Humanity Unlimited Saga

Liberty Station

Freedom Express

Tree of Liberty

Blood of Patriots

Single Novels

Scorched Earth

Storm Divers

The Vigilante Series with Glynn Stewart

Heart of Vengeance

Oath of Vengeance

Bound By Law

Bound By Honor

Bound By Blood

Box Sets

The Empire of Bones Saga Volume 1

The Empire of Bones Saga Volume 2

The Empire of Bones Saga Volume 3

The Empire of Bones Saga Volume 4

Humanity Unlimited Publisher's Pack 1

Humanity Unlimited Publisher's Pack 2

ABOUT TERRY

#1 Bestselling Military Science Fiction author Terry Mixon served as a non-commissioned officer in the United States Army 101st Airborne Division. He later worked alongside the flight controllers in the Mission Control Center at the NASA Johnson Space Center supporting the Space Shuttle, the International Space Station, and other human spaceflight projects.

He now writes full time while living in Texas with his lovely wife and a pounce of cats.

TerryMixon.com

amazon.com/author/terrymixon

facebook.com/TerryLMixon

patreon.com/TerryMixon

bookbub.com/authors/terry-mixon

goodreads.com/TerryMixon